RUN TIME

"I raved about her debut novel *Spike It* and Chris Niles has followed up with a second that is every bit as good. She has a fantastic style which grabs you from the start and puts you firmly in alongside with the main character. You are there with Sam Ridley in every sense of the word. . . . This is a book that is difficult to put down and I cannot wait for the next."

—*Shropshire Star*

"Niles' debut *Spike It* was one of the most refreshing novels to hit the crime fiction shelves last year and she shows it was no fluke with this follow-up mystery again featuring London radio reporter Sam Ridley. . . . Fast, furious, and lots of fun."

—*Lincolnshire Echo*

"Excellent . . . Niles has given her early readers a character named Sam Ridley, a radio reporter who is divorced and degenerate but in possession of a dry wit and an eye for a good story."

—*Luton & Dunstable Herald*

"The ending is a real twister."

—*Sunday Times* (London)

continue

D1059315

RUN TIME

CHRIS NILES

BERKLEY PRIME CRIME, NEW YORK

RUN TIME

A Berkley Prime Crime Book / published by arrangement with
the author

PRINTING HISTORY
Macmillan hardcover edition / 1998
Berkley Prime Crime mass-market edition / October 1999

The Penguin Putnam Inc. World Wide Web site address is
http://www.penguinputnam.com

ISBN: 0-425-17119-1

Berkley Prime Crime Books are published
by the Berkley Publishing Group,
a division of Penguin Putnam Inc.,
375 Hudson Street, New York, New York 10014.
The name BERKLEY PRIME CRIME and the BERKLEY PRIME CRIME
design are trademarks belonging to Penguin Putnam Inc.

PRINTED IN THE UNITED STATES OF AMERICA

10 9 8 7 6 5 4 3 2 1

*This book is dedicated to my parents,
Ian and Helen.*

THANKS:

To Roderick, for graciously bearing everything. To Drew and Ellen, for being consistently fabulous and throwing great parties.

To my editor, Beverley Cousins, for making sense of it all.

And to Ingrid, Fionnuala, Kira, Jacqueline, Mary and Ann—CNN colleagues and tip-top starlets.

Wednesday 8:00 a.m.

I woke in a strange room in a strange town and felt like death. Not just any death. Not some quick-but-merciful-chop-across-the-carotid-artery death. That I would have almost welcomed. No. This was more the slow-painful, expiry-at-the-hands-of-a-torturer-who-loves-his-work death. Slow-roast-over-a-low-flame, hang-'em-up-by-the-thumbnails death.

I suppose the headache had something to do with it, although to call it a headache was to call the Grand Canyon an interesting geological feature. I had a hangover only a football team or a very large mammal could have done justice to. A creature with the body mass of a blue whale could maybe, just maybe, have coped with the nausea, the dry shakes, the feeling that if my brain had the gall to offer any instructions to my body, it would get a "closed" sign in response. My stomach felt as though it were auditioning for the part of a storm-tossed ocean. My tongue was so dry I could have used it to shave paint. My eyes felt as though they were about to make an audacious escape bid from my skull.

Record this day, I said to myself as I edged my fingers toward something that would give me purchase, *because as of this moment, I am never, ever, drinking again.*

It felt good, to make a decision like that, and so early on

in the piece. It gave me the strength I needed for the next stage of the morning's activity, which was to open both my eyes.

The shimmering pain around my head had diverted me from the fact that the rest of my body was in a very odd position. When I prised my lids open and got focused, all I could see was white. White tiles, white porcelain. Something hard and round jabbed into my back. I looked up. A cistern loomed above me. I groaned.

I'd passed out in the toilet.

My arm slithered around the floor, pushed up, found the door handle. It was an odd position to be in, but I was more confident now. I had to show this hangover who was boss. The bowl was close, in case I needed it. I had the feeling I might. My knees found the floor. This was good. This was real progress. Taking all the time that I needed, I hauled myself into a crawling position. The minute I did that I could have sworn that someone began sawing into my skull with a rusty blade. I closed my eyes, tried to get some control. The sawing went on. Back, forth. Ear to ear. Perhaps there were two of them. One pushing, the other pulling. Perhaps even another one, shouting encouragement, like a cox.

It didn't bear thinking about. I stood up.

Uh-uh, said my stomach. *Baaad idea.* I sat down on the toilet. It wasn't much better. I leaned my head against the cistern, to reassure it that everything was going to be okay. It was then that I realised that the room wasn't familiar. The clues were simple but obvious. The room was clean. Tasteful. Both of which immediately ruled out my place. White walls, white floors. A little frosted window, partially open.

The smell was the other thing that struck me. Sweet and fresh. And it was quiet. No humming thrum of traffic. Just birds. Birds singing brightly, without a care.

Nature, I thought. Terrific. Just what I need.

I lay back some more. The ceiling was white, but there were blue and orange spots before my eyes. I thought I could hear The Talking Heads singing in my brain, but maybe it was the hangover.

This is not my beautiful house.

But if not, whose?

I made another manful attempt to sit up. Ignored the sawing in my head. I thought hard. I'll remember everything in a minute, I thought, overcome by a burst of irrational optimism. I sweated my brain. Start slowly. It'll come. Relax.

I put my headache on hold, grabbed the door handle. I pulled the door open slowly. Since I was naked, I didn't want to frighten the natives.

There was a house attached to the bathroom. A nice house, by the looks of things, with hardwood floors and elegant art work. A corridor led to an open-plan living area with a breakfast bar attached to the cooking site. It wasn't entirely unfamiliar. Fragments of the previous evening began to emerge. I remembered a blonde woman called Michelle. And lots of bottles of champagne called Bollinger.

French doors gave out on to a wide wooden deck that surrounded the house on two sides. I opened the doors and went out. The tropical air smelt sweet but the light was way too bright.

In the distance I could see a glint of sunlight on water. I could smell the frangipani, hear the boom of boats on the harbour. I'd seen that harbour, last night. I was in Sydney. Half a world away from my home.

The timpanist inside my brain was sounding long, slow strokes that reverberated around my skull. My cells were screaming for caffeine. I went inside, searched for the drug that helps my brain to work in these situations. There was a jar of instant coffee in the cupboard. I'd make it do. I put some water in an Alessi kettle and plonked it on the stove.

I moved a handbag which had been left sitting on the breakfast bar. It was glossy and expensive and bore the initials of a label synonymous with sophisticated travel. And then I noticed there were clothes on the floor. Tangled clothes. Some of them were mine.

Outside it was clear, inside my brain it was foggy but the caffeine would help, I promised myself. I concentrated on the gurgly sound that the kettle made. Ready to snatch it before it burst forth into song.

Song was the last thing I needed.

I found a cupboard with some cups, put five teaspoons of coffee in one and poured myself a restorative jolt. I looked at the bag as I drank and I looked at the clothes on the floor that weren't mine. The beautiful young woman who'd been wearing them came into clearer focus. Along with me, she had drunk quite a bit the previous night. She'd probably need a gallon or two of coffee as well.

It was the least I could do. A way of saying thanks for giving me a hangover that even I would mark as a milestone.

I poured a second cup. Put it on a tray and took it to her room. Put my hand up to knock. Then I paused. If she was in anything like the state I was, the sight of a naked man might not be what she wanted first thing. I took the tray back to the living room and got reunited with my clothes.

I knocked on the bedroom door. Silence. She was probably still asleep.

I knocked again. Still silence. She'd probably sleep till lunchtime. I should really get going, I thought. Get a place to stay. See some of the sights. Make the most of any weather that wasn't a British winter. After all, I was on holiday. There was no time to waste.

"Michelle, it's Sam. Brought you some coffee. If you feel half as bad as I do, you could probably do with it."

There was no reply. I knocked again, half-hoping that she'd sleep on. The idea of not hanging around picked up speed. Maybe I should just write her a note and leave. Explain that I'd had a really great time and that I'd call her. Last night had been one thing, but what would we say to each other in broad daylight when our lust had faded and the only frisson left was born of awkwardness?

The silence from Michelle's room stretched out as I debated with my inner weasel.

I waited a minute, then I eased the door open with my shoulder because I didn't have a hand free.

When I did that, I knew I should have listened to the weasel.

Michelle was in far worse shape than me. I just felt like death. She was dead.

• • •

Her face bore little resemblance to the laughing woman I'd
met the previous evening. She'd been bludgeoned with something heavy and blunt. The result was pulp. Her features
merged in a purée of blood, skin and gristle. The beating had
been so savage that one of her ears was separated from her
skull, her nose had been flattened. The bedclothes were soaked
in blood. There was blood sprayed around the walls. Despite
this, Michelle had put up little resistance. She hadn't been able
to. Her hands were tied to a rail on the bedhead.

I took it all in and my hands began to shake. I tried to get
some control over my limbs. I took the tray and the coffee
back to the kitchen. Placed them down carefully. Shook my
head to dislodge the horrible image. Went back to where
Michelle lay.

She was so mangled by the beating she didn't look human.
There was no face to connect with my hazy memories of the
night before. There was nothing.

This isn't happening. This isn't happening.

I decided to make a deal with the gods. This wasn't real. I
had had an atrocious, alcohol-fuelled hallucination. And this
was the gods' funky way of telling me to straighten out my
life. Not to have one-night stands. To find a nice woman, settle
down. Participate in a loving, mature relationship. They were
right. Absolutely right. I promised never to misbehave again.

But the deal didn't make the body go away. And in the
humid Sydney heat it had already begun to smell. I gingerly
checked under the bed, half expecting to see blood dripping
from the springs. A ghastly, blood-soaked face stared back at
me. I jumped, my heart set up a steady tattoo. It was the
primitive art statue that'd been sitting in the living room last
night. A statue that I'd touched.

I dashed out on to the verandah, desperate for a reality
check. The world had tilted on its axis. I was in some parallel
universe that looked just like this one except in one crucial
detail. I gripped the balcony rail till the wood hurt my hands.
Acceptance began to seep into my brain. A woman had been
killed yards from where I slept. How had this happened? Why,

even as drunk and jet-lagged as I was, hadn't I heard anything? What the hell was going on?

I checked the doors and windows. As an occasional house-breaker myself, I knew that the place would have posed no serious barriers to anyone who wanted to get in. All those French glass doors, might as well leave them open. There was no sign of forced entry, but the locks on the doors were so flimsy that they would have provided no real challenge to an intruder, especially one who'd remembered not to leave home without his credit card.

The wooden deck gave out on to the garden and a path right around to the front gate. The gate was six foot high and made of wood. In these discrete, leafy streets everyone had a similar fence to the one that Michelle had, shielding them from out-side eyes. The lock was intact. This was bad. This was very, very bad.

I went back inside. The birds were still singing, the air still smelled sweet but the picture didn't hold much charm for me any more.

Very soon the police would come. They'd look the place over. They'd talk to a few people. They'd conclude that most murder cases are pretty open and shut affairs. Most women are killed by men that they know. They'd ask around some more. They'd find that a gormless English tourist had been seen out with Michelle just hours before her death. Drinking, dining, clubbing. The whole population of Sydney'd be lining up to testify. The police wouldn't be looking too hard for whoever had done this.

They wouldn't have to. They had me.

We got drunk together, came back to her place. I wanted to have sex. She said no. A fight ensued. I beat her. I killed her. My fingerprints were on the murder weapon.

And what would I be able to say in my defence? *I didn't do it, officer. You have to believe me.*

Yeah, he'd say as he bundled me into the cell. *And I'm a sucker for Father Christmas and the tooth fairy as well.*

I went back to the kitchen and took a desperate mouthful of coffee. I had to think what to do. I squashed the panic. Told it to wait its turn.

Think, Ridley!

I didn't kill her, that much I knew. It didn't narrow the field because I didn't know what the field was. I didn't know the first thing about this woman. I was tired, hungover and my whole body hurt. Might as well just sit here. Wait for the police to come and collect me. Let them take me off and put me in jail. At least that way I'd get some sleep. In fact, I'd have more time than I knew what to do with. I wondered how often they'd let Simon come and visit.

Simon.

"Oh, Jesus," I said out loud, looking at my watch which told me it was eight-thirty. My kid. He was due here in Sydney any time. He didn't expect to see his father in a striped suit and leg irons. I didn't want him to see me that way.

I had to find some way out of this mess. But as I sat there, I couldn't think of anything at all.

Tuesday 7:35 a.m.

She had boarded my flight in Singapore. A slender, blonde woman of about thirty with a bright, dippy smile.

"Gidday," she said. "I'm Michelle. This isn't strictly my seat, but they put me next to a bad-tempered baby. You don't mind do you?" Her accent was as bold as her expensive purple suit.

"Sam Ridley," I said. I was far from minding.

Michelle had her right arm bandaged so the steward helped her with her other bags. They were expensive, like the suit. The buttons, with the backward "C's" winked at me as Michelle sat down, kicked off her shoes and struggled to get comfortable in the space that airlines seem to think is enough for marathon journeys.

Her perfume was delicate and fruity. She stretched like a cat, sighed, closed her eyes and half-lay there for a few minutes, smiling. I smiled too. Things were looking up.

The first leg of the interminable flight—which to my mind put the "haul" into "long haul"—I had been jammed in by a New Zealand backpacker called Scuffa or Wonga or something equally baroque, who'd explained in loving detail how he'd travelled round Europe for ten months on a laughably small sum of money. That guy knew every soup-kitchen, every rat-infested hostel, every campsite and ditch from Istanbul to Alicante. And he'd not spared me even one of his cost-cutting tips. His insistence on thrift had caused problems. He'd split up with his girlfriend because she'd wanted to go to a hotel one night rather than brave out a force ten gale in his pup tent. "Couldn't believe it, mate," he said sadly, as if his girlfriend had confessed a liking for sacrificing small children to the devil. "And she was a farmer's daughter, too," he shook his head.

I'm English which means that, strictly speaking, I don't have to be friendly with anyone until I've known them at least ten years. I certainly don't have to indulge in casual conversation with people I haven't been formally introduced to. I wanted to appraise Wonga of that but I couldn't get a word in. He was sublimely unaware that our conversation was more monologue than vibrant exchange of ideas. "I pressed on alone, mate," he went on. "I took me Primus stove and I said, 'I'll show you,' and I did. I showed her, too right I did."

I was beginning to think I would have to feign death to get rid of him when, by some freak blessing of the gods, he got off in Singapore. No doubt he planned to traverse the Malaysian peninsula on a skateboard while subsisting on rice husks and curdled yak milk.

Michelle took his place and after our initial introduction, she didn't seem much inclined to talk. She pulled a magazine from her bag and leafed through it. The plane took off and I settled down to try and sleep. There was no sleep to be had. Instead the drinks trolley came around. Grateful for any diversion, I ordered a whisky. Michelle ordered a whisky too. My kind of woman. She sipped her drink. I picked up my book. I'd bought it in a rush as I left Heathrow because the cover looked interesting. The cover still looked interesting. The inside, unfortunately, did not.

The steward brought our meals, ladling the burning hot foil-covered rectangles on to our plates. I'm not that fussy about what I eat, but I thought it prudent to order more alcohol to help that stuff go down. I've read all about it's not wise to drink while flying, how the body dehydrates much more quickly at high altitude, but I've chosen to ignore it. I drink in the air for the same reason I drink on the ground: it helps to pass the time.

Michelle shot a sideways look at me and smiled. She had a nice smile.

"Where're you heading?"

"Sydney."

"All on your own?" Her eyes widened. I kidded myself that she liked the sound of that.

"It's all right," I said. "My mother's given me a note."

We joked and flirted some more. I told her I was a reporter for a radio station in London. I made my life sound like something I didn't recognise. Glossing up the good bits, playing down the bad bits. That's one of the things about being a journalist. No matter how shitty the outfit you work for, the job can always be made to sound like you're Clark Kent to people who don't know anything about the business. My job as a crime reporter for City Radio on the Tottenham Court Road was not going to expose me unnecessarily to a Pulitzer Prize, but it paid the mortgage. And sometimes it came in useful for impressing women.

"Are you working on a story in Sydney?" Michelle kept batting the questions.

It was tempting to make something up. To tell her a lie that would impress her so much she'd want to have sex with me. But I didn't. I was raised right.

"My son," I said. "I'm going to see my son."

She sensed this wasn't flirting territory anymore, so we skirted around the story of my unhappy family. I probably would have told her if she'd asked, there's no greater turn-on for women than a chap who's also a devoted dad, but having just been in the clutches of one aeroplane bore, I didn't fancy turning myself into another.

So I spared her the epic saga of Mary, my ex-wife, me and our son, Simon. Like all great tales, it has drama, pathos and an unhappy ending.

As soon as Mary got custody of our son she decided she would move to the other side of the world. Almost as far away, in fact, as it's possible to get. I don't think she deliberately meant to separate Simon and me by such a distance, but there are some days when, knowing Mary as I do, I can't be sure.

I have to make the best of it, according to the judge who ruled over our hearing. I fought as hard as I could to have Simon stay with me, in London. But the battle was over before I'd even got out of bed. Mary was every inch the successful city executive in her colour-coordinated MaxMara. My suit was old, my iron was broken that day, and my hair looked like I'd slept in it. On top of that, Mary had a big house and a full-time nanny. I had a dingy flat in a part of town the judge only ever heard bad things about on the news. *A child's place is with his mother*, he had intoned sententiously.

That cosy domestic homily meant me trekking out to Australia whenever I could afford it. This was the first time and I was minding it very much. I have nothing against Australia in principle, I just wish it were on the same continent as Britain so I could see my kid more often.

"More wine, mate?" The steward, who could spot a serious drinker when he saw one, waved a bottle in my direction. I shook my head. I didn't want to arrive in Sydney looking like I'd just finished some alcoholic marathon. For once my eyes would be bright and my breath fresh. A model for my young son.

They dimmed the lights on the plane and put a movie up on the screen. My travelling companion settled down for a nap and I dug in my bag for a mint. I wasn't going to see Simon for several hours yet, but it couldn't hurt to begin the de-scruffing preparations early.

The last time I had seen him was more than six months ago. The day he left London for good. I didn't go with him to the airport. I could not have stood the sight of him getting on that plane with someone who wasn't me. Instead, we met at the kiosk in Holland Park. A shabby, prefab building that serves good coffee. It was a gorgeous day as I recall. The sun gently warmed us as we sat outside. Other children, ones who weren't going to be ripped out of the arms of their loving parents, played games with pets and balls.

"Well, kid," I said. "This is it for a while."

He stared at me, his hand plucking at the tab on his Coke

can. I wanted to cry. Instead I looked at the passers-by. An old woman fed hazelnuts to a grey squirrel, making him run up her faded dress to get them.

"You'll be okay. You're going to have a great time," I said cheerfully.

Simon continued to pluck at the metal tab. It made a tight pinging sound.

"What about you, Dad?" he said. "Will you be okay?"

I held his gaze for a few seconds. "Sure," I said levelly. "I'll be okay." Simon took a slug from his drink. He sat the can down very carefully, dead centre of the table, brushed away a few leaves that had settled there. "What will it be like there, Dad?" he asked, his voice cracking a little.

"It'll be great. You're going to have a great time," I said, repeating the same phrases like a demented parrot. "I'll come out as often as I can." The poor kid looked so miserable. He was too young to deal with pain this intense. So, for that matter, was I.

"Why couldn't you and Mum get on?" he said angrily.

"I'll explain when you get older," I said. Maybe I'd have worked out the answer to that question by then.

After that we kidded about a bit, cracked jokes. Dealt with our misery in a guy way. We walked around the park, watched the carp in the Japanese garden, tried to persuade the peacocks to open their tail feathers by doing a soggy rendition of "The Harlem Shuffle."

Too soon, it was time to hand him over. We walked to the western entrance of the park where Mary waited with the car.

"Come and see me soon," he said, hugging me fiercely for a moment. Then he was gone.

Later, as the plane prepared to drop out of the sky on to the tarmac at Sydney airport, Michelle woke. She stretched and smiled at me.

"Is your son meeting you?" she asked.

I just nodded, a big, silly grin plastered over my face.

"You must be excited."

Excited didn't cover it. I was so worked up, I kept forgetting to breathe.

I had a small bag with a few things in it. Passport, tooth-brush, traveller's cheques, boring paperback, guidebook, map, presents for Simon. I grabbed it from the locker and helped Michelle with hers.

The airport wasn't crowded. I was through immigration in a matter of minutes. Feeling rather chipper, despite my lack of sleep, I headed for the baggage carousel where Michelle was already.

"I hate this part," she said. "It always feels like hours. Every time I take a trip I promise myself I'll just take a cabin bag. But when it comes to clothes, I'm weak."

The plane, it seemed, was unloaded in record time. People came, rescued their bags and went. Then more people came and went.

Except Michelle, me and about ten other people who were also looking increasingly exasperated. After about half an hour of this, I would have been prepared to accept a bag that bore even the faintest resemblance to mine. But there wasn't one. The carousel was empty. Soon a representative of the airline came, gathered us together us together and told us the bad news. Some bags had been unloaded in Singapore by mistake and were still there. There were mumblings of discontent from the travelers. Promises by the airline that it would be sorted out the following day.

I was worried about Simon waiting on the other side of the barrier. I took the card handed out by the airline guy, stuffed it in my pocket.

"I'll get this sorted out tomorrow," I said to Michelle. "I've got to go."

She seemed about to say something. But she didn't. She raised her hand and gave me a small wave and a rueful look. I'd forgotten that I wanted to sleep with her. All I could think about was the kid waiting on the other side of the barrier.

"Got anything to declare?" asked the jolly chap at customs.

"No," I said wearily. "Thanks to the airline, I haven't."

There've been few times in my life when I've been so wound up that I feel like I could faint. Important exams, first day on the job, wedding day, waiting for Simon to be born.

Times when you think: *This is it. Adult grown-up stuff. This is important.*

I felt like that as I strode towards the sign marked "Arrivals," my breath shortened, my hands shook. *I'm going to see him, I'm going to see him*, I said, the words marking time with my increasing stride.

I burst through those doors, eyes alight, head held high. Devil-may-care grin at the ready. I scanned the crowd for that familiar, curly head.

All eyes fastened on me as I came through. Smiles poised then dropped as I registered as an unfamiliar face. Those waiting turned away in anticipation that the next person behind me through those doors might be the one they sought.

I scanned the crowd once, twice. My mind unwilling to process the information that my eyes were feeding it.

He wasn't there.

Tuesday 6:35 p.m.

I stood in the middle of the busy terminal, people surging around me and my first thought was that Simon had had an accident on the way to the airport. My son was lying bleeding to death on a road somewhere while nosy onlookers crowded around to get the best view. Maybe a kind person held his head as he breathed his last, reassuring him that he would pass on his final words to his dad. Maybe he'd say that he forgave me for forcing him to make the journey that ended his young life. I could see it in technicolour. Simon was dead or dying on foreign bitumen and it was all my fault. If I hadn't come to Australia, he'd be alive.

But just as suddenly the horror-vision stopped. I pulled myself together. It wasn't my fault. It was obvious that my ex-wife Mary was responsible. She'd concocted some devious plan to keep Simon and me apart for as long as she possibly could. Not content with having him full time, she'd decided to ruin my holiday with him as well. My mind raced through the heinous possibilities. She'd moved house, left no forwarding address to make sure that I never saw my son again.

I dismissed those thoughts as soon as I'd invented them. Mary had a highly evolved sense of cruelty, but she would look you in the eye as she eviscerated you. There had to be another explanation. Most of my flight had already come through. Maybe Simon had come here and waited and when I hadn't showed up, gone away again. I pulled out my trusty credit card—the type that you can use to order cordon bleu meals even though you're perched on a crag at the top of the Andes—and went to find a phone that would accept it. Then I heard my name. An official voice asking me to connect with the information desk.

"I'm Sam Ridley," I said to the woman behind the counter.

"Phone call for you."

"Sam?" The line was bad. Mary's voice crackled and fizzed.

"Well, isn't this a surprise," I said. "You really needn't have gone to all the effort."

"Look, Sam I . . ." the line fizzed some more. ". . . get back."

"What?" I put a finger in one ear to block out the ambient sound of the terminal. "Say that again. I didn't hear you."

"We're stuck," said Mary. She was shouting now. "We're on the Reef and we're stuck. There's been a freak storm. We can't get out today. There aren't any flights."

"Reef? What reef? What do you mean you're stuck?"

"The Great Barrier Reef," said Mary, more slowly. "We came up for a long weekend and now we can't get back. I'm sorry. We'll get there as soon as we can."

"You're sorry?" I said. "*You're* sorry?"

"Yes, Sam. I can't do much better than that."

"How do I get there then? To this reef?"

"What do you mean?"

"If you can't bring him to me then I'm coming to you. How do I get there?"

"You can't, Sam. We're on an island. The only access is by float plane and the sea's too rough. If you could get there then we could leave."

"When will you get off?"

"I don't know yet. It depends on the weather. It shouldn't be more than a couple of days."

I took a deep breath to corral my anger. "Mary," I said softly, "I want you to understand something: Simon is my son too. I know that you often choose to ignore this inconvenient fact, but it *is* a fact. I don't appreciate this. Jesus Christ, woman, I've just flown twelve thousand miles. Is it too much to ask that you could have got him here?''

We were following the blueprints for the Sam-Mary arguments of old. At this point Mary was supposed to call me a rude name and hang up the phone. But she didn't.

The line cleared for a moment. I could hear her sigh. ''Come on, Sam,'' she said. ''Even I don't have any control over acts of God.''

I gave in too easily, as always.

''You really are on an island, cut off from civilisation?''

''In a manner of speaking. It's a luxury resort.''

''Too bad,'' I said. ''So there's no chance of you reverting to savagery.''

''Grow up, Sam. When are you going to realise that the world isn't conspiring against you?''

''When I see some evidence to the contrary.''

''It won't be so bad,'' said Mary. ''Go to the beach, hang out and get some sleep. By the time we get back you'll be fresh and ready to go. Let me tell you, you're going to need your sleep. Simon has an exhaustive programme lined up. He's been planning it for weeks.''

''Yeah,'' I said.

''Let me give you the number here,'' said Mary. ''Call me tomorrow. I should have a better idea of what's happening by then.''

''Is he there?'' I asked.

''Dad?'' The voice came so quickly that he must have been standing right by her shoulder. I imagined him grabbing the phone from Mary's hand. ''Dad? How was the flight? It's a killer, eh?''

''Yeah,'' I said. ''It's a killer.''

''See any movies?''

''Nah. They were all junk.'' It was time to roll out my jolly father routine. ''What about you? Stuck on an island, eh? How about that?''

''Yeah, can't wait to tell the kids at home.'' Home. A tiny

stab of pain. Home meant Sydney. My son was growing up away from me.

"Dad? You still there?"

"Yep," I said. "I'm still here."

"What are you gonna do till we get back?"

"Oh, I don't know," I said carelessly, repeating the options Mary had flung out. "Get some sleep. Go to the beach."

"Don't go to Bondi," he said. "Its so full of tourists and the water's dirty. Go to Palm Beach. It's further north and it's much better. You're gonna rent a car, right?"

"Okay," I said. I had a difficult time fitting me into any picture that had a beach in it, but I was prepared to try, for the sake of my son.

"I miss you, Dad," he said. "Can't wait to see you."

I followed the signs for the airport bus stop. The air outside was warm and still. The sun and clouds were manufacturing a Hollywood-issue tropical sunset—serving up dramatic formations in every shade of fire. The sign told me there was a twenty minute wait for a bus but it was almost a pleasure to stand there watching nature do its bit. I even forgot for a moment about Mary and how much I wanted her to contract a painful, life-threatening disease.

"Sam? What are you doing here? What happened?" It was Michelle. Beside her was a large Maori chap carrying her travelling bag like it was doll's furniture. "Where's your son? Nothing wrong is there?"

"Not as long as someone keeps my ex-wife and me separated," I said. I told her the story.

"Wouldn't that just give you the shits?" she said.

I was about to tell her it hadn't affected my bowel movements in the slightest when I realised this was probably a figure of speech.

"Yes," I said. "It would."

She smiled her dippy, sexy smile. "Let me give you a lift." There was a large blue car standing waiting. The guy, her driver I assumed, had put her bag in the boot. It was there looking kind of forlorn. It was the kind of stylish bag that said I have lots of mates in contrasting sizes. Maybe it was a good thing the rest of my luggage wasn't there. That way nobody could see how well it didn't match.

Michelle opened the car door. Saw me hesitate.

"Come on then, I don't bite. Well, only if you ask nicely." And she grinned some perfect teeth at me.

It was on my mind to refuse. But I decided that would be silly. "Sure. That'd be great," I said as I slid in beside her. I snuck a look at her legs and began thinking of ways to kill the next day or so.

Sydney's usual tourist attractions were not on the list.

Tuesday 7:15 p.m.

The interior of the chauffeur-driven car was leather-lined and spacious.

"Looks like it's my job to improve your opinion of Australia. Fancy some champagne?" She opened a side panel and there some was. Nestled in its own tiny refrigerated compartment. *Why not?* I thought. Got to fill those empty hours somehow.

"What are we celebrating?" I asked as I took a glass from her.

"Does there need to be a reason?" She grinned. I grinned back. She had nice eyebrows. They matched the rest of her body.

The champagne slid down easily. It wasn't French, it was an impertinent Australian upstart that came out fighting. But it was just what I needed. Exactly what I needed.

We escaped from the airport complex and joined a heavy stream of traffic flowing towards the centre of Sydney. We passed shops and houses and warehouses. The novelty of the landscape engaged me in spite of myself. Rows of terraced houses roofed with corrugated iron. It was bright and open and low-lying. Best of all, it was urban. The grass was scraggy and brown in places. Some of the trees looked like they'd won a terrible battle at great expense.

"It's not all like this," said Michelle. "The North Shore, where I live, is a bit more civilised. We'll take the bridge rather than the tunnel—it'll give you a better view." She tapped on the glass and told the driver about the change of plan.

I drank and watched the view go by. Michelle pointed out places of interest. The foreign-sounding names could get no purchase and slid right out of mind as soon as Michelle had spoken them. She chattered about the city as we peeled off beside a clutch of skyscrapers that looked like downtown. A very nice park with a couple of colonial buildings perched on it. Then we were on an elevated highway, skirting skyscrapers with the Sydney Harbour Bridge almost dead ahead.

The impressive scale of the thing, along with the wine, melted my resolve to hate Sydney. It wasn't such a bad place. My son would soon be with me and it'd be an even better place. And in the meantime there was Michelle.

"Don't worry about your son," Michelle said as though she'd read the subtitles on my thoughts. "He'll be here before you know it."

I stared out at the span of the bloody great bridge. We were crossing it now, racing lanes of other cars going in the same direction. From this angle it appeared as if we were trapped in a giant metal cage.

We finished with the bridge. The driver made a left turn and wound through some quiet streets. We were in a classy harbour-front suburb, tucked right under the bridge. Looking back at the Opera House, spread out like the crest of a cockatoo.

"Are there any cheap hotels around here?" I was thinking of my meager holiday budget.

"I'm taking you home with me," said Michelle. "No arguments."

"I really should find a hotel," I said.

Michelle had unlocked a tall gate and we were walking up a path to a wooden bungalow. The driver followed behind with

Michelle's bag. The front door had a stained-glass panel, an art nouveau design etched into it. Michelle fitted a key into the lock. I followed her inside. The driver put the bag down.

"Thanks, Chook," she said, stuffing a note into his hand. "See you tomorrow. First thing."

The driver nodded and tipped a finger to his cap in an ironic salute.

"Cheeky bugger," she said as Chook lumbered down the path, "my staff have no respect."

She guided me down a hallway into the living room. It smelled of polish and frangipani.

"Now," Michelle said. "What about you then? I think you could do with a shower."

"I really must go."

"No you mustn't. You're staying right here. I've got acres of space."

"I should find a hotel."

Michelle ignored me. "You've had a bad start. Let me show you it's not such a bad place. Us Aussies are warm and loving people." She grinned and lifted her eyebrows. Her very fine eyebrows. I shrugged, grinned back, gave in. Michelle laughed her lovely, spontaneous laugh. She really was a good-looking woman and her place, all bare boards and cool colours, was a stunner. I could get comfortable here. A primitive stone figure grinned at me from a side table. I patted its oversized head.

"Why not?" I said.

"Great," she said. "You won't be sorry."

Tuesday 8:23 p.m.

Later, I lay on a recliner on the balcony listening to the sounds of life on the harbour. My clothes were getting the once-over in the washer-drier, Michelle was in the shower and all I had to concentrate on was my gin and tonic and a cigarette.

Michelle's place had a wrap-around porch and a lushly vegetated yard. If you peered hard enough through the trees, you could get a glimpse of the water.

All I had on was one of Michelle's bathrobes, but it was so warm that I didn't need more. I wriggled my toes, sipped my drink and conceded that the situation might be salvageable after all. Simon could be back by tomorrow and in the meantime Michelle seemed determined to distract me.

Sleep grabbed me before I had a chance to protest. One minute I was lying there, then the picture began to get fuzzy, my body started to feel light. I thought I heard voices and then I was sunk in the dreams of tropical paradise.

When I returned to the living room, Michelle was putting on earrings and looking behind the couch for her shoes. The phone rang. She answered it and rolled her eyes at me. I went back to my room and dressed in my clean clothes. I didn't want to eavesdrop but Michelle's voice carried.

"Hi, Vince," she said. "Yes I'm back, darling. Did you miss me after only five days away?" This in a tone unmistakable for its sarcasm. The voice on the other end spoke. Michelle tapped her foot.

"I'm not doing anything," she said. "Going out for dinner with a friend. Nobody you know. What does it matter who it is? I can go out with anybody I like. We're practically divorced, remember?"

"I thought we agreed that I'd call you about my trip tomorrow. Yes, I got everything done. Everything's okay, Vince. It's all set. I took care of it. I'm not completely incompetent, you know. We worked together before, remember? Didn't I do a good job then? Or did you just employ me for my looks?"

The voice spoke some more.

"I don't know when," Michelle said. "I'm not ready. Jesus, I only just got back. Okay, we'll talk tomorrow. I'll ring you."

Michelle came out on the verandah with a sassy smile.

"Sorry for all the yakking. I'm getting a divorce." She slipped a diary into her bag. "And let me tell you it's hard work. But I'm not going to bore you with my problems, I promise. Shall we go?"

We walked down a well-trodden path through the bush to the harbour's edge and neatly connected with a quaint green and yellow ferry. Birds sang and I could smell salt and eucalyptus in my nostrils. The ferry arrived promptly at the time specified on the schedule, a novel experience for me. I helped Michelle over the gangplank as her shoes didn't seem sturdy enough to keep her upright. Her grip was cool and firm.

We sat outside for the gentle journey across the harbour. The sun had gone down but there was no hint of chill in the air. I loosened my tie and looked at the Sydney skyline picked out in lights. As a commute it didn't have the gritty urban texture of, say, the Number 23 bus to Wormwood Scrubs, West London. But I was on holiday. There was no need to be picky.

We passed a small island, a rock, really, with a fort on it. A line of washing hung jauntily above it. We passed other, larger ferries. People on yachts. People on harbour cruises. Drinking, dancing, peering over the edge at the view. The whole city was having fun. I started to feel looser, relaxed almost. No reason why I shouldn't join the fun. No reason at all.

"I've lived here for years, but I've never got over that view," Michelle said, pointing at the distinctive outline of the city. She sat disconcertingly close to me. I could feel the warmth of her thigh against mine. "It's quite something."

"Quite something," I agreed. But we weren't talking about the same something.

A party boat crossed our bow, blasting disco music in its wake. People were hanging over the side. A few minutes later the ferry terminal loomed. A thirties-style building that said "Circular Quay."

Michelle led the charge of passengers off the ferry and grabbed a taxi and told the driver to take us to a place called Darlinghurst. It was a short journey which I think took us near to where we'd driven earlier on the way in, but I didn't even attempt to get my bearings. My body was up and about but my brain was still dozing on the water. I hadn't slept properly for two days.

We drew up outside a small warehouse, painted grey. Inside was a post-modern Italian restaurant with groovily dressed patrons and staff.

"I'm not dressed for this," I hissed to Michelle as the Yamamoto-clad manager led us to our table. My jeans and workshirt made a particularly fetching contrast to Michelle's red party dress.

"Don't worry," she laughed. "This is Australia. Nobody's going to throw you out because you aren't dressed right."

She was right. No one took the slightest bit of notice of the fact that I hadn't caught the latest style bulletin. After I'd stolen a few glances around the room to confirm that people weren't tittering at me behind their hands, I relaxed some.

Michelle was in full-on relax mode. She ordered champagne and the waiter brought small crustaceans which he called yabbies.

"This is my home away from home," Michelle explained.

"I hate cooking, so I come here a lot. It's good like that, they don't care if you're a woman on your own."

The alcohol had begun nuzzling at my insides. So I asked her why she was on her own.

"Usual tragic story," she said. "I'm re-entering the dating market after five years of marriage."

"That's too bad," I said, not really meaning it. Thinking about the short-term opportunities it opened up.

Michelle shrugged. "I'm through with the bitter part. You can't live with that all your life, you'd go crazy," she grinned. "Now all I want is revenge. Fiscally speaking, of course."

"That was your husband on the phone just now?"

Michelle nodded. "He likes to keep in touch. I think he figures I'm up to something. Because he's always up to something he assumes everybody else is as well."

"Maybe he wants to get back together."

Michelle nearly choked on her wine. "Those days are gone. He has a twenty-three-year-old girlfriend to keep him warm. *She* doesn't answer back. Yet."

She poured more wine into both our glasses. "Learning by experience is vastly overrated, wouldn't you say? The old cells don't stand still. Everything's deteriorating and all you have to console yourself with is that you've got smarter as your body edges over the hill."

"You're not over the hill."

"Vince thought so," she said gaily. "He traded me in, the bastard. Tiffany the Trollop is a younger version of me. Bigger tits, smaller brain."

"The man has no taste or judgment," I said, meaning it.

"Oh, he has judgment," she said, grinning. "It's just not connected to his head. Far as women go, anyway. Still," she said as she finished off the yabbies by licking her fingers, "I am finally free of him. Time to start again. It's not too late."

"Indeed not," I said, hoping that her resolution would extend, in the first instance, to me.

The meal was superb and expensive. I decided to cut out a few decisions by having whatever Michelle ordered, so we ate seafood linguine with a peachy chardonnay and I followed it up with a chocolate desert so rich that it contravened every healthy diet law ever written. After we'd sunk a couple of cappuccinos Michelle called for the bill. She paid with barely a glance at the numbers on the bottom line. She left a tip so generous that the waiter put his hand to his heart.

She refused any contribution from me. "It's my celebration, remember?" she said and we stumbled out of the restaurant with about five serving staff urging a speedy return. My head was buzzing from the booze and the rich food. I realised too late that it wasn't mixing that well with the jet-lag. In fact, I felt certain that a physiological fight was about to break out. It crossed my mind that I could prevent this by lying down on the pavement to give my body some rest. A voice inside me urged that I shut down all systems before I did something really silly. I wanted to obey the voice, I truly did. But Michelle had another plan.

"What we need is a night-club," she said. "I feel like dancing."

Ten minutes later we were at The Dancing Queen night-club and cabaret. It was on Oxford Street. I remember that because London also has an Oxford Street, although it varies in tone from its Sydney namesake. In London, Oxford Street is low-rent chain stores and tatty tourist shops. In Sydney, at least the part I was standing in, it was gay central. Gay bars, gay shops, gay restaurants and The Dancing Queen.

"Is this wise?" I said to Michelle as she strode confidently past the bouncer who was dressed, eye catchingly, in full pirate rig-out with the exception of a studded dog collar around his neck.

"It's okay. They know me," she said, pulling me inside, up narrow carpeted steps. The bouncer didn't give us any trouble. He probably thought we were in fancy dress too.

The club's patrons spilled out the doors and down the steps, which gave me some taste of what to expect. As it's name suggested, The Dancing Queen was high drag. Wolf-whistles followed us into the club.

They were dancing to some disco relic excavated from the seventies. Donna Summer, the Bee Gees, something like that. On stage an ironic three-piece girl band mimed the words to dead microphones. They wore white spandex flares trimmed with artificial feathers, matching white wigs and blue glitter eye shadow. The pants were slit to the thigh. A dancing fire hazard.

"Wish I had legs like that," Michelle yelled to me as we threaded through the dancers. "Five days a week at the gym and I still look like the Michelin Man."

That was a lie, of course. Michelle's legs were one of her better assets, as far as I could tell. They were long and well-turned and would have looked great even if they hadn't been set off by all that bank-breaking clobber she was wearing. Her red dress clung to her like a professionally wrapped elastic bandage. She'd covered the real bandage on her wrist with gloves.

A waiter dressed like a French maid took our drinks order and tottered off on platform soles. I sank gratefully into the chair, wondering if Michelle would be offended if I fell face first into the ashtray. *Sleep,* my body was urging me. *Sleep, you stupid bastard. If you don't there will be great pain and darkness will fall across the land and mothers will mourn for their sons.*

Later, I told the voice. I've got the rest of the year to sleep.

The French maid brought our drinks and the band finished its set. One of the singers came to our table.

"Hello, darling," said the white-clad one, keeping one hand on his wig as he stooped to kiss Michelle. "Haven't seen you for a while."

"I've had a lot on my plate," Michelle said. She turned to me. "Harry, this is Sam. Sam's on holiday from London. I'm showing him a good time."

"I hope you can keep up the pace," said Harry, shaking my hand. "She's a wild party animal. Let me get a beer and I'll join you."

"Jesus, what a night," said Harry when he returned. He'd taken the wig off and his hair was covered by a stocking cap. The stage make-up gave his face a cartoonish quality. It was hard to make out his features underneath. "Gracie threw a tantrum in the dressing room. Refused to go on at the last minute. She said the dry cleaner had made a mess of her satin blouse. We told her that it looked okay, but she said it'd shrunk. Made her look fat. Fat! Where does she get the idea? She might as well give up her apartment and go and live at the gym, it's where she spends all her time. Complaining and lifting weights. Her two hobbies.'' He shook his head. ''Anyway, do tell. How was your trip? You're never here any more. I feel like I haven't seen you for ages.''

Michelle shrugged. ''Divorce is hard work. You know Vince, he doesn't give an inch. Everything has to be done the hard way.''

''You know . . . you know . . .'' Harry had hunched himself over and stuck a cigarette between the first knuckle of the first two fingers of his left hand. His accent became rough, his eyes narrowed to slits. ''You know nothing ever came easy to *me*, Michelle. I had to work for everything. Born in a tin shed, I was, on Christmas Day. Born under a lucky star . . . in a shed . . . on Christmas Day!''

''Is that why you think you're Jesus Christ?'' Michelle said, adopting the manner of a journalist and using her glass as a make-believe microphone.

''Michelle, honey . . . now Michelle . . . that's just not fair. I'm a battler, that's all I am. Nothing special. Anybody could do what I did. With a little guts, a little good-old Aussie get up and go. A little bit of nous. A bit of fire in the belly. Anybody could do what Vince O'Donnell has done.''

Harry had achieved the impression of looking modest and smug at the same time and Michelle was laughing so hard she had tears in her eyes. ''You could go on stage with that.''

Harry dropped the act immediately. Sat up straight, put a hand to his heart, his eyes wide open. ''Stage? Stage? Now why didn't I think of that? Thank you, darling,'' he reached over and planted a kiss on Michelle's cheek. It left a smudgy make-up stain. ''Thank you! You've given my life new purpose. Why, hark! There's a stage right here! What say we put on a show?'' He flounced off.

''We've known each other since we were ten,'' Michelle said as if this explained everything.

After a bit Harry came out and did a solo turn—a respectable version of Eartha Kitt's ''I Need a Man.''

Michelle and I drank a little more and then she decided we should dance. It was as good an excuse as any for me to get my hands on her body, so I took it.

It was past one when Michelle started to flag. But still she seemed reluctant to pack it in.

"Let's get you home."

"Don't wanna go home," she said. "I'm living for the moment. That's my new motto. Live for the moment."

"Come on," I said, sliding a hand under her arm. "It's late. Even the moment's turned in."

I helped her down the stairs without thinking that I might need some help myself. Somehow we kept each other upright. The pirate bouncer was still on the door when we left. He'd been joined by someone wearing a Tutu and Doc Martens. It was a warm night. He probably didn't need any more clothes than that.

A taxi whisked us back over the bridge to the North Shore. The bridge was lit from underneath and the city tossed out the kind of spectacular urban-natural phenomenon juxtaposition that I don't get to see on an average day in London. It's true we have the River Thames, which was once probably dignified and majestic. But in rigorous British fashion, we've taken it down a peg or two. Emasculated it as a working water highway, ignored it, turned our backs. Sydney took its many natural advantages and chucked them in your face. *Look at me!* It said. *Aren't I fantastic? Don't you just love me to bits?*

Looking at the lights on the water and the glitter stars tacked on to a black sky, it was a convincing argument.

I helped Michelle out of the taxi. She paid the driver and gave him a tip big enough for him to take his entire family on holiday. We unlocked the front gate and made our slow way down the path and up her front steps. It was quiet. I could hear the hum of the harbour and the trill of night insects. The other houses around us were in darkness.

"You're a good sort, Sam Ridley," Michelle said. She was putting one foot in front of the other in a studious manner. "And I'm not just saying that because I'm rat-arsed drunk."

By this stage we had our arms around each other for ballast. Also because it felt good. She was skinny but she had nice breasts. I tried to pretend I couldn't feel them underneath her jacket.

"Doesn't matter," I said. "I'm the same when you're sober."

"I bet you are." Michelle fumbled in her bag for her keys. It was a small leather bag on a long strap. She had trouble pinning it down. I kept holding on to her, just in case. "But it's like that with some people. Not like my husband. I never knew him at all. Living with a stranger. That's what I realised. Bloody ages his affair had been going on and I had no bloody idea. I trusted him, can you believe that? Talk about a drongo."

"Marriage makes fools of us all," I said, swaying a bit as she put the key in the front door. I put both arms round her. It seemed safer that way. She wrestled with the door a bit until it flew open abruptly, nearly depositing us on the floor. We reached out for each other. An embrace is what I suppose you would call it.

"We shouldn't really be doing this," she murmured after we'd decided that we were more than comfortable this close together. I didn't answer. My full attention was concentrated on the smooth line of her neck, the smell of her perfume. I nuzzled like a newborn lamb.

The reptilian part of my brain had taken charge. Suddenly I was as sprightly as a sixteen-year-old. Ready for anything. I should have been sleeping. I should have been preparing for my son's arrival. I should have been tucked up in my solitary bed in a cheap but respectable hotel dreaming happy, family-values dreams. But I was doing none of those things.

Michelle took my hand, slipped off her shoes and guided me towards the living room. Once there I reached out for her again but she stepped back. It wasn't too late to back out.

"Nightcap?" she said. There was a good bottle of whisky sitting on the kitchen bench. I said yes. I went to the French doors, opened them up and breathed in the smell of the water. Forced myself to think about something other than sex.

She came up behind me, I could hear the clink of glass against ice. I kept facing forward. She stood behind me, put one hand holding my glass around my chest and kissed the back of my neck.

I took the glass so she could concentrate. Her hand reached round and started on the buttons of my shirt.

I wanted her very badly. I needed somebody to hold on to. I needed somebody to make up for the disappointment I felt at having travelled all this way only to find myself as alone as when I'd left London. I wanted to tell Michelle this, because I knew she would understand. But she was too busy, taking off my clothes. Taking off her clothes, guiding me down, promising me sweet, sweet things.

I decided I would tell her later.

Afterwards I lay on the couch, not finding sleep. It was afternoon London time, that probably had something to do with it. The ice in the whisky glass had melted, but I decided there was no sense in letting it go to waste. I finished it off while I watched Michelle doze, her breathing light. There was a throw rug on the back of the couch and I put it over her. She murmured something about getting into her bed. I walked around the house, glass in hand. Enjoying the feeling of the bare boards on my feet. I finished off the whisky.

The funny thing about getting drunk is that one moment you're utterly in control of your senses and able to debate things like the opt-out clauses in the Maastricht Treaty and the next minute you're wishing the room would stop spinning.

I suddenly felt very ill and much in need of the bathroom. My brain felt as though it had been shredded with a grater. I staggered down the hallway towards the bathroom accompanied by a loud buzzing in my ears.

I looked at my face in the mirror. Took in the rough shave, the bloodshot, unfocused eyes. I looked like a mess. But then I'd been awake since the beginning of time. I searched the bathroom cabinet for some painkillers. There were none. Lots of vitamins but nothing to help someone in my state.

Then the buzzing got louder. All I could think of was lying down. I sat on the toilet. It wasn't enough.

Without a thought for how it would look, I collapsed on the floor.

Wednesday 8:25 a.m.

I had woken up in a strange apartment with a dead body in the master bedroom. The right thing to do was to contact the police. Show them the body and let them get on with it. Who knew? Maybe they'd believe my pathetic story and let me go after a few questions.

Yeah right. As I mentally rehearsed my interview with the investigating officer I realised how flimsy my story was. No cop would buy it for a minute. Going over it all in my head, I wasn't even sure if I did.

I rehearsed the correct steps once more. Call the cops. Tell them your story. Let them get on with the job.

The doorbell rang. A loud, intrusive sound that clanged through the whole house. I sat dead still. My heart got up and did a hundred-metre dash.

The bell faded to silence. I waited. It rang again. It was followed by brisk knocking.

"Michelle? You there? It's Chook."

I remembered Michelle had arranged with the limo driver to take her to the gym. And here he was. About to catch me red-handed.

"Michelle? Come on, mate."

The knocking stopped. He was coming round the back of

the house, I could feel it. I couldn't move. I couldn't think.
Any minute now he was going to come in and find me. And
find her. Then the police would come and take me away.
They'd hang a number around my neck and take my photo
from lots of unflattering angles. And I would be branded. Rapist. Killer. Scum.

Without thinking about the consequences of what I was doing, I slowly put on my shoes. Picked up my bag. Slipped
down the corridor till I thought I heard Chook round the back.
Made for the front door. Slipped out of that house.

It was bright and hot outside. The sunlight smacked me in
the eyes. I fumbled for my dark glasses. Put them on and
immediately felt safer.

It was a false feeling.

He launched at me at waist level. A flying tackle that hinted
at many years in the back row of an enthusiastic rugby team.

I was face down on the ground with the wind knocked out
of me. My bag went flying. My arm was twisted under me at
an odd angle. The thing was trying to grab my other arm. I
could tell right away that I was in great pain.

"What have you done to her?" he said in my ear. He was
very close behind me.

I jerked my head back. My hard skull hit the soft cartilage
in his nose.

He rolled off me and squealed in pain. A surprisingly high-
pitched sound for such a big man. But I didn't stick around
to analyse his discomfort. I was on my feet, grabbed the bag
and was out of there.

I didn't fancy a sprint through the streets of those sleepy,
affluent suburbs in full view of sleepy, affluent suburbanites.
The path which led down to the ferry was my only choice. It
had shelter. It had paths that forked. Michelle had pointed out
to me the previous night that if you took the left-hand fork it
led to rather an interesting nature path. Much of Sydney harbour was surrounded by Crown land, she had told me, meaning that it belonged to the government. I ran like a hare down
that path, thanking the government for giving me such a con-
venient means of escape. I didn't know where that escape was
leading me, but that was for worrying about later.

The path traversed a steep hill which jutted out into the
harbour. It was rough in places, I should have adjusted my
speed accordingly, but with Godzilla on my tail I figured flirting with a sprained ankle was the least of my problems. I
practically fell down some steps, across a bridge over a steep
gorge. Chook had lost some ground, but he hadn't given up,
of course he hadn't. I couldn't see him, but I knew he was
there, he ran with heavy feet.

My breath came in short gasps, my lungs had not yet recovered from having the air knocked out of them. My lungs
hurt. My hangover hurt. And a sharp pain niggled under my
rib-cage. I ignored it, knowing it would be nothing compared
to the sharp pain I would feel if Chook caught up with me
again. I tucked my bag under one arm, pressing it tight into
the source of the stitch.

After about a hundred yards, there was a fork in the path.
Straight ahead was concrete. Left was well-trodden dirt. I took
left. The path was hemmed by large boulders. Much higher
up, houses perched. The path became tarmac again, and I
could see the harbour on the right. Here the land became flat-
ter, the trees more spaced out. I picked up speed, which
seemed advisable because Chook was gaining now. He was
pretty quick for such a big chap. No doubt the rugby had
something to do with that as well.

I chanced a look back. He was a mere ten feet behind me.
There were buildings around us now. A yacht club and a ma-
rina and, further around the bite-sized bay, a ferry terminal.
People sat on benches in the sun.

I noticed a path leading up the other side of the valley. It
seemed the only way to go, so I took it. My lungs felt flayed,
but I ran hard. No time to be worrying about inconsequentials
like lack of fitness.

Up ahead I faced another choice. The sealed path went to
the right, a dirt track to the left. I snuck a look back, Chook
wasn't doing so well on the hill. There was blood streaming
from his nose and people were staring. He'd pressed a handkerchief to his face to stem the blood, but it had held him up.
He came to a sharp bend below a rocky outcrop. It put me
out of sight for a brief time. I plunged off the track. Ran a

few yards, ducked in behind a bush. And waited.

It worked. He didn't look to the right or left. He plodded on up the hill. I waited some more. After a few minutes he came back. Met a woman coming up the hill. Asked her if she'd seen me. She said no. He retraced his steps.

I sat behind the bush for some time although I knew the area would be knee deep in cops at any moment. It was too hot and my head hurt too much for me to think clearly. Instead all I felt was surging waves of lethargy. I didn't want to deal with this. I would stay behind this bush until the problem went away. Then I would come out and resume my life as a normal, law-abiding citizen.

Some time passed. Could have been two minutes, could have been three hours. Or maybe it was just the time it took me to realise there wasn't much mileage in the fantasy that the god who rights injustices would blast into town and set everything straight on my behalf.

I rummaged in my bag. I'd bought a joke hat for Simon in London. A baseball cap with antlers. I ripped the antlers off. I put the cap on, pulling it down low over my eyes. Readjusted my glasses. It was the sort of look that would make mothers sweep their children away from my oncoming path. But it would have to do.

I rounded up my valuables—travellers' cheques, credit cards. Realised they probably weren't much good to me now. All I had was the cash that I'd brought with me from London. I fished in the bag for my passport. It wasn't there. I took everything out of the bag and shook it upside down. Nothing fell out. I went through everything more carefully. Still nothing.

"Shit," I said, out loud. "Shit, shit, shit." I knew I hadn't taken it out of my bag since leaving the airport. I'd left the bag at Michelle's place while we went out last night. The passport couldn't have fallen out while I was escaping because it was zipped in a side pocket. I remembered doing that.

As I filtered those options through the alcohol-sodden sponge that was my brain, a third, less pleasing notion came to mind.

If the passport wasn't in my bag, then who had taken it? And what did they intend to do with it?

Wednesday 9:17 a.m.

The bastards were laughing at me, that was the problem. I strode along the track to the ferry terminal in the next bay and I could hear them. Chortling, guffawing. At first I thought it was the gods, having a jolly good yuk at my expense, because they like to do that. I know they're not always on my side. I know they get titillation from my discomfort. Then I realised the sound was a kookaburra. A bloody laughing bird. It didn't put me in any better frame of mind. It seemed to be a symbol of something. My churned-up brain couldn't think what.

Still, at least the lethargy was gone now. Replaced by an overpowering urge to break someone's skull. All I had to do was find out who that someone was.

I pulled my hat down over my eyes and walked harder.

There were no cops at the ferry terminal. I was taking a risk showing up there. But hell, life was risky, I thought as I brazenly handed over the money for the fare. The ticket operator didn't even look up.

I sat at the stern of the ferry, staring out the way we had come and avoiding the eyes of the other passengers.

Circular Quay thronged with morning commuters. They charged down the gangplanks and out to waiting buses, taxis,

and trains. There was a single cop, strolling the promenade
that linked the ferry terminal with the Opera House. I melded
into the purposeful crowd. We strode as one along the quay
and through the ticket gates, past the fast-food stands and
buskers and out underneath an overpass.

There was a taxi outside and without thinking, I grabbed it.
Anything to get out of the radius of the cop.

"Where you go?" the driver asked.

My brain raced, but someone had lifted the back wheels off
the ground. There was no purchase.

"Where you go?"

"Oxford Street." I said the first thing that came into my
head.

"Where on Oxford Street?"

"The bottom."

"Okay then," he said starting the engine, jerking the car
into gear. "Where you from?" he asked as, without looking,
he spun the car out into thick traffic. Horns tooted, breaks
squealed. "You tourist, or what?"

"Just a tourist," I said grimly, wrestling with the seatbelt
that had suddenly assumed much greater significance.

"I live here now," he said, angling the mirror so he could
look at my face. *Terrific*, I thought. *Memorising my face for
the line-up parade.*

"I am new Australian," he went on, changing lanes without
indicating. "Born in Croatia, but I live here now three years."

"Lovely," I said as, to my immense relief, I got the belt
fitted. "Just got our driver's licence though, did we?"

"Driving is my life," he said, nodding solemnly, slamming
on the brakes to avoid colliding with a truck that had stopped
at the lights. "I am proud to be driver in Australia."

"Your driving could well be my life too," I mumbled. We
were circling round a park now. It felt like not every wheel
was in contact with the road. I gripped the door handle. It
came loose in my hand.

"That's Hyde Park," said the cabbie. "You know, like England."

"Lovely," I said again, not really concentrating on the bo-
tanical splendour.

"You like Australia?" he demanded, dropping a couple of gears and sliding in front of a Honda Civic.

"Yes."

"What about that bridge? You like our bridge?"

"It's a very nice bridge, indeed. I'd like it even more if you would slow down."

"And the Opera House? You like our Opera House?"

"Wonderful. A masterpiece," I said as the driver overtook the bus on a blind corner. Wheels squealed, more horns tooted. The driver seemed oblivious to every vehicle on the road.

"That's good. We have many fine buildings in Sydney. Fine buildings. Fine parks. And the beaches, pouf!" he said, swerving slightly as if to emphasise the magnificence of it all.

I closed my eyes. I was going to die, but that would probably be a good thing. Death would be more comfortable than prison.

"I bring you here then," said the cabbie, depositing me near The Dancing Queen with a flashy but illegal U-turn. I couldn't be sure, but I thought I could smell burning rubber.

"I've had many, many hangovers in my life," I said, handing over the fare, "but this is the first one that has been frightened away."

"You're gonna like Australia," said the driver. "It's the Lucky Country. That's what they call it." He blasted off in a cloud of blue smoke.

The Lucky Country? I thought. *Hey, it's working for me.*

It was dumb, I realised as I stood there on the busy thoroughfare, to come back to the place I'd been last night with Michelle. It was the first place the cops were going to look.

To cunningly outwit the forces of law and order I crossed the road, took a side street and walked until I found a small coffee shop.

Feeling irrationally safe behind my dark glasses, I ordered a double espresso and a croissant and sat in the window on a shaky plastic stool. The place was tiny and packed. Like any Italian coffee shop worthy of its name, it was decorated with boxing memorabilia. People in business suits rushed in, ordered coffees and rushed out. Others, more casually attired, sat hunched over papers and cigarettes. Several people sat out-side on the narrow pavement. I watched it all. I couldn't have felt more foreign if I'd just landed from Mars sporting shiny green skin and eyes that bobbed on stalks.

"Mind if I share?"

A young man with wild hair pulled at the stool next to mine and sat down. He stirred his coffee while he dialled his mobile phone and arranged to meet someone later in the day. Sud-denly I realised how badly I needed a shoulder to cry on. There was a phone booth outside. It wasn't too late to call one of my colleagues in London.

"Hello, Sarah Williams speaking."

"Sarah, honey it's Sam. May I have a word with your fa-ther?"

"Dad! Phone!" Sarah yelled, forgetting to take the receiver away from her mouth. My headache came sliding back. In the background I could hear a loud thudding sound which Lyall's kids prefer to listen to instead of music. There was more yell-ing before the stereo was turned down. My friend Lyall was relaxing in the bosom of his family.

"Sam?" It's hard to get Lyall worked up over anything, but even he sounded faintly surprised to hear from me.

"Hey. How's it going?"

"The usual. Wars and rumours of wars. Sydney okay?"

"Not so great," I said. "Got off to a bit of a bad start. Can you call me back? I haven't got much money." I gave him the number. In a matter of seconds the phone rang.

I told him everything. Lyall listened without interruption. It's one of his special skills.

"Jesus Christ," he said when I'd finished. "How do you manage it?"

"Events conspired against me." I could feel a whine creep-ing into my voice.

"Sam. Listen to me. You're in serious shit. You must go to the police. This is not a multi-choice situation."

"I can't go now I've done a runner. Besides I was setup."

"Who, Sam? Who set you up? The only person you know in Sydney is now dead. She's not doing any arranging."

"I don't know," I mumbled. "It feels strange."

"Of course it feels bloody strange." Lyall was speaking slowly now. I've heard him use the same tone with his teenagers. "When was the last time you woke up in a house with a dead woman? For God's sake, Sam. Get a grip."

"Where's my passport then? Someone took my passport. They've planted it in the apartment. I know it. And my fingerprints are on the murder weapon. I touched this little stone statue last night."

Lyall sighed. "Your fingerprints are all over the apartment, Sam. And you misplaced your passport. It happens to thousands of tourists every day. It's the very least of your worries."

I was silent. Lyall was right. Lyall was always right.

"You may be right," I said after expensive transcontinental phone moments had passed.

"I *am* right," Lyall said firmly. "I'm seldom, if ever, wrong. And you haven't taken in a word I've said."

He was right about that too.

"Sam. Listen to me. No. Listen to what you're saying. So someone set you up. Whom might that someone be?"

"I don't know . . . the husband?"

"There's no husband alive that can manipulate his wife into picking up a stranger at the airport . . . How would he have done that, do you suppose? A remote-control chip in her brain?"

"He knew I was there though because he called her. Maybe he killed her in a jealous rage and set me up as part of it."

"Didn't you mention that he already had a girlfriend?"

"Yeah . . . but . . ."

"Jesus Christ, Sam. Look—" Lyall stopped. Swore again. Gave up the fight. "I know a guy. Aussie guy. He stayed with us once, couple a years back. Said to look him up if I was ever down that way. Hang on and I'll find his number."

"Right," he said when he got back to the phone. "His name is Oswald Booker. But he answers to Ozzie—don't they all?" He gave me the number and an address and I wrote it on my coffee shop paper napkin. "He might be able to talk some sense into you."

"Thanks."

"You're a stupid shit, Ridley."

"Yeah, I've heard it said."

"You heard it right. Keep your head down. And call me. Anytime. Even from jail."

"I will."

I put the phone down. Dialled the number Lyall had given me. An answer machine was taking calls.

"Yeah, gidday," said a deep, slow voice. "Ozzie here. But not here, if you get my drift. You're talking to a machine. So tell it what you want me to know and I'll get back to you."

I debated leaving a message, decided against it and hung up the phone. Stayed in the booth for a few minutes more resting my head against the phone. Hoped that the whole horrific scenario would vanish.

A cop walked by. Saw me coming out of the phone booth.

"You alright mate?" he asked. I jumped.

"Yes. Felt a bit dizzy," I lied. "It's the heat."

"Take it easy," he said. He was very young, pink skinned, concerned. "I'd buy a hat."

"Thanks. I have one."

I walked quickly away, pulling the hat out of my back pocket and jamming it back on. I Looked about as innocent as a cat in a roomful of feathers.

I walked up Oxford Street, sweating a rich, fearful sweat. Lyall was right. I should go to the cops right away. Explain everything. Beginning to end. *But* said another voice, *when a beautiful rich woman is murdered, they want to get the scum who did it right away. They won't be straining any muscles trying to find alternative offenders.* I knew my passport was in Michelle's flat somewhere. I could feel it in this tricky place in my gut that only ever speaks the truth. My passport, my fingerprints on the murder weapon. My vital fluids. I'd had sex with her, for God's sake.

It was a case that said "open and shut." It was a case that said "Sam Ridley is guilty." And I didn't want any part of it.

I turned and walked back down the way I had come.

Wednesday 10:03 a.m.

The Dancing Queen had the seedy air of any establishment that's not used to day-time scrutiny. As I plodded up the stairs I noticed that the carpet was frayed and the paint faded. It smelled of a pungent cocktail of cigarettes, booze and sweat.

The door was open, so I went right in. The room was dark. The windows had been painted over. The chairs were up on tables and the place was deserted except for a middle-aged man sweeping the floor.

"Hello," I said. "I'm looking for someone called Harry. He works at the club. He's a singer."

The sweeper did not respond. He went on switching his broom back and forth. It was probably not my place to judge, but he didn't seem to be making much of an effort.

"Excuse me," I said, a little louder this time. "Can you help me find this person Harry?"

The place was silent except for the swishing of the broom. I'd given up hope of a reply when he finally spoke.

"You see anyone here?" he growled. "See anyone 'cept us?"

"No."

"Well, he isn't here then," he said, and went back to the sweeping.

Normally, I'm a placid sort of fellow. But I just wasn't in the mood to be jerked around. I put my foot on the broom. Looked the geezer in the eye. Grabbed the broom handle.

"Go on then," I said. "Give me a clue."

He stared at me sullenly. I stared right back. I felt like a prat wearing my sunglasses indoors. But I tried not to let it show.

"Annabelle's Café," he said, "round the corner. First left. First right."

"Thank you so much," I lifted my foot from the broom head. "See how much easier it is when you make an effort to be nice."

Annabelle's looked like the waiting room for a Village People audition. It may have been early in the day, but nobody had stepped out of the house without making that extra effort. My simple, sporty look stood in stark contrast to the bushy moustaches, studded braces and general air of fantasy dressing that appeared to be the norm amongst the clientele. I found a spare table.

"Help you?" the singsong voice belonged to a waiter who wore a mini-apron over brief cutoffs and a muscle tee-shirt.

"Coffee, please," I said automatically.

"Right with you," he said, spun on his heel and wiggled away. The coffee was back a full forty seconds later.

"I'm looking for Harry," I said to the kid. "He works at The Dancing Queen. You know where I might find him?"

"Sorry," he said in the same tone of voice he'd taken my order in. "But I've just started. I'll ask Gordon, the manager."

Gordon, a husky-looking guy, dressed, I was thankful to note, like me in denim, didn't know much more.

"Saw him in here yesterday," he said. "They usually come in in the mornings, after the club shuts. Not today though."

The coffee had fired a few brain cells. They were putputting along like an old banger, but at least they were in motion. A name emerged from the haze that had been the previous evening.

"What about Gracie?" I asked. "His singing partner."

"Gracie's easy," Gordon said. "He's always at the gym. Round the corner. Down the hill."

I followed his instructions. It was downhill all the way. But the day was heating up. I took my jacket off and stuffed it in my bag.

The gym wasn't hard to find. It had a ten-foot neon sign outside, a stylised bicep.

"Is Gracie here?" I asked the gym receptionist.

She leaned over the desk and yelled, "Norm! Seen Gracie today?"

Norm, who looked like he could probably get a job advertising anabolic steroids, had been standing near the door. He hulked his way over to the desk.

"Bloke wants to see him," the receptionist said, nodding at me.

"What for?" Norm looked suspiciously at me.

"Important family business."

"This way, scum." Norm led the way into the gym. He didn't actually use the word scum, but his manner implied it. The huge bulk of his torso looked funny from behind. His arms swung out from his sides, like they were too small for his body.

I've become familiar with the insides of gyms. Normally, I avoid exercise because I hate it, but recently I injured my shoulder so I've been communing with weight machines for a couple of months. It hasn't improved my attitude to exercise, I still hate it. I can't wait until my shoulder is better and I can get back to neglecting myself again.

Gracie was at the far end of the room, delicately squeezing his thighs together while strapped to a machine designed to keep them apart. His one-piece leotard was striped purple and green.

"Hi," I said after Norm had pointed him out to me. "I'm looking for Harry."

The thighs continued pumping. In and out. Harry was right. Whatever other problems Gracie had, fat was not one of them. With his slender limbs and waist, he could have passed for a teenage girl.

"Can't you see I'm busy?" He didn't look up. In and out the thighs went.

"If you tell me where Harry is, I'll go away."

Breathing "a hundred," under his breath, Gracie stopped. Reached down for a water bottle and took a swig. I watched his Adam's apple bob up and down. He finished slurping, wiped his mouth carefully with a purple and green striped towel and looked at me for the first time.

"I don't believe I've had the pleasure," he purred and reached out to shake my hand. "Fancy a juice?"

The gym had a juice bar at the top of several flights of stairs. It was a light and airy room, mostly glass, with a good view of the city. Gracie ordered something green and disgusting.

"So," said Gracie. "What's Harry got that I haven't?"

"Do you know Michelle O'Donnell?"

Gracie batted his lashes. He had eyes like a Bambi deer. I bet they went down a storm at the club. "A little," he said.

"I need to contact Harry to pass on a message from her," I said, which was about as true as I could be under the circumstances. "It's extremely important."

Bambi, I mean Gracie, continued to stare at me. I wondered if I would have to tell him that I wasn't the sort of guy to get serious after one wheatgrass juice.

"Harry's incommunicado today," he said finally. "He's at his day job. Can't be disturbed."

"What do you mean?"

"He's a make-up artist. Today he's doing a fashion shoot on the Hawkesbury River."

He saw my blank look. "You know, near the Barowra Waters Inn. Ever been there? It's divine. Frightfully expensive, of course, but then it is Australia's best restaurant—"

I closed my eyes. Took a deep breath. I was about to go down for murder and this guy was talking restaurants. Perhaps this really wasn't happening to me after all.

But I opened my eyes and Gracie was still there.

"Gracie," I said gently. "He can't be out of reach. Surely there's someone on that boat with two-way radio or a mobile phone?"

"Well, if there is, I don't know who," said Gracie.

"Do you know the name of the boat?"

Gracie shook his head. "I'm not being much help, am I? But he'll be back tonight. We're on at the club, as always." He got up. "It can wait, can't it?"

"No. It can't."

He shrugged a shrug that said it wasn't his problem. "Must fly. My t'ai chi class starts in five minutes. Ciao." He waved and was gone.

"Ciao," I said, then I put my head in my hands.

I could have wept as I sat there at that sunny table. If I thought it would have made any difference, I would have.

"What did you say your name was?" It was Gracie, back.

"The lonesome stranger."

"Well," he said. "Call me if you want to be shown the sights. We've got it all here, you know. Every single little thing. And I'm a fabulous guide. You know where to find me." He sashayed off, waving a hand above his head.

Wednesday 10:57 a.m.

Oswald Booker lived in a squat terraced house in a suburb not that far from Oxford Street. I walked there following a small map I'd brought with me from London. Wide, one-way roads cut swathes through what would otherwise have been genteel residential districts. Dilapidated warehouses, tiny car-repair yards and second-hand shops combined to give the impression that the area hadn't yet found its personality. The houses had that desperate air of owners who'd bought hoping that the neighbourhood would "go up." If it was going up, it was taking its time about it.

Oswald's house made no concessions to gentility. The look said "shabby." And it said it with pride. The grass was uncut, hedges untrimmed. The paint job looked like a fond memory and even my untutored eye could tell that the overhanging roof had a list not intended by its designer. The only thing the picture really lacked was a rusting appliance on the front lawn.

I knocked smartly on the door. The reply was some time in coming.

"Yeah?" said an unkempt man, dressed only in a shirt, boxer shorts and odd socks. He squinted in the bright light.

"I'm looking for Oswald Booker."

"Yeah, mate," he said, scratching his head. He had fairish hair and it stood on end.

"Does he live here?"

"Yeah, mate."

"Can I speak to him?"

"You are," Oswald grunted. "Sorry. Not used to hearing that name. Only me grandma calls me that and she's dead."

"I'm sorry to hear that."

"No worries," he said. "She had a good innings." He opened the door and stood aside to let me in. "The receiving room's that way." He pointed down a long, dark hallway to what appeared to be the kitchen.

There was a woman dressed in a suit trying to wrest a piece of bread out of the toaster. Her hair was dyed black and she wore a white medical smock.

"This is Cheryl," said Oswald Booker. "Flatmate." Cheryl lifted one hand. It was holding a knife. I said hello.

"I'm a friend of Lyall Williams. He said you'd stayed with him in London. He said to look you up—do you think you should be doing that?" My eyes had strayed to Cheryl. She had begun digging in the toaster with the knife.

"It's stuck," she said plaintively.

"Give me that," said Oswald Booker. He took the toaster, turned it upside down and rapped it smartly on the underside. The toast fell on the floor. Oswald Booker picked it up, handed it to Cheryl.

"See, I told you a bloke about the place would come in useful."

"Thanks, Ozzie," she said, sarcastically. She took the toast, flung it neatly into the rubbish tin at the other end of the room. "Who says those years of netball were wasted," she said, brushing the toast crumbs off her hands. "Gotta go. Keep your head down, sweetie," she said and patted Oswald Booker on the head.

"I need coffee," said Oswald after she'd gone. "What did you say your name was?"

"Sam Ridley . . ."

The phone rang.

"Could you answer that?" he asked. "Tell whoever it is

that I'm not here." He'd unearthed a packet of coffee and was searching amongst the clutter on the benchtop for something to put it in. I picked up the receiver.

"Is Ozzie there?" demanded an angry voice. An older man.

"He's stepped out."

"Who is this?" The voice was so loud that Ozzie could hear it. He flinched.

"Ah . . . this is," I looked to Ozzie for clues. He was miming the toast incident. I took a stab. "I'm a friend of Cheryl's," I said.

"Can you tell Ozzie that I want to speak to him," said the caller. "It's Gavin, he knows what it's about." He hung up.

I relayed the message.

"My best mate's old man," Ozzie said. "I didn't think he'd be going into bat for his son. Like some coffee?"

"Love some," I said. It had been at least half an hour since the last infusion, I was sure my caffeine levels were getting dangerously low.

Ozzie was slopping some strong black stuff into a large chipped mug when the phone rang again. I looked at him, he nodded. I picked up the phone.

"Mr Booker's residence," I said in my best imitation of an English butler.

"Don't bullshit me, Ozzie!" the voice on the other end, young, female, was so loud I felt a piercing sensation in my inner ear. "You arsehole," she shrieked. "How could you fuck her? How could you? I'm going to make you pay for this, I swear to God. You'll be sorry you ever met that bitch. You'll be sorry you ever clapped eyes on her. You'll be sorry you were fucking born—"

"Thank you for your call," I interjected smoothly, "I'll be sure to see that Mr Booker gets your message." I hung up.

"You're a natural at this." Ozzie ran his fingers through his hair. "Jeez, I didn't think Paula would be so wound up."

I had taken maybe two sips of coffee when the phone went again. Ozzie let the answer machine pick up. A young man's voice. He was also plain mad.

"Ozzie, it's Matt. Your former best mate. I'm gonna kill you, Oz, you lying scum. And if I don't succeed in doing that,

I'm gonna make sure you never work again. You're finished in Sydney, mate, so you might as well pack your bags and leave right now. Oh, by the way, hope you enjoyed screwing my wife. Didn't realise she was such a goer, or you for that matter. Who'd have thought it, eh? Underneath that pug-ugly exterior lurks a genuine Casanova.''

Ozzie reached for the phone, changed his mind. Sat back. Took in more coffee. Got up, left the room. Came back fully dressed.

"I've come at a bad time . . ." I said.

"Nah. As good a time as any. Let's go out for breakfast. We're not going to get any peace around here." He pulled a baseball cap over his spiky, unwashed hair, stepped into jeans and a pair of boots that lay on a kitchen chair. "I'll deal with all this shit later. Right now I could do with a fry-up. Can't think without some grease in my stomach."

He drove a large silver Volvo estate with a cage separating back from front. In the back were several silver suitcases.

"Lyall told me you're a cameraman."

"Not if my former best mate has his way," he said. "My career is bloody over. Might as well move to Wollongong and do bloody flower shows."

"He'll cool off," I said. "Give him a few days to get over it."

He laughed at that. "A few days? You don't know Matt. He'll carry this to his grave."

The café was about three blocks away. We could have walked it. Ozzie parked illegally outside.

"Ciao, Mario!" he said to the proprietor, striding in with one hand raised in the American high-five salute.

"Ozzie, my friend." Mario was short and dark-haired. He wore black with a matching van dyke beard.

"Coffees all round, I think." Ozzie had the air of someone who came here often. "And a little shot of something to make it . . . interesting. Fuck it, the sun's over the yard arm somewhere in the world. And I've had a hard night. I don't care who knows it. My mate Sam here knows it. Sam, meet Mario."

Mario and I shook hands. Ozzie's nervous energy appeared

to fizzle out. He slumped into a chair, grabbing the menu with one hand and an ashtray with another. "Jeez, I'm all out of fags, can you bloody believe it?"

"Mate, I'll send someone next door. You sit here. Don't worry about a thing," said Mario soothingly. A café proprietor who had evidently just descended from heaven.

Mario brought us two coffees and two shots of whisky. Ozzie downed his in one. I did the same. It torched every tissue, but it brought an artificial calm.

"Sorry mate," Ozzie said. "You're not seeing me at my best." He rubbed a hand over his eyes, blinked fiercely as if by doing so, his troubles would all be sorted.

Mario came back with a packet of Camels. I eyed them hungrily. Ozzie offered them around and we threw ourselves into the procedure of lighters and ashtrays.

"God that's good." Ozzie sucked on his Camel like he was taking his last breath. "Want any food?"

I shook my head.

"Nah, me neither. Thought I did, but these'll hit the spot. So, Lyall said you need a hand?"

"You've spoken to him?"

Ozzie shrugged. "He rang me first thing, scummy bastard. Got me out of bed. Still it was good to hear from him. He said you'd be in touch and that you'd explain everything. And I should believe what you say because you're an honest sucker."

"He said that about me?" Perversely I was thrilled. Coming from Lyall that was high praise.

Ozzie nodded. "Yeah, touched my heart as well. So I'm listening. Explain away."

I explained. Ozzie smoked thoughtfully and didn't say a word until I'd finished.

"Lyall said you had a knack for it," he said finally. "He said I should knock some sense into you. Said it'd be hard but I should give it my best shot. So here it is, mate, I'll say this only once: Get a good lawyer then go to the cops. You're screwed. Any minute now you won't be able to move in this town. The only people not looking for you will be looking for me. Which will put me in no position to help you." Ozzie

tapped his long fingers on the cigarette packet. "Jesus Christ."
He was staring over my shoulder.

"Cops?"

"Worse, Matt and Gavin." Ozzie looked up behind me.
Grabbed his hat. "Time for us to vamoose," he said quickly.
"Mario, old mate—borrow your car?"

Mario peered out through the window, frowning. "What's
going on?"

"Explain later, mate."

A muscular blond man was climbing out of a smart car,
straightening his suit. With him was an older chap, grey-haired
but no less smartly dressed. They looked like father and son.
The two who'd called this morning.

"It's a good yarn, Mario," said Ozzie, leading the way
through the kitchen, "and it'll improve in the telling. You can
have my car, and you can't say fairer than that."

Mario rolled his eyes, but dug in his pocket for his keys.
He and Ozzie exchanged keys, slapped each other on the
shoulder.

"Nice to meet you, Sam," said Mario waving cheerfully.
"Come back in the evening. I do a great scallop linguine . . .
loads of garlic, a touch of white wine . . . just the right amount
of . . ."

"We'll discuss recipes when we get back," said Ozzie.

There was one car parked out back—a shabby orange VW
combi van. It looked as if it'd done the hippy trail and back.

"Looks like we've both got the knack for it," I said. Ozzie
crunched reverse and we were out of there. Ozzie turned on
the radio, tuned it to a talk station.

"So this woman, Michelle. You don't know anything about
her? You didn't have a little pillow talk before you shagged
her?"

"We chatted a bit. But she didn't tell me much."

Ozzie swung the van into a stream of fast-moving one-way
traffic. I had to shout to be heard over the roar of the ancient
engine. "I don't know what's going on."

"I feel the same way, mate. Events beyond my control are
propelling me." Ozzie kept checking his rear-view mirror for
the angry yuppies. "Maybe it's something in the line up of

the planets or something. What sign are you?"

I was saved from replying by a radio station news jingle. Listen up, it said. We'll tell you something you can't afford to miss. I turned up the volume.

"Michelle O'Donnell, the estranged wife of property king Vince O'Donnell has been bludgeoned to death at her home in Neutral Bay," the newsreader began. "The attack occurred in the early hours of this morning. Mrs O'Donnell had spent last night at La Carravagio restaurant in the company of an unidentified man. The man was seen leaving Mrs O'Donnell's house early this morning. Police want to speak to him in connection with last night's events.

"Vince O'Donnell, the colourful property developer has been questioned by the police. Mrs O'Donnell's driver, Charles Neil, discovered the body and chased a man from the scene. Police say they have not established a motive for the attack.

"Jesus—that's you?" Ozzie looked at me with new respect.

I nodded dumbly.

"Vince O'Donnell's wife. She's like society. You've hit the big time."

"Is that bad?" I was feeling slightly sick from a combination of Ozzie's stop-start driving technique and the news I'd just heard. Michelle was no longer something I could pretend would go away. All I had to look forward to was the prospect of it swelling like some cancerous Incredible Hulk.

"Very, very bad. Give yourself up right now."

"I can't."

"Then get the hell out of town. If you're not going to give yourself up, the only option is to run like hell."

"I don't have a passport."

"How'd you get here without one?"

"Someone took it."

"Someone took your passport?"

"It doesn't matter," I said sadly.

Ozzie shook his head slowly. "You're toast."

"I don't appreciate that analogy."

"We don't have the death penalty here, mate. But the place where they'll put you won't be much fun."

"That's why I need to get myself some leverage."

"What sort of leverage?"

"I don't know yet."

"And you want my help?"

I said nothing. I had no right to ask someone I didn't know. But I was desperate. Ozzie looked at my face. He saw that I was desperate. He sighed.

"I'm not getting involved in this. God knows I've got enough troubles of my own."

He was right. There were laws against helping people like me now. He could go to prison.

"Tell you what I'll do," Ozzie went on. "I'll drop you off somewhere. I've got to go home and pick up some gear. Then I'll take you to the New Harbour site. It's on my way."

"What's New Harbour?"

"It's your girlfriend's husband's work," Ozzie said. "He likes to build."

We returned to the restaurant where Mario had not only seen off Ozzie's friend and his dad, but parked the car at the back of the restaurant. Then we drove to Ozzie's house and he loaded some more silver cases. Then we drove north.

As we crossed the Harbour Bridge, Ozzie gestured off to his left to a swatch of green land that had the beginnings of construction scars etched on to it.

"Vince O'Donnell bought some defence land cheap because the government's strapped for cash. Plan is to turn it into a complex of hotels, apartments and shops. I've seen the plans, it's bloody ugly, the locals are furious. It's going to block their views, which in this town is a worse crime than murder."

"That's comforting."

"Sorry, bad example."

"Can't someone stop him?"

"The biggest union has refused to supply labour, so they're using scabs. The union has a picket. There's some talk of court action. They've only dug the foundations, so it's not too late to put the kaibosh on it all."

I peered out at the building site. I could see earth-movers and trucks and ant-like figures moving about.

"Jesus, I'm late. But look, I'll just drop you over there. It's as good a place as any to start. And you never know, there might be some aggro. There's nothing like a poncy North Shore-ite when it comes to protecting their perch on the side of the harbour." Ozzie jostled confidently with the other drivers on the bridge, we scooted out the other end and turned left. In a few minutes we were on a suburban street, clinging to the side of a steep hill, the harbour low on our left.

"See, the planning laws in this town don't always work," he said pointing to a multi-storey apartment block right on the water's edge. "That thing should never have been built. But money finds a way."

"What's Vince like?"

"Never met him personally," he said. "But I've been at a couple of press conferences. He's a bit of a larrikin. One of the lads. Likes to make a big deal out of his poor background. Born poor, no money for shoes, that sort of thing. Don't know whether it's true or not."

"Why would he make it up?"

"Because in our country, unlike yours, you get more kudos if you've been able to pull yourself up by your boot straps. Aussies love a story about a working-class joker made filthy rich by the sweat of his own brow. It's our version of the national myth. That's why Ned Kelly—who was, let's face it, just a cheap crook—is a folk hero. We love a battler, y'know. Someone who triumphs against the odds, no matter what side he's on."

"I'll take a measure of comfort from that."

We were winding around suburban back streets. The sun didn't let up. The monotonous hum of the air-conditioning reminded me that I could do with about three years' worth of sleep.

The building site was protected by a high metal fence and a set of iron gates. Between them and several men with placards stood three cops. A couple of women had brought coffee and scones in a basket and were handing them out.

We couldn't see much of the New Harbour development from outside the gates. The ground dropped away steeply. But

Ozzie told me that fourteen storeys were planned, so no doubt the neighbours would be seeing far more than they wanted to soon enough. Ozzie hoisted his camera out of the car for added credibility. We wandered over to the pickets.

"Morning," Ozzie said. A couple nodded in response. I hung back. I didn't want to get too close to the cops. Fortunately they were concentrating on the pickets.

"Coffee?" said a bright voice. I turned to see a small middle-aged woman handing a cup in my direction. I took it. It was a Pavlovian response.

"We serve anyone who turns up here," she said. "The more people who turn up, the more we can show those bastards. The TV crews love it if they get a free feed. Scone?"

I said no. Ozzie chatted with one of the picketers. Scanned the area through his viewfinder.

"What's happening today?" I asked the scone woman.

"Today we go for Vince O'Donnell's balls," she said gleefully. "Sure you don't want a scone? My daughter made them this morning."

I shook my head.

"Nothing much will happen here. We're going to be in court this afternoon. We want the judge to overturn the planning consent."

"What are your chances like?"

"The court will realise that it must listen to the voice of the people!" She'd raised her finger and was stabbing it in my direction. I stepped back. The mood she was in, I could lose an eye. "This project was ill-conceived from the beginning. Sydney's gone tourist mad. This country doesn't make anything any more. We ship our raw materials to Japan and God knows where, when we could be processing them here and making ten times the money. Then we fall back on tourism to make up the shortfall. Always taking the easy way out, the quick buck, this government. They never think about our future. Well, we're going to make them. We're going to squeeze them till their eyeballs pop out of their skulls. More coffee?"

Ozzie returned. The woman handed him a cup and a scone. For the first time I noticed security guards standing inside the gates. Beefy guys who looked like a good bit of violence would set them up for the day.

"Not much happening here," said Ozzie. "Bit of a scrap this morning when the scabs arrived. Quiet otherwise. It's been the same for days. The blokes reckon they're way behind though. Haven't been able to get enough scabs to fill their quota. And they're working on a pretty tight budget."

As he said that, a car drew up. It was a black Range Rover with tinted windows. The security guards rushed to open the gates, but they weren't quick enough. The car had to stop. The cops moved in to keep the picketers and the car apart, but some got through, including our scone lady. Shrieking four-letter words, she tipped coffee over the car and rubbed a jammy scone across the windows. Ozzie swooped into action, his camera as close as he could reasonably get it. Other pickets attacked the car before the cops grabbed them and pulled them back. They made a gap big enough for the car to get through. The pickets surged through after them, but were pushed back by the security guards. There was shouting, abuse, more scuffles. Then the gates shut.

"Who was that?"

"Vince, for sure," said Ozzie.

We walked back to the car. Ozzie took a cassette box and wrote on it. The scone woman followed us.

"I need to find out where Vince was in the early hours."

"Vince?" asked the scone lady, breathless from her exertions. "Why he was at home last night. We had a protest outside his house. He was having a dinner party. He wasn't very thrilled. He had some big star guest . . . that football player . . . what's his name? . . . can't remember. Anyway . . . he came out to try and scare us off. We just said 'tough.' And when all his fancy guests arrived we just waved placards in his face. He interferes with our quality of life then we'll interfere with his. Rob Bennett. That's his name, the football player. They say he earns five million a year. For football."

"What time did you stay till?"

"Oh, let me see. The last guest would have left about four-thirty. We stayed on till just after that. I think that's why I'm feeling a little tired today."

"Are you sure?"

"Of course."

"There's no way he could have left?"

"We'd have seen him. Besides he came out and had a slanging match with us at about three-thirty. That's when the cops got involved. Are these pictures going to run on the news tonight?"

"Sure," Ozzie said.

"What time? I'll set my recorder."

Ozzie told her the time and she left.

When we got out of ear shot, Ozzie said. "You weren't thinking that Vince had done his wife?"

"I'm keeping an open mind."

"Because that's a pretty cool alibi," Ozzie said, pressing the point unnecessarily.

"I know."

Ozzie packed the gear up and we got back in the car.

"Come on," Ozzie said. "I'll drop you somewhere. I've really got to go. I'm already late for work. At the rate things are going, it might be the last job I do in this town."

Wednesday 11:43 a.m.

Ozzie lifted his cap and ran his hand through his dark blond hair. "Jeez, it's a tale of woe from beginning to bloody end. My best mate Matt married a Pommy . . . sorry, an English woman. Her name's Catherine."

He'd looked like he wanted to tell me his tale of woe. And I needed a diversion. So I'd prompted him.

"Matt met her on holiday in Bali. They hit it off right away and next thing she's back here and she's Mrs Matt. They had a small wedding, on the beach at Balmoral, she looked gorgeous. We had a great time getting pissed on champagne, Matt spared no expense. I was best man. The weather was beaut, everything was perfect.

"Things were fine for about three months. She got a job, they were happy together. Then slowly, bit by bit, his interest trailed off. He was working long hours, going off for the weekend with the boys and leaving her home on her own. He's an ambitious bastard, Matt. He's news director of Channel 14. It's a good job for someone who's just turned thirty. Anyway, Catherine began to feel neglected. I dunno, if she'd been an Aussie, or maybe a bit more outgoing, she might have been able to fend for herself. But she'd just moved here and she didn't know anybody except Matt's mates. Except me, really.''

A child could see where this story was heading.

"So you offered her comfort?"

"It wasn't like that. She's a good mate. She has a great sense of humour. She's fun to be with. I found she calmed me down and I suppose she liked me, too. Matt was never around, he didn't mind us spending time together. I suppose he figured someone like me wasn't going to be a threat. So we hung around—going out to restaurants and theatres and stuff. I'd never been to many plays and she knew all about them. And I taught her how to windsurf.

"Earlier this week Matt was out of town with work and Catherine was left at home as usual, so I asked her to come to my parents' beach house up the coast. We went up there and mucked about. Didn't do anything special, just relaxed. Trouble was, Matt came home early and found that Catherine wasn't there. He called around and found out where she was and drove up and confronted us. We were walking back from the beach and I had my arm around her when he arrived, and of course Matt jumped to conclusions. We argued, he grabbed Catherine, didn't even give her time to pack, drove off like a maniac. She was crying. I was left standing there like a right berk. I had my arm around her—nothing wrong with that. I'm the affectionate type and I love women. Matt knows that more than anyone. I tried to explain but he wouldn't listen.''

"So this is all a failure of communication?"

Ozzie nodded miserably. "Now everybody's after me. Matt, his bloody old man, my girlfriend. Although I don't suppose she's my girlfriend any more. It's a bloody mess, I don't mind telling you.

"You should get it straightened out. Explain that you took pity on her because he was away so much. Tell him that you're his friend and friends don't sleep with each other's wives.''

"Oh, we slept together, alright,'' said Ozzie. "But Matt doesn't need to know that.''

We rounded a corner and the sun glinting off a glass building sent a flash of pain through my skull. Ozzie was threading the car under the massive stone pylons of the Harbour Bridge. It crouched over us like a giant child's toy.

"So what are you going to do? Are you in love with Catherine?"

"I dunno mate. I felt such a fool. And now I don't know what she thinks of me. I'm not the catch that Matt is."

I drew a deep breath and tried not to think about the absurdity of the situation I was in: on the run from the law yet still finding time to dispense advice to the lovelorn. "I'm sure she has her own views on that. Why don't you ask her?"

Ozzie looked pleading, like a little boy. I gave him my best I've-had-years-of-experience look. Never mind that that experience had left me with a thoroughly broken marriage and a series of unmemorable affairs, I could still do the look.

"You think?"

"Can't hurt."

"Yeah, s'pose you're right. Look . . . I've got to go now," he said, stopping the car. "You gonna be okay?"

"I'll be fine," I said. Alone in a town where I know no one. Wanted for a murder I didn't commit. Sure I was going to be okay. Stupid question.

"Train station's right there. It'll get you into town. And . . . here . . . take my mobile number." Ozzie ripped a page out of the diary he plucked from his pocket. "Ring me if you get stuck."

The train platform was a simple above-ground affair. I sat on a bench and looked at the view. There wasn't much way to escape it. Everywhere you looked you were battered by beauty. It depressed me still further. I turned away. Concentrated on a magazine stand that displayed a series of tacky picture rags, the sort that feature stories about movie stars in their "beautiful mock-Tudor homes." Here was a measure of comfort; this was life more on the level I was accustomed to.

The magazine that caught my eye showed a lithe blonde woman perched on a reproduction Louis XIV chair, which probably would have looked dull except that she was wearing a bright-pink lycra aerobics outfit and a fluffy headband and enough make-up to plaster a house with. Still, the legs were good. I peered a little closer. Her name was Tiffany Jones, part-time model and air hostess and the woman rumoured to be the next Mrs. Vince O'Donnell.

"Well, well," I muttered. Pulled the magazine out of the rack and turned to the page where Tiffany featured. The article gushed about her flat in Double Bay. It spoke of her hopes for her career and said archly that Tiffany refused to be drawn on her "friendship" with Vince O'Donnell.

"Hey you!"

I started guiltily. Expecting hordes of cops to be surrounding the newsstand.

"You gonna buy it? Or you just gonna wear out the pages?" The magazine vendor glared at me.

"How much?"

"Two dollars."

I handed over the money.

The train came. I got in, not really knowing where I was heading. I looked around furtively in the carriage. Nobody seemed to notice me. There was hardly anybody in the carriage anyway. Apparently everyone in this city drove cars. I returned to my magazine as we chugged sedately back over the bridge and into the centre of town.

Tiffany was featured in various rooms of her house: wielding a whisk and bowl in the faux-farmhouse kitchen, recreating the Zsa Zsa Gabor look in the bathroom in fluffy house gown and mules and, my personal favourite, poised on an air mattress in the swimming pool in a wet, pink bikini. Further into the copy came mention of a "wacky" incident in Tiffany's "chaotic romantic life." Vince had recently taken Tiffany to her favourite restaurant, a place called Deep Blue. It was her twenty-second birthday and she'd bought a white dress from Gucci. They ordered champagne and sat at the best table in the house. The oysters were just being transferred from the waiter's tray to her plate when estranged wife Michelle had stormed in, screaming something at Tiffany that a family magazine could not repeat and threw a pot of blue ink over her expensive dress. Tiffany did not take it very well. She got up, grabbed Michelle by the hair and pushed her backwards so hard that she fell over. Michelle got a sprained wrist and

Tiffany got a dent in her hair-do. The restaurant, not appre-
ciating that any publicity was good publicity, banned them
from going back. Tiffany did not wish to be drawn on the
subject, as far as she was concerned, it was history. "I want
to concentrate on my career now," she told a pliant reporter.
"I want to become an actress." The article went on to mention
a soap opera that she had auditioned for.

The train stopped at the central railway station, which
seemed as good a place as any to get out. I found a news
kiosk where I bought a pen and a notebook. Then I went to a
phone booth. It had a phone book inside and a working phone.
I took a couple of minutes to be impressed. Such symbols of
civility have long since ceased in London.

I dialled a couple of T. Joneses who were listed in Double
Bay. I got the Tiffany I'd seen in the magazine on the fourth
call. I told her a lie. Actually, I told her a pack of lies. She
told me to come on over, she was happy to be interviewed for
Hello! magazine.

Right, I thought as I hung up. All I have to do now is find
out where Double Bay is.

I located it on my folding map. I found I could get close
enough by train. I bought a day ticket, because it was cheaper.
Just because I was on the run from the law was no excuse to
be needlessly extravagant.

Double Bay had a village atmosphere, if you can imagine
a village solely populated by people wearing Versace and driving Ferraris. I was mildly shocked by the ostentatious display
of wealth, it's something the English have never been very
good at, even in London where lots of lucky sods are wading
knee deep in the stuff. Double Bay, by contrast, looked as
though it had had long experience in not hiding its light under
a bushel. Firm young women with big sunglasses, big carrier
bags and little skirts sashayed down the streets. Expensive foreign sports cars idled by, slowed down by the traffic and the
sight of the legs on the pavement. The boutique shops boasted
the names of Europe's top designers. We could have been in
one of the more brassy resorts in the South of France.

Tiffany's place was a few minutes' walk from the train station. I was sweating by the time I got there, and not just from the heat. Tiffany might have been questioned by the police. They might have already shown her my passport photo. She could finger me as soon as she opened the door. I fired that thought. Start thinking like that and I'd never get anywhere.

Instead, I took a deep breath and pressed the buzzer on her front gate. It clicked open almost immediately and there she was, welcoming me to her tasteful abode. I showed her my press card. She didn't look at it too closely.

"Mr. Perry," she said sweetly. "Won't you please come in?"

Wednesday 12:17 p.m.

She looked good in her blonde hair and long legs. Lots of cool skin, a light tan and not a line nor a pouch anywhere.

"You must be Miss Jones," I said in an obsequious, slobbering way that she was no doubt used to hearing from men. And I didn't have to try too hard, she was gorgeous. Vacant-looking, but then you can't have everything.

"Do come in," she smiled professionally. I followed her into a small world of greenery and sparkling water.

The pool was the most eye-catching feature of her garden. It was small and inviting and kidney-shaped. The sun danced on the surface the way sun and pools usually interact. The bottom of the pool was a complicated mosaic in contrasting shades of blue. I wanted to jump in and lose myself in its crystal depths. Instead I sat on a wooden chair that Tiffany directed me to.

"Can I get you something?" She flicked her hand like a hostess in a fifties American sitcom.

"I'm fine, thanks. Just a few minutes of your time. This is a preliminary interview only . . . to lay the ground work . . . so to speak."

Tiffany sat opposite me. At her elbow was a tray with a pitcher of what looked like iced tea. She poured herself a glass.

Looked around, realised she'd forgotten something. Excused herself and went inside.

The sun was killer bright. Did it never let up? I was grateful for my Raybans. I closed my eyes.

I heard a sound. I opened my eyes. One of the Greek statues around the pool had come to life. A perfectly formed kouros with chest and stomach muscles so well defined he was a walking anatomy lesson. I blinked. Rubbed my eyes. The statue began to assume life-like qualities. It wore cut-off jeans and carried a net for scooping insects out of the water. Slowly, steadily it dipped the net into the water. Just as slowly and steadily it brought it out and shook it. There was almost no sound except the waves plashing against the side of the pool.

Tiffany returned. She carried cigarettes. She offered me one and although they weren't my brand, I suddenly realised I could not go on unless I had one right then and there. The first drag was sheer delight.

"Don't mention this in the article," Tiffany said, waving her cigarette. "Officially, I don't smoke."

"Officially, neither do I," I smiled ingratiatingly. "Perhaps we could start with a little bit about how you got started in the business. As a model."

As she launched into her version of Tiffany: The Wilderness Years, I tried not to let my mind wander. But it was hard. The temperature was conducive to an empty mind and the light scent of tropical flowers didn't help. Tiffany's garden was so dense with growth that I half expected to see David Attenborough pop out from behind a fern.

The pool attendant had finished debugging the pool and was fitting chlorine into the dispenser. I prayed to the gods that we could change places. I'd be good, I promised the celestial guys. I'd give up my crummy reporter's job and do something worthy with handicapped children. I'd quit smoking and donate all the money I saved to cancer research. I'd spread sunshine and joy wherever I went. I'd even start being nice to my neighbours.

My reverie was interrupted when I noticed Tiffany looking at me very oddly.

"You're not taking any notes," she said coldly.

"I . . ." I fished around for my notebook. It had been there a minute ago. Tiffany continued to stare.

"My research tells me that you have established certain 'friendships' with influential people in Sydney society," I said ponderously. Is there any one person who has . . . er . . . helped you more than most?"

Tiffany's eyes narrowed. "What are you getting at?"

"A . . . er . . . mentor."

"You mean Vince? I don't talk about him. My private life is private. Absolutely off-limits."

I cleared my throat. "Have we discussed the matter of the . . . er . . . fee?"

"Fee?" Tiffany managed to look surprised and greedy at the same time.

"Just to cover your expenses. And the inconvenience of having a photographer in your house . . . a nominal fee."

"How nominal?" she shot back.

"Well . . . er . . . thirty-five thousand pounds is about average . . . I'm not sure what that would be in Australian money . . . seventy thousand dollars . . . roughly speaking."

Tiffany worked quickly to conceal her joy. "That's negotiable, I assume," she said coldly.

"Yes . . . er . . . yes it is. It depends on the circumstances. What we ask in exchange is that you give a frank and wide-ranging interview. And of course you get to vet the copy before it goes to print . . . Anything you don't like . . ." I trailed off. She was going to kick me out and call the cops any minute. Nobody was that stupid. Not even a part-time model/air hostess.

Tiffany stared at me. She stubbed out a cigarette and lit another barely taking her eyes from my face.

"What do you want to know?" she said.

I accepted a glass of iced tea. Tiffany seemed determined to give value for money.

"We met three years ago," she said. "I was 'Miss Enterprise New South Wales' that year. I met Vince at a party. I'd heard about Vince, of course. He's pretty well known around Sydney. We hit it off. Of course, technically he was still married at the time."

"Tell me about the dinner at Deep Blue."

"That was totally hyped. I just gave her a little push, that's all. She had no right to be there. Vince had explained the situation to her. She didn't care about him, anyway. Don't know why she suddenly came over like the possessive wife. She wasn't, believe me. She only wanted the money."

"What money?"

"His money. The divorce money. She didn't care about Vince. They didn't have a marriage in the proper sense. They hadn't slept together for years."

Amazing that that old line still works, I thought.

"All she wanted was what she could get as a settlement. Mind you, if I were her, I'd be worried too. I mean, she isn't getting any younger. It's sad, really. But I suppose she's going to find it hard to grab another rich husband. And no skills to speak of. I mean, there's no question that she could support herself." Tiffany's beautiful lip curled.

"He says she's always coming back with more demands. His money's tied up in the business. She wants more and more. She doesn't know when to stop. Still, I suppose she's got to provide for her old age." I wondered how Tiffany was going to feel when she hit thirty.

"How do you feel about that?"

She blew smoke out of her perfect mouth. "They're spending more time together now they're getting divorced than they did when they were married," she sniffed.

"Divorce requires more dedication than marriage," I said.

Tiffany looked at me blankly, then turned her attention back to her cigarette. "Not that I care, particularly. I have my own life. I have no reason to be jealous of someone like her. She's on the way out."

She patently didn't know that Michelle was dead. I wondered why Vince hadn't phoned her. Or maybe this was all a big act. I've been taken in by pert young women before.

"How did Vince feel about her money demands?"

"He was resigned to it. He said women were always trying to take him for a ride. It wasn't enough that he supported them in style for years, he had to go on paying after they'd gone.

Take his first wife, Noreen. He had to work like a slave for years to pay her and the two kids off.''

"So Michelle wasn't the first?"

Tiffany smirked. "My dear, Michelle was a secretary who got ideas. And that's all she was. A jumped-up secretary who went after a married man.''

"And you didn't?" I couldn't resist one small barb.

"It was different. Their marriage was a sham." No shadow of self-knowledge crossed Tiffany's beautiful but empty face.

"What's Vince's first wife like?"

"I don't know. I've never met her. She runs a shop. A dowdy dump of a place. A bit like her. Anyway, I thought this interview was supposed to be about me."

I asked her a few more questions for form's sake and then made my goodbyes. She escorted me to the gate.

"When will this be done?" she asked.

"Another fortnight or so. We'll do the interview in depth and bring a photographer." I couldn't conjure up a pang of guilt about toying with her this way. Mean-spirited, spiteful and shallow, Tiffany gave mistresses a bad name.

"By the way," I said. "I tried to call you last night, but you weren't in."

She looked puzzled. "I was here all night. Studying my lines. I've got an audition next week."

So Vince hadn't invited her to his dinner. Why not if they were such a hot item? Or maybe Tiffany hadn't wanted an invite. Perhaps she'd popped across the harbour and beaten her rival to death.

It was something to think about.

Wednesday 1:20 p.m.

Double Bay didn't look like the kind of place that would welcome someone like me but I stayed there anyway. I found another phone booth and got some change and tried to locate Michelle's friend Harry. I called the coast guard. I called the navy. I called The Dancing Queen to see if someone had arrived who could tell me Harry's last name. In desperation I called the restaurant Gracie had mentioned to see if the people from Harry's photo shoot had plans to drop in for lunch. They didn't.

I gave up. Found a patch of shade while I smoked a cigarette. Took my options out and looked at them from every angle. After I'd done that they still didn't come to much. I went back to the phone booth, checked the book and found the address of Vince's first wife. She was listed in a place called Rose Bay. I cross-referenced with my map and found that Rose Bay was just along the harbour from Double Bay. So many bays—Vince must have trouble moving without running into one of his ex-wives.

I began walking towards the main road in search of a bus stop.

Noreen O'Donnell's shop was one of those places that sells clothes to wealthy, middle-aged women who already have too

many choices to face when they get up in the morning and
deal with it by stocking up on variations on the things they
have already. The place was full of sensible stuff like blazers
in peach, beige and navy, ankle-length pleated skirts and silk
shirts with ties at the neck.

A well-preserved woman who was dressed along similar
lines came forward, smile at the ready. She had black hair and
wore spectacles on a chain. But there was a sexiness about her
that her attempt at an up-market librarian belied.

"Can I help you?"

"I'm looking for Noreen O'Donnell," I said.

"That's me." Her voice didn't match her face. It was low
and rough and she hadn't bothered to knock the corners off
an extremely broad accent.

I gave her a fake name. Told her I was working on the New
Harbour story. She smiled in a bored way. Turned her back
to dismiss me.

"I can't help you. My husband and I split up years ago.
We don't see each other and I don't know anything about his
life."

"Do you know Michelle?"

"Of course. She was my husband's secretary before she
took my place."

"Did she still work with Vince?"

"What's this got to do with anything?"

"I want to know what her other interests were."

Noreen smiled. "She didn't have any other interests. She
was a trophy wife. It's a zen-like condition—all you have to
do is be." She reached out absently and straightened a jacket
on a railing.

"Does Michelle have any enemies?"

"Decency and common sense."

"What about people?"

Noreen spread out her hands. "Look, I knew her once, years
ago. All I know now is what I read in the gossip columns.
Now please go . . ."

"Hi, Mum." A tall girl in school uniform whirled into the
shop with a brown paper bag. Kissed her mother lightly on
the cheek. "Got your salad, Mum," she said. Her long black
hair was tied back. It went well with the school colours of

aqua and maroon. The first impression was of clean-cut youth, until you saw the two gold rings in her eyebrow. She stopped, saw me, and paused. Looked at her mother for clues.

"Can you feed Cocky?" asked Noreen. For the first time I noticed a large cage with a sulphur-crested cockatoo in residence.

"Yep," the girl said, producing another bag. "Picked up his stuff on the way here."

The phone rang. Noreen answered it.

"Should I know you?" asked the girl. She was anxious to talk because her mother wasn't. I said a little thanks to the gods of teenage contrariness.

"No," I said. "I'm new in town. I was talking to your mother about your father's second wife."

"That must have been fun," she said as she poked black seeds through the cockatoo's cage. "We've been laughing ourselves sick." The bird grabbed the seeds deftly and greedily. They were cracked and swallowed in two economical movements. The girl cooed and whispered endearments. It sounded as though she hadn't heard the news.

"You don't like your father's wife?"

"I hate her. When my father left I got my Barbie doll, which coincidentally looked just like Michelle, and stuck pins in it hoping it would bring my father back. Must have worked, mustn't it?"

"What do you mean?"

"The divorce. Now my father is treating her the way he treated my mother. You can't help but laugh."

The bird screeched, reminding me harshly that in addition to all my other problems, I still had a hangover. It felt like a toxic waste dump had lodged in my brain and was being squeezed out through my nostrils. I was sure the bird was grinning at me. This country; even the fauna was hostile.

"It's Dad's usual *modus operandi*. When he found out that bitch queen wanted big bucks he had a private eye follow her and find out what she was up to—"

"Caroline!" Noreen crossed the room quickly. The girl stopped.

"What?" she said in the whiny voice that all teenagers have made their own.

"Be quiet."

"Who was the private eye?" I asked.

"You don't owe him anything, Mum," said Caroline.

"There is such a thing as family loyalty," Noreen hissed. The expression on Caroline's face said *not in this family* about as plainly as if she'd put it on a billboard and I wondered that this woman who had been treated so badly by Vince was still prepared to go on protecting him.

"Why did Vince put a private eye on Michelle?"

Caroline looked at her mother, defiant. Her mother moulded her expression into impassivity. *Go on, tell him*, it seemed to say. *I don't care one way or another.* That went on for about ten seconds then Noreen backed down.

"Caroline, please. Michelle's dead."

Caroline's mouth formed a perfect O. She stopped pushing the bird food through the bars of the cage and the bird squawked in response.

"Dead dead?"

"That's what that phone call was just about. The cops want to speak to me."

Suddenly it was time for me to go. But I didn't want to. I wanted to hear what would be said next.

Caroline turned to her mother, her eyes alight. "Who killed her? Was it Tiffany? She hated her."

"Caroline!" her mother wailed. "Please have some respect."

"Why? She never respected us." She turned back to me. "Yeah, I could see that vacuous bitch doing the job. She hated Michelle, especially after that business at the restaurant with the blue ink."

"Enough of this," said Noreen. "Please leave. Right now."

I glanced at Caroline. She grinned, happy with the chaos she was creating.

"Get out," said Noreen. "Please."

"The private eye?" I gave Caroline my most conspiratorial smile.

"Just go," Noreen moved towards me. I backed back.

"His name is Marvel," Caroline called after me. "And he works in King's Cross."

Wednesday 2:22 p.m.

King's Cross was the city's red-light district and not too hard to find. The train stopped right in the middle of it. It perched on a hill looking down on the city skyscrapers. Geographically superior, but not morally, judging by all the invitations I saw that could plunge a man deep into vice.

The Yellow Pages furnished Marvel's address. I walked down the main street past peep shows, X-rated cinemas and fast-food joints, looking for Marvel's office. After a couple of passes I spotted it over a Lebanese burger bar. In lieu of a sign B. S. Marvel had taped his business card to the front of the door. It was grubby and the tape was peeling. I pushed the door open and climbed some rickety steps. There were two doors at the top. One advertised Lusty Louise's School of Pain and the other had another of Marvel's cards taped to it. It was clear he didn't have a big office budget.

The place smelt of onions and fried animal and maybe I was just imagining this, but I thought, somewhere in the background, I could hear the sound of leather whipping flesh.

I knocked and went in.

A middle-aged guy sat behind his desk, feet up, forcing a burger in his face. He wore a khaki shirt and trousers and tomato ketchup on his nose.

"Hi, don't get up," I said pulling up a chair. "You must be Marvel. I'm Ridley."

I'd obviously interrupted a private moment. Marvel, still unable to speak because his jaws were working on the meat, put the rest of the burger down, but he kept stealing loving glances at it as he chomped.

"Don't let me stop you," I said brightly. "When you're done I want to talk about Vince O'Donnell. And by the way, you've got ketchup on your nose." Marvel chewed some more and gulped loudly. He wiped his nose with the packet that the burger had been wrapped in. The ketchup gave way to a shiny grease slick.

"You should always chew your food properly," I said. "Otherwise it just sits in your stomach and rots. And that's bad. Snakes can deal with it, but the human digestive system can't. That's why we have teeth."

Marvel glared while he swallowed. His Adam's apple worked hard. It was painful to watch. Politely, I looked away.

Marvel got up. He went from the room. I considered going through his files but decided against it. If he'd gone to the loo to freshen up, he wouldn't be long. I was right. He was back in less than four minutes.

"Whaddywant?" Marvel croaked as he slid back into his saggy chair. He patted a few wisps of hair in place. It was a tender gesture—like he was praising them for putting up such a valiant fight when the rest of the follicle brigade had long since decamped. His shapeless face was still damp from splashing water on it. His breath was so bad it could have doubled as defoliant. I was willing to bet that rogue beef slice was still lodged somewhere near his larynx.

"You work for Vince O'Donnell?"

"I work for lots of people. Who are you?"

"Ridley."

"Who I work for is not your business, Ridley."

From another room I heard a brisk crack and a responding yell that sounded more pleasure than pain. Lusty Louise's school was in session.

"You were hired to follow Vince's wife, Michelle."

Marvel's eyes were not giving anything away. He glanced at the burger.

"Go on, eat it," I said magnanimously. "Don't mind me."

The burger stayed untouched. Through the wall I could hear a grown man say, "I've been very, very bad. And I must be punished." There followed a sharp, thin crack. A Proustian Madeleine experience for me. The old school days with the old school master brandishing the old school cane. But this was no time for reminiscence.

"Michelle is dead," I said confidentially. "She was murdered last night after she'd arrived home from Singapore. I'm sure I'm not telling you anything you don't already know but I want to find out who killed her. Any thoughts you'd like to share?"

Marvel's hand flitted to his non-existent hair. His expression, which looked like mild indigestion, didn't change.

"I know her husband paid you to follow her."

"Paid is the verb in that sentence. What I'm paid to find out I don't pass on to mangy bastards who barge into my office."

"That's not fair. I knocked."

Marvel folded his arms across his chest. He'd been watching too many tough-guy movies. I could have told him that to pull that look off you needed to be a hulking six foot four and have at least two prison-issue tattoos under your eyes.

"Get out."

"Don't be like that. We can help each other. All I want to know is if there's anybody, apart from your client, who'd want Michelle dead. Anyone at all. Off the top of your head."

"You're wasting my time."

"Tell me how many days you tailed her."

"Bugger off."

"Why did she go to Singapore?"

Marvel stood up. Gestured not very politely towards the door. Somewhere, in another room, I could hear Lusty Louise's client howling like a dog. If he spent a morning with me, I could teach him about real pain.

"Tell your boss I'll find out what happened," I said before I shut the door. "I'm the persistent type."

"Want some health-preserving advice?" growled Marvel. "People who persist with Vince always wish they hadn't."

I decided to wait around and see if Marvel did anything rash. I went down the street a little and into a café that had a reasonable view of Marvel's front door. I ordered a coffee and a sandwich. The café was dark and not salubrious. Everybody in it looked as evil and guilty as me. The racket from pinball machines and one-armed bandits was almost too much. I groped for my coffee. The combination of the gloom of the bar and my sunglasses made me almost blind. Outside sailors and tourists cruised the streets looking for diversion in massage parlours and video arcades. Office workers slouched into coffee bars and Lebanese takeaway joints. Interspersed with the sunny seediness were upmarket minimalist restaurants where professionals kept power-lunching appointments.

After a couple of truly awful coffees, Marvel came out of his office blinking in the strong sunlight. He'd put on a jacket but it was too small, his stomach fell out the front defying the cheap fabric to contain it. He popped a cigarette and shuffled towards me. I doubted he could see through the smoked glass of the café, but I slunk in my seat anyway. Marvel ambled on. I paid my bill and went after him.

The pace wasn't too hard to keep up with. We were heading south from what I could tell, away from the harbour. There was a slight incline. We crossed a road that doubled as an overpass. Marvel walked straight and didn't look back. He behaved more like he was out for the good of his health. Maybe he was. Maybe he'd outguessed me and I was being led into a trap. I slackened off, looked around. There were no heavies with pork-pie hats and machine guns ready to drill me full of holes, just a couple of people with a bag of laundry heading into the laundromat. Some more cluttered outside a coffee shop.

We continued this way for about ten minutes. The only thing that changed was the surroundings. The streets became more uniformly residential. The houses became larger. The street that Marvel stopped in was expensive. The terraced houses were carefully decorated in matching shades. The wrought iron on the balconies was lovingly intact. Apart from a kid delivering circulars and us, there was no one else on the street.

Marvel approached a semi-detached place. It was painted light blue with dark blue and pink trim. The path was lined with roses. Marvel went up to the door and knocked. He lit another cigarette while he waited. There was no reply. He knocked again. Smoked and tapped his foot. Looked around. I slunk back further out of sight. He knocked a third time but it was apparent that nobody was coming to the door. Marvel walked back down the path, craned his neck to see if there was anybody at home upstairs. If there was they didn't come to the window and wave.

Marvel walked down the path, shut the small iron gate behind him. He was heading back towards me. I made a note of the street name and made myself scarce.

I rang Ozzie from a phone booth about two blocks away after I'd seen Marvel trundle back off in the direction of his office.

"How's things?" I asked Ozzie and immediately regretted it.

"Bloody awful, mate. Things could not be worse. Matt tracked me down at work, there was a bloody great row. He threatened to knock my lights out and he would have done if my sound man hadn't restrained him. He tried to reason with him and Matt knocked him out. He's had to go hospital to be checked for concussion. And my news director is mad as hell. The boss of a rival station bursts into the bloody newsroom and tries to knock out a freelance cameraman. I mean, how does that look?"

"It looks bad, Oz. It looks bad."

"Bloody oath. It looks terrible. And I'm being blamed for it all. Not only that but now everybody knows. I'm the laughing stock of Sydney. I'll never live this down. I'll have to emigrate to the bloody Norfolk Islands."

"People change their minds. In a week you'll be a legend in your own news hour."

Ozzie was taking no comfort. ". . . and I can't get hold of Catherine. I've rung her five times. I think she's avoiding me. Paula's trying to track me down but I'm avoiding *her*. But

I'm going to have to face her today because she's got some gear that I need. It's a disaster. My life has collapsed in a morning. So, what's up with you?''

"I was hoping you could tell me. I haven't heard the news.''

"Hang on,'' said Ozzie. "I'll go to the newsroom and get on a terminal . . . see what the wires are saying . . .''

He shut up for a minute or two. I could hear the reassuring background hum of a busy newsroom. What I wouldn't have given to be in my own busy newsroom, several thousand miles away, right now.

"Let's see,'' Ozzie said. "Cops have questioned the driver and he's given them a full description of the person he chased from the house. Late thirties, dark hair, blue eyes, medium build wearing jeans and a pale-blue shirt. Strewth, that's about as close as it gets. It's not good Sam. They've released your name.''

"What about my picture? Is there a passport snap or something?''

"Uh, hang on, I'll check what happened with the midday bulletins.'' Ozzie put the phone down and again I could hear the newsroom sounds through the phone receiver.

"No. Not yet, mate.''

"Well, that's something,'' I said.

"What are you going to do now?''

"Go to court.''

"Court? Why? That's the surest way to run into cops.''

"The appeal against the New Harbour project is there today. I remembered that Michelle spoke to Vince on the phone last night. She said something about working with him. Maybe it's to do with that.''

"It's the quickest way to get caught.''

"Not if my photo hasn't been released.''

"Just because it hasn't been released doesn't mean the cops don't know what you look like.''

"I'm taking applications for better ideas.''

Ozzie clicked his tongue. "Can't think of one.''

"Nope, me neither.''

Wednesday 4:15 p.m.

The cool inside of the court building was a welcome contrast to the big, bold sun outside. A young man in a good suit sat behind the information desk. He directed me to the New Harbour hearing.

The building had an institutional smell, a combination of floor polish and disinfectant. I found it reassuring. It took me back to another time when I had fewer mistakes to look back on. When I was a young reporter chasing a beautiful girl.

I had met Mary, my wife, when she was still at university, and I was working on a local radio station in London. We met in court. One of her tutors had been convicted of arson after having what his lawyer described as a spot of emotional trouble. He'd taken off all his clothes and run amok in the university laboratories with a bottle of Napoleon brandy, a bowler hat and a ceremonial African spear. After he'd transferred the brandy from the bottle to his bloodstream he broke into a chemistry lab where he was found by a security guard in front of what he explained was "a small fire to warm an old man's bones." The guard got him out before the place burned down. Pressure of work was the explanation for his rather unacademic outburst. It was the end of the summer, and the professor had not been looking forward to the start of term with any enthusiasm. God knows how it even came to court, but it did. And it was a gift for an arrogant young prat like myself. Covering that same story now, I'd have tempered my response. I'd have felt sympathy for the guy. I'd have known that life is a capricious mistress and sometimes it's too hard to keep a respectable grip on things with all the bullshit that one has to deal with on a day to day basis.

But not then. Then I was twenty-three and I didn't know anything. Worse, I had no concept of the scale of my ignorance. At twenty-three it was a hoot. A good headline, a pun-laden prize to be laid at the feet of my editor.

Mary caught me smirking in the courtroom one day, whispering with a fellow reporter. She glared at me, raised a finger to her lips. When I got out, she was waiting to flay my hide.

"You people make me sick," she said. "This is a jolly big laugh to you, isn't it? What if that were your father, or someone you cared about?"

"I'm sorry, but there is a funny side."

"My friend has been nursing an extremely ill wife for the last seven months. Which part of that exactly do you find amusing?"

"I'm sorry," I said again. But I was barely listening to her words. All I could see were her eyes—so blue they were almost black—and her hair—so black it was almost blue. Just like a cartoon babe. Off she went again, about the responsibilities of the media.

"You're right," I said when she'd paused for breath. "I'm an oaf. Let's discuss it over a drink."

The blue-black eyes widened even more as she took that information in. "I don't fucking believe it," she said finally. "Have you heard a single word I've said to you?"

I opened my mouth to tell a little white lie, then thought: *No, Ridley. You want to get this one off on the right foot.*

So I smiled my best smile and said, "I'm sorry, no I didn't. You see, I think I just fell in love."

I shouldn't have said it, of course. It was stupid. It was corny and, even worse, it was such a shoddy cliché. But I was only twenty-three. She didn't take that into account. She thought I was making fun of her. Without another word she stalked off.

It was too late for me. I was cast adrift. I went home that night, started making plans. I pictured the wedding we would have, the house we would live in, the kids that would save the world from every manner of pestilence and disease. By the time the next morning rolled around, I had our future sorted. When I thought about it, which was every waking second, it was with the words "happy" and "everafter" tagged on.

She was in court the next day to hear the verdict—the lightest sentence possible given the extraordinary nature of the circumstances—and she didn't look my way once.

This time I was waiting for her when she came out of the courtroom.

"They've taken a poll which shows that two out of three people believe I can be a complete prat at times."

She didn't say anything. She didn't slow down. I had to almost run to catch up with her.

"Let me buy you a drink."

"I've got to be somewhere else."

"A very small drink?"

"I don't think so."

"Then how about we get married and live in a little cottage on the edge of a wood? Somerset, Wiltshire, somewhere like that. I'm not fussy as long as it's got an open fire."

She'd stopped at a pedestrian crossing. She turned to look at me, foot tapping, arms crossed, lip curled.

"Do I look like the kind of wally who would fall for a stupid line like that?"

She was even more beautiful with a sneer. It gave her perfectly proportioned face hauteur.

"If you let me buy you a drink, I promise never to use it again—on you or anybody else."

The sneer relaxed a little. The pedestrian light changed from red to green but she didn't walk. I kept my mouth shut. Sometimes it's better that way.

"Alright," she said after what seemed like a million years had passed. "I'm undertaking this strictly as a social service. If I let you buy me a drink you must promise to put that awful line in cold storage, where it belongs. Perhaps future generations will resurrect it as an example of how primitive we once were. But right now I don't think it should see the light of day, do you?''

We had that drink and then a couple more. Found we had quite a bit in common—two people with a peripatetic childhood and no real place to call home. We sorted that one right out by moving in together and getting married. I made the money while she finished her masters degree. Then she went out into the bad world and started using her clever brain to trade stocks and shares.

It worked for a long while, her and me. And then it didn't. I can't place where it went wrong, but I know that one day I woke and knew that I'd missed a thousand opportunities to put things right. She stayed with me perhaps longer than she should have. Then there was someone else. Someone as successful and bright as she. Someone with a future and who didn't take her for granted. Which was why, all those years later, I was in Sydney.

As I opened the door to the courtroom, I thought how right it was to blame all my problems on Mary.

Wednesday 4:20 p.m.

The courtroom was packed. A lawyer was on his feet mumbling about planning regulations and end-use applications. I recognised some people from the building site this morning, a few of the union picketers and the woman who'd served scones and coffee. I squeezed into the back row next to a nattily dressed guy who was taking notes in a leather-bound notebook with a Mont Blanc fountain pen.

It was pleasant there. Just the right temperature. And I had a place to sit down. It wasn't exactly mother's womb but it wasn't so bad either. With the soporific words of the lawyer to lull me, I fell asleep.

I woke up because people around me were trying to get past. I guessed that some time had elapsed.

"What'd I miss?" I asked Mr Mont Blanc.

"A good night's sleep by the look of things," he said over his shoulder.

"What's happening about New Harbour?" But he was gone. Swarming towards a tall guy who had got up from his seat at the front of the courtroom. I could tell he had authority. It wasn't just the cut of the suit, it was the way he held himself. Expecting attention. Reporters swarmed around him, notebooks held aloft. Microphones pointed at his face. Over-made-up women caught him by the arm. They had on enough slap to be TV reporters. They wanted him outside on the front steps, speaking into the camera. But the print and radio folk had the upper hand. Hemmed in by them, the man stayed where he was.

"Johnno," said an attractive young redhead with a microphone, "what will it mean for your political position if the court rules against New Harbour?"

"Well, Jane," he turned to look at her, smile cranked up to the max, "I'm not making any predictions about how it'll go. That's for the court to decide. However, I'm confident, that New Harbour will go ahead. An independent analyst's report shows that Sydney is drastically short of luxury hotel rooms. If we're going to woo the high-spending end of the market, we need more facilities, it's as simple as that. As Minister for Tourism, I can't afford to ignore this trend."

A babble of voices shouted more questions. "What about the residents?"

The minister smiled sympathetically in the way that politicians do when they're going to explain something that only they understand fully. "Well, Tone. You know as well as I do that the residents have had every opportunity to make contributions to this project as it progressed through the planning stages. I think the residents will find that when the building is up and running, that it isn't as bad as they think. Don't forget, they've only seen the plans. The building proper hasn't started yet. They don't actually know how the building is going to affect their views and I think they'll find themselves pleasantly surprised. Not least by the amount of money that wealthy tourists will bring to their area."

"What about the environmental damage?"

"What environmental damage?" asked the minister. "There isn't going to be any. The developers liaised very closely with the planning department when the plans were drawn up. None of the city's or the state's environmental laws have been breached, and those laws are some of the toughest in the world. The government knows that it has a world-class asset in Sydney Harbour. We'd be foolish to jeopardise that in any way. Now, if you'll excuse me. . . ." He began to make his way to the courtroom door. My neighbour, the man in the waistcoat, was standing in his path.

"Frank," the minister nodded and made to step around him. The man called Frank stood loosely in his path, hands in pockets. He hadn't contributed to the reporters' scrum but I had a feeling he was about to.

"Will you resign if this judgment goes against you?" asked Frank.

"The action's being brought against New Harbour, not the state government," said the minister, still smiling.

"It's your baby, though," said Frank. "You pushed for the re-zoning."

"I wish I had as much power as you imagine, Frank."

"Will you resign?"

The minister smiled. "No. But I might sulk for a while." He clapped Frank on the shoulder to let him know he'd cracked a joke. "I am the state government's representative in this matter. It's not a personal crusade, okay? It's my job."

Other reporters followed him as he pushed through the doors.

"Who's that guy? What'd I miss during my power nap?" I asked the guy in the waistcoat.

"That guy is John Holden and the judge has reserved his decision," he said. "Needs to review the evidence. You're new around here?"

"Just visiting." He told me he was Frank Webster and he worked for a daily paper. I told him a lie about who I was and what I was doing. We followed the crowd out to the steps where John Holden stood in the sunshine answering the same questions for the television cameras he'd answered inside. I stayed as far away as I could, no sense in showing up in some cutaway shot on the evening news.

"What's your interest in this?" asked Frank Webster as he searched his pockets for his keys.

"I've been roped into an involuntary busman's holiday." It was stupid even speaking to the guy since any moment now I was likely to be dragged away in chains, but I felt like a politician on the hustings. I had the irrational urge to spread the gospel about my niceness before the world knew me only as the guy who liked to end his dates with the ultimate climax.

"Is Vince O'Donnell crooked?"

If Frank Webster was surprised by the sudden turn in the conversation, he didn't show it.

"We would all like to know that. As far as I can tell he bends but doesn't break the rules. He is a curious chap. Extremely shrewd and part of that shrewdness is to do with fighting another day. I think he knows if he breaks the law somewhere it will catch up with him. There've been too many greedy Australian entrepreneurs who got caught like that and are now spending the best years of their life making wickerwork. Vince doesn't want to end up like that."

John Holden had finished talking to the cameras. The crowd on the steps seeped away. "Are you doing a story on him?"

"You could put it like that," I said.

"Then you should stay awake. Otherwise you might miss something." He waved cheerily as he left.

I watched John Holden get into his ministerial car and gradually the crowd of reporters dispersed. It was hot on the steps. The whole city was much too hot for my liking. I moved into the shade. People walked by; barristers in robes, juniors wheeling boxes of files. Women in short skirts and high heels. I stood and wished for a cigarette. Anything to help me think. I couldn't think, that was the problem. I closed my eyes. Felt a hand on my arm. It was Ozzie, looking worried. "Everything okay mate?"

"Couldn't be better."

"Yeah," he said. "I know the feeling. Want to come for a ride? I need your help."

"Why not?" That's the one good thing about being on the run from the law; it frees your schedule right up.

"I've got to see Paula. Can't put it off any longer. It might get ugly."

"Paula?" We walked towards the Volvo, which was parked at the curb.

"Remember I told you about her? She's sort of my girlfriend. Was. Before Catherine."

"Sort of?"

"You know. We've hung around a bit. No commitment

though. Never said anything about commitment. Haven't made her any promises that I can't keep."

"I hope you're not going to ditch her with those exact words?"

"Why? What's wrong with that?"

"Take it from me. There are gentler ways."

"You married?"

"Once. A long time ago."

"Paula has pretty well got the picture anyway. She called me this morning. Don't think there's going to be much explaining to do."

"Think again. She'll want to hear it from you."

Ozzie looked at me in astonishment, as though I'd just suggested that Santa Claus didn't live at the North Pole with a bunch of elves. "She's pretty low maintenance. A good bloke. Likes a drink. Nothing to write home about. I mean, she's not Catherine. Catherine has class. The only reason I'm going over there now is because she's got some gear of mine. Otherwise I'd just leave things to blow over. But I need that gear for a job."

We drove in silence for some time through the inner city and back out to the eastern suburbs. I tried to get orientated. Persuaded myself that I recognised some of the landmarks. Everything still looked the same.

"Where are we going?"

"Bondi."

I settled back. I could have done with five or six cigarettes, a gallon or so of Scotland's finest and some sleep. In that order. Instead I wound down the window.

We crested a rise and Bondi Beach lay before us in all its sexy, world-famous glory. The sand was just as white as the pictures I'd seen of it. The sea was just as blue. The colour hurt my eyes. The perfectness of the vista hurt my brain. People lay sprawled on the sand, crouched on surfboards, paddling in the shallows. Their most pressing concern was probably deciding what to have for dinner that evening. As I looked at it I had a deep desire to rush into the sea, stroke out as far as I could and never come back.

Suspected murderer Sam Ridley eluded a massive police

manhunt today. He was last seen at Bondi Beach swimming strongly out to sea. Police are combing the southern beaches where they expect his body to wash up.

I wondered how that would play with my son and decided not very well. I sighed deeply. I was too tired and too old. I wanted out of this situation. But the gods, wherever they were, weren't accepting petitions from tired journalists. At least I didn't see any fiery chariots descending from Mount Olympus with a snake-wearing goddess at the wheel pointing her finger at me.

Ozzie had peeled off to a side street and we were climbing a hill. We stopped outside an apartment block angled, like those all around it, to the best view of the sea. He killed the motor. Two kids zoomed by on skateboards, shrieking because they'd worked up a head of speed that they hadn't bargained on. I watched them till they were out of sight.

"I'll wait here. Call me when you need me," I said.

Ozzie turned to me, a look of panic on his face. "What do I say?"

"What do you want to say? Are you breaking up with her?"

"Yes . . . no . . . I mean yes. Of course I am. I'm breaking up with her . . . not that we were ever a real item as such—"

"Don't say that. Don't say 'I never made you any promises.' Women, for some reason, don't see that as an excuse for bad behaviour. Be gentle."

"I can be gentle."

"Good. And don't rave on about Catherine. Try and keep her out of the conversation."

"No Catherine. I can swing it."

"And don't, whatever you do, tell her you hope you'll still be good friends. For some reason women can always tell when you don't mean it."

"That's all?"

"That's all. And above all, don't forget to be yourself." I put my hand on his arm and smiled smarmily. But Ozzie was too tense, the irony was lost.

"Doctor Love's surgery is closed for the day," I said, stretching out. "I'm going to catch some sleep."

"Take the phone," he said, handing me his mobile. "I may need some help carrying the gear down."

I took his phone. But I didn't fall asleep. I looked out on the strange landscape—the suburb parked next to a beach, and I tried to make sense of this strange world that I was plunged into. Michelle was dead, her soon to be ex-husband was having trouble with the authorities and his mistress had the sort of grudge that stood out like blue dye on a white dress. Why were Michelle and Vince so matey if they were pitching up for an acrimonious and expensive divorce? And what had Michelle meant about working together with her husband? Noreen, wife number one, said Michelle had been Vince's secretary, which tallied with what Michelle'd said to him on the phone. Was she somehow involved with the New Harbour project? And if so, what had she "taken care" of in Singapore?

The car became too hot, my brain too cramped with questions that didn't have matching answers. I wound down the window and smelled the fused perfume of tarmac, tropical flowers and salt water.

I was having the sort of confused, panicky dreams that are more tiring than being awake when the phone went. For the second time that day, I awoke in heart-stumbling panic. Where was I? Where was that irritating noise coming from?

It was Ozzie's phone, which had slipped on to the floor.

"Sam. Come on up mate. It's number 13b."

I stumbled out of the car, blinking. Found the steps. Counted them on the way up. There were eighty-two. Knocked.

A slim woman in cutoffs answered the door. I could see why she fell into the "good sport" category. She was attractive in an offbeat way—short light-brown hair, nose slightly crooked and a small, well-shaped mouth. At the moment the mouth was turned down at the corners.

"You must be the help," she said tartly.

"I'm Sam." I put out my hand and smiled. She took it half-heartedly.

"Ozzie's in the spare room sorting out some of his stuff.

He's going to need you to carry it, or so he said. I think you're really just here to give the ferret moral support.''

Her flat had very little furniture. One sofa and an antique Indian coffee table. Instead of a stereo she had a soapbox-sized ghetto blaster. The radio was turned low. Paula had spent her money on Oriental rugs and elaborately framed prints of the Buddha. But you hardly noticed what was inside because the view was so spectacular. The whole of Bondi lay before us. I stood, staring. Drinking in the colour.

"The view's the only reason I live here," said Paula. "Me and the roaches. There's so many of them I make them chip in for rent.'' She was dry, laid back. If she were a forties' movie star you'd have called her laconic. Not pretty exactly. Poised.

Dead ahead of us on the north side of the bay was a large brick Victorian building. From inside it poked a tall modern building about ten storeys high. It was as if some malevolent giant child had skewered a graceful old toy with a brash new one.

"What's that building?''

"A reminder that you should never trust politicians,'' she said. "It used to be a boys' school but it went out of business. It was sold to a developer who found some loophole in the planning regulations. Hence the absurd addition. It's apartments now. Okay for the yuppies living there because they don't have to look at it.''

"Was the developer Vince O'Donnell by any chance?''

"I think so,'' she said. "It was put up about seven years ago. A bit before my time.'' She seemed to thaw a little. "What brings you to Sydney?''

"I'm on an action-packed adventure holiday.''

"Sit down if you like, you look done in.''

So did she. Pissed off and done in. Yet she was making an effort to be nice to a stranger. I admired her grit.

"You know him well?'' she asked, indicating the bedroom where Ozzie was sorting through some things.

"No.''

"Well let me tell you, he's a stupid galah who doesn't know

what's good for him." She blinked away tears and made a sound mid-way between a sob and a laugh.

"What is good for him?"

"Me. I'm good for him." She said it fiercely. I had the feeling Doctor Love was back in business. "See, he thinks he should have some blonde gorgeous ornament on his arm. I don't know why he thinks that because he knows that ornaments don't give much in the way of laughs. He'd be bored in a fortnight. But he can't ditch this stupid idea. He can't see that companionship and compatibility are part of the whole damn thing. He just has this stupid romantic idea that he has to have a fucking princess." Paula stood up. She had strong, smooth legs. Athlete's legs. "Sorry, I've got to have a fag." She disappeared into the kitchen. I could hear things being thrown around. A television was turned on. There was no sound from Ozzie in the bedroom.

I wondered if I'd ever have the energy to get off the sofa.

The radio was playing Van Morrison. "Jackie Wilson Said." All the years I'd listened to that song I'd never been able to figure out what it was that Jackie Wilson did say. So many things I'd never done. At least prison would give me a chance to catch up on them all. Maybe I'd be one of those prisoners that gets advanced degrees and then comes out to an entirely new life. When I was ninety-five.

It was not a comforting thought.

The afternoon sun cast its golden benediction on Bondi. The beach was still crowded. Swimmers clustered together in areas bounded by flats. Surfers further out, waiting for a ride. Dusky sunbeams sloped in Paula's windows and I watched motes dance in the beams. I closed my eyes for a few seconds, just to see what it felt like. It felt good. There was orbital sound—Paula venting her anger on small kitchen appliances, the murmur of the radio announcer—but the longer I laid my lids together, the further it leached into the background. I was tired. So very tired. My body melted into the chair.

I awoke with a start. The familiar feeling of dread woke with me. Something was very wrong. If only I could remember what it was.

I opened my eyes. Paula stood in front of me with a softball bat. She was half-crouched. Ready to strike. The bat pointed at my nose.

"I saw you on the news," she said. "Don't move, I've called the police."

Wednesday 5:57 p.m.

I opened my mouth to speak.

"Don't," she warned, waggling the bat. "I don't want to hear from you. So just shut up and sit there until they get here."

"What are they saying about me?"

"I said shut up!" The bat looked like an extension of my nose now, it was so close. Pinocchio Ridley.

Paula was pale. Nervous but determined. I had no doubt that she would use the thing to swat me and that it wouldn't be pleasant. I don't like it when my body is hurt.

"Did you?"

"Did I what?"

"Kill that woman?"

"No."

"I don't believe you."

"Apparently, you're in good company."

She seemed a little thrown by the fact that I wasn't protesting my innocence. The bat wavered. "The police'll be here any minute."

"I can hardly wait."

I strained my ears for the wah-wah siren sound, but heard nothing. Incongruously, it seemed, the radio was still on.

Crowded House this time, with a smoothly crafted ballad. I wondered where Ozzie had gotten to. I wondered what would become of me. I thought of my son and I felt like crying at the unfairness of it all.

"What the . . . ?" Ozzie had obviously been down to the car and come back. He stormed my self-pitying reverie. Phone clutched in one hand, eyes a little wild.

"Stay back. This man is wanted by the police. He killed a woman."

"No he didn't," said Ozzie, bless him.

"How do you know that?"

"He told me."

"Jesus and you believed him? I feel better about you ditching me now. You're soft in the brain."

"Paula, honey. This situation is much more complicated than you think . . ."

"That's what you told me about Catherine," hissed Paula. "Stay well back or I'll give your mate a dent in the skull that it's going to take a very qualified surgeon to rectify."

"Honey—"

"Don't honey me!" Paula shouted.

"This isn't about Sam, is it?"

"Ozzie, you bring a fucking criminal to my house. You put my life in danger. You put my fucking health in danger by sleeping with that stupid Pommy bitch. I'm starting to conclude that you don't care for me at all, Oswald Ainsworth Booker."

Ozzie advanced slowly. "Why don't you put the bat down and we'll talk about it. Sam isn't going to hurt you."

I could hear the sirens now. And I thought about how long it would take Paula to get enough swing up to really hurt me with the bat.

The sirens were louder. Crowded House stopped singing. Paula's jaw was set in a tight line. It was time for me to go.

I snatched the fat end of the bat and pulled. Hard. Paula lost her grip and stepped forward. Using the bat to demonstrate, I waved her back. She looked frightened, but she kept her mettle. "You gonna bludgeon me like you did that woman?"

"No. This is just so you don't hinder what I hope will be a speedy getaway."

I backed towards the door. Ozzie stepped out of my way, blocking Paula's path at the same time.

The sirens came closer.

"Ozzie don't be such an idiot. He's spinning you a line, probably like he spun that woman a line. He's a deranged maniac." But Ozzie continued to stand between me and her. I handed Ozzie the bat.

"For God's sake," hissed Paula and she lunged around Ozzie at me. Ozzie's hand came down to stop her but she wriggled free. She went for my throat, tried to stick her fingers in my Adam's apple. I was surprised at how much it hurt. I grabbed her arms, tried to lever them away. Her grip was fast. I could feel my air supply drying up. I gagged. My face felt hot. My organs and tissue insisted that air be delivered immediately. I scrabbled ineffectually at her arms. She glared at me from much too close a distance.

Then it stopped. Paula was being lifted away by Ozzie. He grabbed her around the waist with one arm. Hooked one of her swinging hands in his. She kicked out but he held fast. He tried to talk to her, she wouldn't listen. I gave myself some distance. I coughed. Breathing felt good. Must remember to appreciate the little things. I coughed some more, rubbed my throat. Then went for the door.

"Keep in touch, mate," Ozzie said.

"Thanks."

I dived down the stairs. Two cop cars had just turned into Paula's street.

There was a back path, so I took it.

Wednesday 6:31 p.m.

Paula's flat was one of a modern block of six. Hers was on the first floor. Out the back was a communal garden arrangement with a few straggly plants. A high wooden fence separated the block from an almost identical one facing. The fence had cross bars and I made good use of them. Up and over and a less than graceful landing on the other side.

The yard was deserted. A good thing. I took the side path and promptly collided with a woman carrying a load of wet laundry. She screamed and swore. I swore and tripped. And then I apologised. My mother brought me up right and she always used to say that a mark of a gentleman was that he retained his manners when under pressure.

The apology didn't appear to compensate for the pile of twisted and now dirty laundry.

"I'm calling the police," snarled the woman.

"I think you'll find someone's beaten you to it," I said.

I could hear heavy, police-like footsteps next door. I ran down the path to the gate and leapt it by miles. To my left, another cop was taking the corner. I took the road straight ahead. It was uphill but I scarcely noticed; adrenalin, the panic's companion, turbo pumped through my veins. I ran like an eighteen-year-old star athlete.

Police followed me on foot and in vehicles. I took a side street. And another. I was in an alleyway, narrow enough for only one lane of traffic. Lined by garages. In England it would have been tarted up as a mews. Australians were content to leave it as a place for their cars.

There was a garage door open and I took it as an invitation. I went through it, out the back door, also unlocked. I crossed the yard, climbed another fence and crossed another yard. That fence was made of tin. I cut my hands as I swung over it and crash landed on the other side.

Police sirens grew louder.

This garden presented an interesting contrast to the suburban layouts I'd just trawled through. It was overgrown, the grass hadn't been mowed and there were no shrubs or vegetables.

All there was was a huge pine tree and an old house that looked like it hadn't seen paint since the day it was built.

I kept to the fence, figuring it would lead me out on to another street. I needed to get away from the deserted suburban landscape. Find some people to merge anonymously with. Goddamn suburbs. I hate them.

The big old house didn't look inhabited. I crept all the same. Knowing my luck the police would come abseiling out of the sky at any moment. The house was a trim fit on the swatch of land. The property had probably been sliced down the sides as the fortune that built it had dissipated.

The narrow path was overgrown. Weeds and webs swatted my face. I put my hand to my eyes to clear them. I could hear shouting and the sounds of car doors slamming, running feet. Slowly, I was being surrounded on all sides. There were probably hundreds of them and only one of me. And I didn't know where I was or what I was doing.

I pushed on through to the front garden. It was similarly overgrown. A privet hedge protected passersby from looking in. The hedge was D-shaped. There was a hole on one of the short sides of the D, no doubt made by generations of kids passing through to visit their neighbours. I squeezed through. A tight squeeze. I was in another backyard. The house next door was smaller, more modern. There was a big, old-

fashioned car in the driveway. It was in first-rate condition.
The doors were open. Somewhere, I could hear a young
woman's voice yelling, "Hamish, if you don't come here this
minute, you're going to go without dinner, do you hear me?"

I scanned the yard, I couldn't see anyone but the voice
sounded like it was coming from inside. I took a chance,
scooted across the lawn and opened the boot of the car. It was
big and bulbous. I climbed inside, holding the boot down as
tight as I could without closing it.

"There you are, now come on, would you? Jenny is waiting."

I heard two sets of footsteps. One big and purposeful, the
other small and pattering. The boot smelt slightly of petrol. I
hoped nothing was leaking.

Something light and plastic clattered on to the concrete.
"Pick it up and come on," said the adult. "We're already
late."

A gate creaked and the woman said, "Oh, hello."

"Gidday." It was a cop, I could feel it. I huddled into a
smaller ball, my hand gripped the inside of the boot catch till
the knuckles were white.

"We're looking for a man who was seen in this neighbourhood a few minutes ago." He gave her a description that
sounded roughly like me.

"Oh," said the woman. "Is he dangerous?"

"He killed a woman."

So much for the presumption of innocence. *I did not!* I
wanted to shout. Instead I gripped the car boot tighter. The
muscles in my hand starting to cramp.

"Oh dear. Well, I haven't seen anyone around here . . . and
I've been here all afternoon . . . Hamish darling, do get out of
the dirt. We're going to be eating soon."

"Mind if I look around?"

"No. Please do. I'll show you."

The adults went away. I lifted the boot and saw the child
crouched in the flower beds. He yanked a geranium, studied
the roots as if they were the most absorbing thing he'd ever
seen.

"If you see this man, don't go near him," the cop said when they came back a few minutes later.

The woman laughed. "There's no chance of that."

"We'll pick him up pretty soon. He can't go far."

That's what you think, buddy. I felt a childish sense of glee as the woman got into her big, old car, started the engine and backed out of the drive. I imagined the cop waving as he watched the car disappear down the road.

It wasn't the most comfortable of journeys, but it wasn't too long, either. We dipped and climbed, we took a few turns. I rattled around in the back. Then we slowed down, took another couple of turns and came to a halt.

"Bring your train," the woman said. I pictured her unbuckling her son from his car seat. "Look, there's Aunt Jenny waiting at the restaurant. Wave to her."

Their voices faded. I waited for a while and then lifted the boot lid a couple of inches. I could see the sea. I lifted the lid of the boot some more. I could smell the sea. It was Bondi Beach, the same beach I had seen from Paula's window. One of the most famous beaches in the world. Here I was at last— at a tourist mecca and in no position to buy even a postcard.

I remained in the boot for some time because although it was getting on for dark, Bondi Beach was crowded. Jam-packed with fun-seekers who'd think it suspicious if they saw a grown man clamber out of the boot of a car.

I hadn't taken my son's advice about staying away from Bondi, but I was sure he would sympathise if he knew my predicament. I flexed my legs, which were starting to cramp. I peered out on to the beach and watched a young couple with boogie boards brush the sand off themselves and settle down for a quiet snog. As he ran his hand up her smooth thigh she slapped him away. It gladdened my parental heart; she couldn't have been more than fourteen. A gaggle of young women went by on rollerblades. They all wore short shorts and bikini tops and they shrieked and flapped their arms like birds as they tried to stay upright. An elderly couple strolled by arm in arm eating ice-creams. I could hear stereos playing and babies crying. People laughing, drinking and having care-free fun. I hated them all.

The petrol smell was starting to make me feel lightheaded. I tried breathing through my mouth. I turned over so that the car's spare tyre was puncturing my other side. After what seemed like an eternity had passed, I heard the rumble of diesel engines. The hiss of hydraulics and the clatter of feet on steps. It was accompanied by the babble of Japanese. Then the light went from around the car. Well-clad bodies streamed past on their way to dip their Manolo Blahniks and Patrick Cox loafers in Bondi's platinum sand. It was the opportunity I needed. Their eyes were glued to the sea and even if they saw me hop out they would just attribute it to another strange *gaijin* habit.

I hopped out nimbly, brushed myself down casually as if I did this every day of the week. An elderly Japanese man noticed me. He looked puzzled then smiled uncertainly. I bowed and mumbled the few words of Japanese that I learnt when once getting drunk with a salaryman. He bowed back then followed his companions to the beach. I watched for a minute as they made the edge of the sand and like some formal dance routine, began grouping and regrouping in picture-taking formations.

Then I got the hell out of there.

Wednesday 7:02 p.m.

Bondi had a shabby lack of gentility that appealed to me. I liked the tatty tourist shops, the souvenir stalls, the racks of discount clothing, the cheap burger bars and kebab joints. If you discounted the jaw-dropping beach, ocean and cliff combination, you could almost have been in an English seaside town.

The other thing I liked about Bondi was I didn't have to go far to find an unsalubrious bar. It was dark and rough and the music was so loud the first place you noticed it was bouncing off your rib-cage. It was just what I needed.

"Pint of lager," I shouted to the barman.

"We only sell schooners," he shouted back.

"I'll have one of them then," I said recklessly. What did it matter? Might as well live a little.

The beer came in a huge glass and I gulped it needily. It didn't put the world to rights but it was the next best thing. I found a quiet corner of the bar and looked about. It was a cavernous spot filled with men in singlets, short shorts, rubber flip-flops and unflattering hair. There were a few women about but they didn't look like the types you'd take home to meet mother. There was a television locked to one wall with a grill over the screen. It was tuned to a sporting event. My own personal sporting event probably wouldn't feature large on this crowd's horizon. I felt safer here.

I sipped the second half of my beer more slowly and pretended I was planning a strategy.

I didn't expect Ozzie to come racing to my rescue once more. The police would have him down at the local station as fast as his legs could carry him. I hoped he had the presence of mind to convince Paula to leave him out of the story. But Paula didn't seem in a conciliatory mood.

Either way, I was utterly on my own. The picture of me in prison fatigues was coming into ever-clearer focus. I suddenly missed my friends in London, my grotty flat, my uneventful life. I missed it with a strength that I didn't think was possible. *I want my old life back.* I wanted to howl those words like a spoilt kid. I craved it, yearned for every monotonous moment. I wanted everything to be just like it had been before I met Michelle. I cursed the airline that had put us on the same flight. When this was over, I'd sue.

The hangover which I'd pushed to the back of my brain had begun to edge forward again. I tried to think of something constructive to do, but nothing would come. I tried to think of anything at all. My cognitive reasoning had drained away. All I could hear was the voice of my ex-wife admonishing me for my many faults.

I got out my wallet and found the piece of paper that I'd written Mary's telephone number on. I studied it. An admonishing voice was better than none at all.

I got some change out and went in search of a phone booth.

"Hello?" Mary's voice sounded thin and far away.

"It's Sam."

"You needn't worry. We're getting out of here as fast as we can. Looks like tomorrow at this stage."

Shit, I thought. "Terrific," I said. "Look, something's come up."

There was a slight, suspicious pause then: "What is it?"

"I need some information about a company owned by Vince O'Donnell. He's a property developer."

"What is this about?" Mary sounded irritated.

"It's about life and death," I said. "Please."

"Life and death? What do you mean?"

"Exactly what I say. I'm a journalist, remember? I use words with precision."

"Whose life and death?"

"Please, Mary. Can't you just do it for me?"

"What do you want to know?"

"Anything. What sort of shape he's in. Anything at all you can find out. Can you do that?"

"No," said Mary sharply, "I can't just do that. I left my crystal ball back in Sydney."

I took a deep, shuddering breath. She picked up on it, even though the line was poor.

"What's going on Sam? Are you in some kind of trouble?"

"Did I not just say the words life and death? I need your help Mary. I can't put it any plainer than that."

Mary clicked her tongue. It's her way of saying she's supremely pissed off. "Alright," she said. "I know someone who might know. I'll ring them. But you owe me."

"I've already given you my first born."

"Oh, please, let's not go into that."

"Mary?"

"What?"

"Don't let Simon watch any news bulletins."

"No chance of that, we haven't even got power. Sam, what the hell is going on?"

"It's complicated."

"Try me."

"The cops think I killed someone. A woman."

There was a long silence. "Oh Jesus," she whispered. "What happened?"

I rattled off my by now well-practised version of events. Mary, to her credit, didn't even ask if there was any basis to the cops' suspicions. I wanted to marry her all over again.

"Sam, I'm giving you the name of my lawyer. She's very good. Ring her immediately and then go down to the police and make a statement. We'll post bail, we'll get you out and you can go about this the proper way. This gallivanting around the city is absurd. Do you hear me, Sam? It can only make things worse."

"It's too late for that," I said.

"What do you mean it's too late?"

"I can't do that now."

"Can't do that? What do you mean you can't do that? Of course you can bloody do that."

"I was set up."

"What a stupid bloody notion. Set up by whom? You don't even know anybody in Sydney. You'll go to prison."

"I'm hoping to avoid that."

"You don't avoid prison by hoping, you idiot. You avoid prison by hiring an expensive lawyer."

"Alright," I said. "Give me her name. I'll call her later tonight."

"What are you intending to do now?"

"Oh, I don't know. A seafood meal and a stroll along the promenade perhaps. I'll see how the mood strikes me."

She recited the lawyer's name and number and I copied it down.

"I'll ask around about Vince but I really don't see what this is going to do."

"Great. Anything at all. Gossip, anything."

"You're not going to go to the police, are you?" She sounded weary.

"Not yet."

"That's one of the reasons I divorced you, you know. You never listened."

"Well, Mary, I'd love to stay and thrash this out, but I have authorities to evade. Perhaps you can come and see me in prison and we'll do a proper post-mortem on our marriage."

"Fine," she snapped.

"Sorry," I said. Squabbling is a reflex reaction with Mary. "You'll hit the phones?"

"There are days when I wish I'd never met you, Sam."

"You say the sweetest things. Gotta run."

I put the phone down. There was something surreal about arguing with your ex-wife while on the run from the police. Maybe that was why I felt so strange when the conversation ended. But then conversations with Mary were often like that. She could do kindness and recrimination in one sentence without even using a comma. A woman of class. And a pain in the neck.

Wednesday 7:31 p.m.

I walked. Head down, hat pulled over my eyes. Vaguely making for the Victorian building that I had seen from Paula's place. I had no real plan, it was the only thing I could fasten on to. It could be seen all over Bondi.

My stomach reminded me that I hadn't eaten. I stopped in at a kebab stand and ordered the first thing on the menu. The evening news was on and there I was. They'd gotten hold of my passport photo, which is the kind of thing that can do irreparable damage to your self-image. I glanced at the screen, startled. By now the police would know everything about me. I could imagine Interpol computers chattering at each other, spilling their guts about my vital statistics. Where I lived, who I worked for, how I spent my time.

I attempted to cheer myself up by noting that I looked nothing like my passport photo. To add to my meagre list of blessings, the spotty youth ladling greasy meat into a pitta pocket didn't even glance up at the television. He wiped his nose on his hand before he passed the kebab over, but I was prepared to forgive him even that as long as he didn't look at the television. I pushed my glasses further up my nose.

The kebab tasted reassuringly like bad kebabs the world

over. It barely touched the sides on the way down and lounged in my gut like a malevolent toad.

I walked briskly.

The sun had lost little of its heat, even though it was heading towards the horizon. A layer of sweat bubbled up underneath the layers of dirt, fear and fatigue. I was the walking dead. I hadn't slept properly, I hadn't showered. All I could hear was Mary's voice dishing out advice. She was right. I needed a lawyer and I needed one sharp. There was no sense in continuing this ridiculous charade. I was alone in a city that I didn't know.

The building was late Victorian I guessed. It was built of a pale-coloured brick and it faced south on to Bondi Beach. It was probably about five storeys high, with narrow windows. In the centre a crenellated turret rose another couple of floors. The modern building had echoed that turret with one of its own in blue glass. It must have been nice for the people living there. They got great views which didn't include their building. Inside I could see expensive cars and well-kept shrubs. A high fence rimmed the property and the gates were securely closed. I couldn't get in and realised that I didn't particularly want to.

On the street outside was a bus stop. I sat on the bench and looked at it, seeking inspiration. None came.

Cheap, flowery cologne irritated my nose. A pair of blinking watery grey eyes stared into mine. They belonged to an elderly woman in a flowered housecoat.

"If you're waiting for a bus then you're out of luck," she said. "This service doesn't run in the evenings any more. They cut it back." By the sound of her voice she was from England, but a long time ago. Her vowels had stretched in the meantime.

"Thanks," I said, not meaning it. "I'm waiting for a friend."

"You're English?"

I nodded, wishing her a thousand miles away.

"You look familiar. Where from?"

"London." I shut my eyes, waiting for the tumblers to fall. She looked like the type who watched the evening news. I had a vision of knocking her down to make my getaway. I was becoming a hardened criminal.

"I'm from Kent, near Margate."

"Fancy that." I actually wanted to scream at her to go the fuck away. But I concentrated on keeping calm.

"Haven't been back in twenty-five years," she said with a hint of pride. "No reason to. The family are all here. I miss it, though. Sometimes. Not the weather of course."

"Of course."

"You look like someone on the telly." She peered at me again. I smiled winningly.

"Lot of people say that. I must have one of those common faces."

"What are you doing here?"

"Looking at property. I want to buy a place around here." The state I was in I didn't look solvent enough to buy a beer, but she didn't appear to notice any inconsistencies. "I'm very interested in this building, actually," I said, pointing at the old school.

The old woman snorted. "It's a bloody disgrace. Old place like that should never have been touched. At least England has respect for its history."

Jolly old England. What I wouldn't have given to be there.

"It's going to come to me soon," she mused, "who you look like, I mean."

Oh, I hope not, I thought, while smiling pleasantly.

"Well, it's been nice chatting," I said, getting up as though I meant to go.

"Yes," she said, her brow creased in concentration. I made a small prayer to the gods to deliver me from interfering old busybodies. I ambled off down the hill. A chap without care whose only big decision was where he would spend the cool half-mil that he wanted to plonk into property. I began whistling a little tune then decided that it was laying it on a bit thick. I turned back. The old woman was still there, looking slightly forlorn. Then she realised where she'd seen me. She put her hand to her face. Turned, hurried back to her house.

I broke into a run. I had to get the hell out of Bondi.

I kept off the main roads but had no clear idea of where I

was going or why. Nor any expectation that I would get there. The cops would be here in five seconds flat. I stopped running. There was absolutely no point. Then I had an idea. A Japanese tour bus had saved me once before, perhaps it could save me again. I headed back into the centre of Bondi.

It was a wild idea and I had no thought of how I would convince a bus load of tourists that they should give me a lift back into town. But I hung on to it. Because a plan, however bad, was a prophylactic against the insistent tide of hysteria that threatened to overwhelm me.

I merged with the crowd on the main street and breathed relief. I love crowds. No one looks at you, no one bothers you. There's only jostling to deal with, and I can manage that. I crossed the main street to the car park which bordered the beach.

There were three tour buses in the car park. They were empty, their inhabitants scattered for the moment, soaking up the remnants of the day. Patently, getting in the bus itself would draw the sort of attention that I was hoping to avoid, so I tried the luggage compartments. Crouched down between two of the buses I had some sort of cover. I wrestled with the handle. The door slid open smoothly. The space was full. I moved on to the next one, where the story was the same.

"Hey you!"

A bus driver had rounded on me. Hands on hips, he had stopped in surprise at seeing someone having their way with his vehicle. He lunged for me, but my responses were getting quicker. I stepped to one side and then ran. I made for the promenade, which was full of joggers and rollerbladers and people moving as fast as me. I kept to a walk-trot pace, so people would think I was an eccentric jogger who hadn't bothered to go out and buy the gear. I needn't have worried, the driver was not interested in a full-scale chase. Once he'd seen me off he went back to his bus.

I reached the south end of the beach. It was practically dark now, but there were still people swimming in the tidal pools. *Fun. Is that all you people think about?* I thought crossly as I climbed up the hill. I was just putting one foot in front of the other, with no long-term objective. Then there was a bench to sit on, so I sat. Looked out to sea. The ocean rose and fell in a soothing fashion, but it didn't soothe me. I sat stubbornly resistant to its charms. All I could think about was death.

"Samuel Ridley." The voice came out of the half-darkness, I couldn't see who it belonged to. I jumped. Began to turn to get a fix on the sound when a firm hand clamped my shoulder.

"Well, well. Fancy seeing you here."

Wednesday 8:00 p.m.

My heart lurched. I felt sick. I wondered if I should run but realised it was pointless. It was over. I didn't even bother to turn around.

A shape materialised, breathing heavily, sat down on my bench. The shape of the well-dressed journalist called Frank Webster whom I'd last seen at the court building.

I opened my mouth to say something, but my vocal chords had packed up and left without saying goodbye. All that came out was a dry gargling sound. Frank Webster's grin put me in mind of a wolf gazing on a plump young chicken. It was the smile of a reporter when he's about to hit on a big story. And I was the story.

"I'm dying to shoot the breeze with you," Frank said as he got comfortable in a proprietorial way. Took out a small can of cigars and lit one slowly and lovingly. Didn't offer me one. "Imagine my surprise when I get back to the office after meeting you in court to find that the person who passed himself off as a fellow reporter is wanted for murder."

I shrugged modestly. "I'm multi-functional."

"I'll just bet."

"How did you find me?"

"I listen to the police radio. I heard them say you'd been

spotted out here and so I came out to see what I could see. I've been hanging around all afternoon. At first it was just a good excuse to get out of the office. But now I'm kind of interested.

"I'd almost given up hope, then there you were—jogging along the promenade," he beamed, proud of his cleverness, his sheer luck. "You've taken to Sydney like a local. What do you think of our fair city?"

"It hasn't been fair to me."

"Give it a chance, you've only been here a day. Perhaps you can pull off an armed robbery tomorrow to lift your spirits."

"I'm not a criminal."

"What were you doing at the court?"

"I wanted to see what I was up against."

"Up against?"

"I didn't kill Michelle."

"I love it." Frank was writing his story in his head as we spoke. Figuring the angles, phrasing the headline. I've done it myself a million times. "Who do you think did? The husband?"

"She did say she wanted to get his money."

"There isn't any," Frank said, studying the tip of his cigar. "The New Harbour development is Vince's last chance. And he has quite enough on his plate without taking on the additional shit which arrives when your wife is murdered. I think that kind of rules him out, don't you? So let's talk about you. What did you have to gain?"

"Are we on the record or off?"

"Haven't decided yet."

The sea was drawing in the colour of night, getting darker and calmer. Ship lights winked on the horizon. I imagined running away to sea.

"I didn't have anything to gain. I had everything to lose. I came here to see my son."

"Human interest. Excellent." Frank balanced his cigar on the arm of the bench and brought out his notebook. It had his initials embossed on the cover.

"I met her on the plane. We had some laughs. I didn't kill her. I quite liked her, actually."

"Ah," Frank sighed, "your eyes met across a crowded baggage carousel. This is good. My readers will love this."

"Then I got drunk and passed out in the lavatory." I tried to imagine how my defence lawyer would construct a credible case from that sad piece of information. It didn't look good even to me.

Frank's grin widened. "Corker," he said as he wrote neatly on the pad. His script was old-fashioned, ornate. "Actually on the dunny? Or the floor?"

"The cops will have you if you print this."

"I didn't say I was going to. Yet."

"Are you going to turn me in?"

He laughed outright at that. "Why on earth would I do that?"

"Civic duty. Respect for law and order."

Frank laughed some more. "You don't know much about Australia, mate," he said, his accent broadening. "We love outlaws, cobber. We lionise them. They're our bloody national heroes."

"I'll do you a deal," I said. "If you help me, I'll give you the story."

"How far do you think you're going to get? You're number one on the hit parade."

"That's why I need help."

"I'll have to talk to my editor."

"Keep your editor out of this. Make up your own mind."

Frank closed his notebook slowly. Placed it in his pocket. Crossed his sharply pleated trousers.

"There's no risk to you," I said. "All I'll need is information. And whether I'm right or not you'll get the story."

"So you said. They arrest you it'll be *sub judice*. I'll be done as an accessory. Bang goes the brilliant career."

"I'm not going down for this," I said. "I didn't do it."

Frank leaned back against the bench and surveyed me, eyes narrowed. "Why didn't you get on the first plane out of here? Why are you being such a jolly good sport by hanging around?"

"I was dropped on my head as a baby."

"Too bad. That's not a reason."

"Someone took my passport. The police found it in the flat and now they know all about me. So you can understand why I'm a little tense."

Frank sat up. His instinct told him that maybe there was a story that was worth something.

"That's as good a place as any to start," he said.

Wednesday 8:14 p.m.

"**P**olice want to question British tourist, Samuel Ridley in connection with the murder of a Sydney woman in her Neutral Bay house last night." A honey-voiced radio newsreader was busy nailing my coffin.

"Michelle O'Donnell, estranged wife of property developer Vince O'Donnell, was bludgeoned to death. Police believe she met Mr Ridley on a plane flight back to Sydney from Singapore. The two spent the evening together and were seen going back to Mrs O'Donnell's house. Vince O'Donnell has offered a reward of thirty thousand dollars for any information that leads to the killer's capture," the presenter went on. "His lawyer made this statement outside Sydney Police Centre today."

"My client has co-operated fully with the police," said the lawyer. "He has spent two hours answering questions. He is as anxious as anyone to find out who is responsible for this vile deed—"

The reporters' voices clamoured. One was louder than the others. "Where were you last night, Vince?" she shouted.

"I—" began Vince. Someone cut him off. His lawyer.

"My client has given his testimony to the police. He has contributed thirty thousand dollars as a reward. He has nothing further to—" This time it was the lawyer's turn to be cut off.

"Can I just say one thing?" asked Vince.

"How does this affect the New Harbour project?" someone else yelled.

"Can I just say one thing?" Vince insisted. The crowd laid off. There was silence, which Vince stretched to dramatic effect.

"I just want to say that I am devastated by the death of my wife, especially in this barbaric manner. I may never come to grips with the loss that I feel. Michelle was an extremely special woman. Funny, generous, smart—"

"That why you left her?" came the same voice from the back.

"As I was saying, no one who knew her would have wanted to hurt her. It's true, that our marriage didn't work," Vince went on. "But lots of marriages don't work and for lots of reasons. But, my God, this is—" He paused, took a deep shuddering breath and then put his hands up to his face. "I'm sorry," he said. "This is . . . I can't . . . I've got nothing more to say."

"He does a good grieving relative," said Frank. We were in his Mini, heading west. The story switched back to the studio. The newsreader gave out my description and a telephone number that potential Samuel Ridley spotters could call in on.

"They've had your photo on the news," said Frank.

"I know. I saw it. We need to talk to Michelle's lawyer. She must have one if she's divorcing."

"Want to stop off for some hair dye?"

"No, I do not."

I heard a police siren.

"Strewth, that was quick," Frank said.

I turned around. A police car was hard on our bumper.

The police officer inside waved us on to the side of the road.

The cop switched off the siren as he pulled in behind us. Other cars whizzed past, drivers staring rudely at our predicament. I shut my eyes, not wanting to know what would happen next, praying to the gods for miraculous, flashy deliverance.

Slowly, too slowly, the cop got out of the car, walked forward to where we were parked. Bent at the waist. I felt as if his action should have had a soundtrack accompaniment. Something ponderous with timpanies. Something that spelled out doom.

Frank rolled down his window.

"Good evening, officer," he said, his tone jovial. "Frank Webster, *Sydney Star*. What can I do for you?"

The cop looked at both of us. He took his time. I tried to arrange my face to how an innocent person might look. It wasn't easy. I felt guilty.

"Licence please," he said.

"Certainly, officer," said Frank expansively, chuckling as he reached into his wallet. I thought he was overdoing it a bit.

Frank located his licence and passed it to the cop who stared at it intently for longer than it probably deserved. He handed it back. I looked around nervously for the back-up which was surely being called right now. I could imagine lines of police cars speeding to the spot to take us off to prison. Then there'd be the helicopters who'd shoot at us from the air if we tried to get away. There was no escape. They were probably erecting the barricades right now.

No, I knew I would go peacefully. I didn't have the heart for a high-speed chase. That's how it would end—not with a bang but a whimper. I slumped in my seat.

The cop bent down, looked in the car. "Your lefthand tail light isn't working, mate," he said at last.

"Oh my God, it isn't?" exclaimed Frank. "I had no idea."

"Get it checked out," said the cop. "Soon." He slapped the roof and walked away.

Frank and I sat there, not comprehending that we'd somehow got off. We sat while the cop started his car and we waved while he drove off. And then we sat some more.

"Well," he said finally. "That's got to be a good omen. Think I'll buy a lottery ticket this week."

Frank's flat was a converted warehouse near the centre of

town tucked in behind a highway and a brewery. I could smell both as I got out of the Mini.

"You look like you could do with a shower," Frank said as he unlocked the front door.

His bathroom was a moulded white plastic modular affair. No windows, no natural light of any kind. I showered in the dark, grateful for a small space in which to think about nothing. The shower was strong. The drumming rhythm quieted the voices in my head. It eased out the tension that had congregated in my shoulders and spine. It made me feel, for a few sweet minutes, more like a human than a hunted animal.

Frank had opened a bottle of wine and was sorting newspaper clippings. The television was on with the sound turned down. The only other light in the room came from a standard lamp, antique by the looks of things. The rest of the apartment was a mixture of bachelor modern and eclectic hand-me-downs. The most striking feature was the sound system. It was sleek and Scandinavian and its accessories dominated one long wall. Frank's collection of CDs, records and cassettes could have stocked a fair-sized shop. They were stacked in piles like mini skyscrapers, perched on shelves, tumbling out of boxes. They were about to take the place over. Just holding back the tide of plastic was an elderly upright piano. It looked well-used. Classical sheet music piled on top.

"You're not tempted by the reward?" I asked as Frank handed me a glass of wine. "Thirty thousand dollars buys a lot of shorthand notebooks."

"Money can't buy happiness," Frank grinned. "Cheers."

The wine warmed me, made me feel better. I sat down on the floor beside the clippings file. "Didn't know newspapers still used these things," I said, holding up a story about Vince O'Donnell.

"They don't. We have a technophobic colleague to thank for this. Bernie Jennings didn't trust computers. He cut and pasted the old-fashioned way. He was obsessed with Vince. Followed everything he did. Concocted grand conspiracy theories about him. Figured if he stuck on his arse long enough Vince would make a mistake and Bernie would be there to trip him up."

"And was he?"

Frank shook his head. "Bernie died on the job. It was a tragic accident."

My heart leapt. "Do you think Vince had anything to do with it?"

"Not unless he was pulling beers at the Great Western pub the day Bernie took his final liquid lunch. He drank five schooners then got up. Said his goodbyes and pitched over. Flat on his face. Some poor bloke tried mouth to mouth, which was a really heroic gesture considering how much Bernie'd had to drink, not to mention the two meat pies he'd eaten for lunch. But it was too late. Bernie had drunk his last."

Frank had sorted his old colleague's stories into two separate piles.

"Here we have Vince's career in chronological order," he said. "Take your pick."

I chose the pile that had a photograph of the Victorian school building at Bondi.

We settled down to read.

Frank's former colleague had been obsessive about tracking Vince's career. His clippings were extensive. On the day when work had started demolishing the school he'd kept the whole page. It was a sliver of life preserved from that day. There was a large photo of some minor dignitary posing with a shovel. A surf carnival, a photograph of a missing office worker, a clever child admitted to university at thirteen.

That was seven years ago, almost to the day.

Several firms had put up for the tender, some of the newspaper articles carried sketches of the planned developments. Vince's original proposal didn't bear much resemblance to what he had ultimately erected, and for that he came in for some flak. But he grinned and bore it. That's what progress is about, he said. And progress is good for Sydney.

I skimmed the rest of the material. It was essentially the same story told over and over again. Vince keeping one step ahead.

"Did Bernie Jennings have any theories about this guy?" I asked Frank.

"Just one. That he was the anti-Christ."

"Did he ever get anything concrete."

"He followed him about for years, poking into his business affairs. Obsessive almost. Problem was that Vince has a thing about keeping inside the law. He employs platoons of lawyers to find ways under the fence. Nobody's ever been able to touch him. Not in the way that would hurt him anyway."

There were photos of Vince. I looked through them slowly. Vince on building sites, Vince on his yacht, Vince and Michelle at society parties, chatting with government ministers, socialites, media stars. I went through them two or three times trying to glean clues. His smooth, sun-tanned face gave nothing away. I collected the clippings up. Stacked them neatly. Tried not to think about the sense of futility that had begun to settle on me like a noxious gas. The newsreader in my head had abandoned the script and was starting to sound a bit like Mary. *It's useless*, she said. *Give this up now*. I looked at the phone. Mary was right. I had to start behaving like an intelligent adult. I had to get a lawyer, go to the cops. Have them take my statement. The courts would let me out on bail. I couldn't do this thing on my own.

"Well?" Frank asked. "Did that lot spark any ideas?"

"One of these articles mentions Vince's son."

"Darryl O'Donnell, there's a name to conjure with. Now let me see." Frank sorted through the clippings. "Here we are." He laid a clipping out in front of me. It was of Vince at a building site, checking plans with a man in a hard hat. Darryl, a large, well-built man with a silly haircut and dark glasses stood behind him, glaring.

"Apparently he's quite the one with the ladies," Frank murmured. "Amazing what money can do. Look at that stomach and imagine what he'll be like when he's fifty."

Darryl's stomach protruded firmly, as if he had a large ball underneath his shirt. His jowls were attempting to reach his shoulders.

"Does he get on with his dad?"

"The expression right-hand man was invented with Darryl in mind."

"Where would we find him?"

"Usually in the bar at the Hilton drinking cocktails and

pulling sheilas. He likes the ones who don't speak English because there's less chance that he'll have to use words bigger than two syllables. But tonight I happen to know he's at a reception at Darling Harbour.'' Frank smiled. ''I put the time I spent hanging around on Bondi Beach to good use.''

''What will I do while you're circulating with a martini?'' We were back in the Mini, speeding towards Darling Harbour, wherever that was, with a female opera singer blaring out of the speakers.

''Relax, take in the sights. You're on holiday, remember?'' Frank began singing along with the music. He had a good tenor voice.

We deposited the car in an underground car park and followed the signs towards the Convention Centre, a circular building that along with the rest of the construction in the harbour looked only a few years old. The city skyscrapers were bunched on the skyline across the water.

''Sam! What the hell are you doing here?'' I cringed. Looked around. A rangy figure with a television camera balanced on one shoulder hurried over.

Oswald Booker was back in my life.

Wednesday 9:20 p.m

"Jesus," he said, "I was worried. How did you get away from the cops? Who is this guy? Why didn't you ring me?"

"For all I knew you were in jail for harbouring a dangerous criminal. And this is Frank."

"Nah, mate. Paula told the cops she'd seen you running down the street. She'd called me and I'd rushed over to help her. Do you think I could have been wrong about her? I mean it's true she doesn't have Catherine's class, but she is a damn good sport. And I'm sure she likes you, despite what happened. I mean, it was me she was getting at, not you."

"Ozzie, Paula's good opinion is the very least of my worries right now."

Ozzie looked relieved. "Yeah. Course it is. Sorry. You don't know how to run sound do you?"

"I'm a radio journalist. I've got a fair idea."

"It's just that right now I'm in a bit of a bind. I'm supposed to shoot this bloody do for the late news but my sound man's got a concussion, thanks to my former best mate, Matt. Think you could stand in for him? I can carry all the gear myself but it's a bit of a hassle, you know? Will you do it?"

"No, I won't."

"Come on. It's not hard. I'll show you how. It'll take five minutes."

I took a deep breath. "Ozzie I haven't had much experience being on the run from the law, but I'm fairly sure it doesn't involve mixing with the great and good at cocktail parties." I looked at Frank for confirmation, and wondered if the pressure Ozzie was under had become too much.

Ozzie shrugged. "Nobody takes the slightest bit of notice of crew," he said. "It's the best disguise you can have short of wearing a paper bag over your chops."

I looked at Frank for confirmation. He grinned. "It's your funeral," he said. "I get the story either way, remember?"

I suppose all the running around and hiding out in fume-soaked car boots had softened my brain because I found myself saying "yes" out loud at the same time as my inner voice was shouting, *What? Are you crazy?*

I ignored the inner voice. I had information to seek. Vital information that would save me relocating to a small room with bars on the windows. This was no time to be timid.

We went inside. The crowd was well-lubricated and noisy. Ozzie scanned the room through the viewfinder, muttering something about the indignity of a cameraman of his calibre working a job like this. I held the fluffy, phallic microphone at a professional angle and kept my head down, concentrated on watching the needle on the sound monitor dance.

"I've spotted Darryl," Frank plucked at my elbow. "He's out on the deck mauling some poor woman."

"Darryl? Darryl who?" asked Ozzie.

"Vince O'Donnell's son. He's the reason we're here. Come and stick your camera in his face. Maybe he'll say something that he didn't intend to."

"This isn't my brief." Ozzie, I could tell, had the feeling that life was something that was now well beyond his control.

"You might get a scoop. There's no story here," said Frank nodding at the party. "Just a bunch of galahs getting pissed."

Frank dived into the crowd. Expensive smells wafted around me, expensive fabrics brushed against my dirty shirt. Frank forged on. We made the edge of the crowd, drank the cooler air on the balcony. A dark-suited man stood with his back to us. One mitt caressing a bottle of beer, the other a skinny woman in bright-blue sequins. She giggled, he pawed. It wasn't pretty.

"Darryl? Frank Webster, *Sydney Star*. Can I have a word?" Darryl turned. Lifted his face from his partner's décolleté. Focused on Frank. Ignored Ozzie and me. Ozzie was right. Although I felt as though I was outlined in neon and had cymbals between my knees, to the rest of the world I was non-existent.

"No." Darryl turned back to the twinkly skyline view.

"Your stepmother's dead, Darryl. How do you feel?"

"I prefer to do my grieving in private," Darryl sneered. Slurped at the neck of his bottle. He was a tall chap with sunburned cheeks and the haircut looked even more unflattering in person, cut short and straight on top and sides, long and limp down the back.

"How's your father bearing up?"

"Ask him."

"He must be relieved. This way he doesn't have to face an expensive divorce," said Frank, bravely, I thought. Darryl didn't look like the kind of guy who would consider opposing viewpoints for the sake of stimulating debate. But Frank's words didn't seem to connect with Darryl. His eyes were glazed. If you pressed me on it, I'd say there was more than just designer beer zinging around his bloodstream. He put his giant hand to the girl's nape. She seemed frozen, like a character in a play when the spotlight has shifted to someone else.

"Any theories about who would want her dead? Besides your old man, I mean."

If Frank's intention was to antagonise Darryl into letting something slip, it didn't seem to be having the desired effect. The lad wasn't quite all there. Far from taking offence at the question he seemed to have forgotten that Frank had even asked it. Darryl checked his bottle which turned out to be empty. Handed it to the sequin girl who trotted off to get a full one. Then he pushed himself off the railings with both hands and lurched into Ozzie's personal space.

"Wanna be on the evening news?" Ozzie squinted into his eyepiece.

Darryl reached for the microphone that I was trying to hold equidistant between the two speakers. He snatched it away from me. Held it close to his mouth.

"Get fucking lost. Or I'll find a fancy new use for this." He said it loudly. The effect was like canon shot in my ears.

"Is this your way of saying hitmen are cheaper than lawyers?" Frank said crisply.

Darryl turned away, yanked the microphone out of its socket and tossed it over the rail. Ozzie winced as he heard the thin clatter of expensive equipment hitting concrete some feet below.

"Hey!" said Ozzie. He looked like he was about to thump Darryl. I put a hand on his arm.

Frank remained cool. "I'll take that as a no comment."

His sarcasm enraged Darryl. "You people fucking make me want to chunder," he spun back, his voice almost a shout. "My father didn't do anything wrong. Bloody women were always trying to bleed him. He put up with her for far longer than he should have, the bloodsucker. All she did was spend his money. Her half-cracked business ideas." He plonked his beery face in Frank's. "I'm just surprised my father's stayed here all these years with the trouble that he gets. I'm surprised he hasn't upped and left you carping pygmies to it. Gone somewhere where they respect entre . . . entrepren . . . people with vision."

"Were they in business together?"

"What?"

"Your father and Michelle? You said he supported her business plans. Was she working on the New Harbour project?"

"No, now fuck off."

"But you said . . ."

"I said, fuck off."

The sequin girl returned with a new bottle and Darryl drank deeply, his Adam's apple bobbing. The girl looked at us, shrugged in half-sympathy and picked up her champagne glass.

We went inside.

"My microphone," moaned Ozzie. "It was brand new. Cost me bloody thousands."

"I'll buy you a new one."

"You don't get paid in prison."

"I'm not going to prison." I said it with a defiance I didn't feel.

"Ozzie!" The woman squeaked in surprise. Put her hand to her chest and spilt some of her champagne in the process.

"Catherine, what are you doing here?"

"Well, I'm . . . well. You know. One goes to parties."

Catherine was tall and thin. Too thin for my liking, but her breasts were big enough for me to overlook her other faults. She wore a lacy red dress that was gratifyingly see-through in parts. Her brown hair was long, glossy and straight. In one hand she cradled a cigarette and a glass. The other was flapping as if the room had suddenly become too hot or too small.

"Matt's just over there," she said, pointing with the champagne-glass hand.

Ozzie didn't look in the direction of her hand. "I want a word."

"Not now."

"Why not now?"

"Because it's not right. I'm here with Matt, Ozzie. And he'll kill you if he sees you."

"Well when?"

"Look. I don't know when. I'll phone you tomorrow."

"I can't wait, Catherine. We've got to talk. Bugger Matt." Ozzie's emotions threatened to overwhelm him. Catherine squirmed in true British fashion and said nothing. She looked down her cleavage. She took a step back. Opened her mouth to say something and decided not to. If I had to put money on it, I'd say she was planning to tell Ozzie that his idea about riding off into the sunset with him was not going to fit with her very tight schedule. But not now. Now she was going to leave him dangling.

"I've got to go," she said.

"Why didn't you return my calls?"

"I've been . . . you know . . . busy."

"You've been busy?"

Catherine had the grace to look ashamed. As an excuse it

didn't quite rank up there with "I was walking my iguana."
But it was close.

I checked the room for someone who might be paying too
much attention to our cosy little group. Someone like Catherine's husband. The last thing we needed was an ugly scene
involving former friends.

"Come on, Ozzie. We've got to get back to the office."
Frank laid a firm hand on Ozzie's shoulder. He'd reached the
same conclusion as I had. "We've got work to do, remember?"

Ozzie's eyes were dull. "Okay," he said.

Relief softened Catherine's features. "Tomorrow," she
said. "I'll ring you tomorrow."

Frank and I got out of there as fast as we could. I took the
camera off Ozzie, he seemed too faint to carry it. On the pavement outside I picked up the remains of the microphone. Ozzie
allowed himself to be led to his car.

"I don't understand what's happened. She's changed. She's
not like she was the weekend we were together."

"The glow of passion's worn off, eh?" Frank said.

"I bet the family's got to her," he said. "That's it. The
family has threatened her. They've got to her and told that if
she leaves Matt they'll . . ."

"They'll what? She's not married to the mob. She's
changed her mind, that's all," I said wearily. The camera had
become heavy. I had to struggle to keep up with Ozzie, who'd
suddenly picked up some speed.

"No she hasn't. Not Catherine. She needs time to think
things over, that's all. I understand that. It's a big step, breaking up a marriage. She can't decide to do it on the basis of
one dirty weekend. And I'd think less of her if she did."

We'd reached Ozzie's car. Ozzie unlocked the boot, took
the camera off me and stowed it in a metal box. "No, she
needs time to think and I'm going to give her time. I don't
want this thing to be a rush job. It has to be thought through
if we're going to base this relationship on anything solid." He
took the microphone shards, barely registering the damage and
chucked them in the back. "Space is the key to this whole
thing," he declared triumphantly as he shut and locked the

boot. "I'm going back to tell her that I understand what this is about. I'm going to tell her that I understand her wanting to think things over."

"Ozzie," said Frank, pinching the bridge of his nose. "Is this such a good idea, mate? You've got to get that tape back to the studio. Somebody wants those pictures for the late bulletin, remember?"

"It'll only take a minute," Ozzie said, a shade truculently. We watched him stride off through the gloom.

"I can say one thing for Ozzie," I remarked as we made our way back to Frank's car, "he makes me feel a whole lot better about my relationships with women."

The Mini was parked at a rakish angle. Frank shoved a tape in the machine and a woman began singing very high. A different woman to the one I'd been treated to on the way over.

"What'll we do now?" he said, jerking the car into gear and forcing the poor little engine to do too many revolutions. We spun out of the car park and out on to the street. A sleek black car went past.

"Michelle's lawyer," I said. "She must have had a lawyer if she was divorce—"

"Aha!" said Frank. "John Holden. What a happy coincidence." The car in front turned into the convention centre. John Holden got out, straightening the lapels on his dinner jacket. Frank's abrupt stop was complete with screeching tyres. I shuddered.

"Wait here," Frank said, leaping out.

"Don't worry. I feel an irresistible urge to lie low."

"John, a word?" Frank covered the ground between them smartly. John Holden turned around. Forced his face into a smile.

"Frank, what can I do for you?" he said genially.

"How is the scandal over Vince's wife's murder going to affect government support for New Harbour?"

John Holden sighed, pushed a hand through his well-cut hair.

"We don't support Vince O'Donnell. We sold him the land, that's all. We sold the land to free up some cash. The reason I was in court today was to explain why that decision had been reached. Whether Vince O'Donnell is charged with murder is quite immaterial. Two separate issues, Frank. Anyway, I understood he'd been released.''

"It's one more controversy that the government doesn't need. Your record isn't good and you're heading for an election. Mud sticks.''

Holden laughed gently. ''I'd expect you to understand that more than anyone, Frank. Since you're usually the one throwing it.''

"What if Vince O'Donnell goes belly up?''

''I've been in politics too long to play the what-if game with reporters.''

Holden reached in his pocket, brought out a packet of cigarettes, lit up. Offered one to Frank who shook his head. Holden's aid made a conspicuous job of checking his watch but Holden ignored it.

"What's this really about, Frank? You got something on Vince?''

Frank grinned broadly.

"What have you got?''

"Buy the *Star*, Holden. It's first with the news. But if I were the government I'd be getting as far away as I could. The votes don't want to see you associated with a big fat failure like New Harbour. Or worse.''

Holden laughed lightly. ''When there's a job on my policy staff I'll let you know.''

"I'm giving you this advice for free. Michelle O'Donnell's death is going to open a can of worms.''

"It seems pretty straightforward to me. She was less than discriminating about who she picked up for the night. Anything else is just wishful thinking on your part. You hate Vince and you want to see him fail.''

"And you don't?''

"My job is a pretty thankless task where people like you are concerned. Always the naysayers. You forget that when the Opera House was built people hated it. What would the city be without it now?''

"Don't tell me Vince's shoddy buildings are going to stand the test of time,'' Frank laughed.

"How do you know?"

"My innate good taste."

"You'd have preferred that the contract went to some Japanese consortium? You know what would have happened then. They build the things like hermetic cells. No jobs for Aussies, Frank. No money for the local economy, it all goes straight back to Japan. Personally, I don't have an opinion about Vince one way or the other. All I care about is jobs for Australians. And you can't fault him in that department."

"Yeah," Frank drawled, "he's true blue."

Holden flicked his cigarette away. It was still glowing. The aid put his foot on it. Holden had spotted somebody over Frank's shoulder, he lifted his hand in greeting. Excused himself in that smooth-but-curt way that politicians do when they no longer have a use for you.

"Happy hunting," he said over his shoulder.

Wednesday 10:06 p.m.

"What was all that about?" I asked as Frank climbed back into the car.

"Just stirring," Frank said. "Making a few connections. Maybe Michelle was involved with New Harbour somehow."

"We don't know that for sure."

"No, but I like winding Holden up. He doesn't show it but he's terrified about the next election. And any contribution I can make to his lack of sleep is okay by me."

"So it's personal?"

"Not particularly. I quite like Holden actually. He's capable and smart. But that New Harbour land should never have been sold to a developer. It should have been left as it is. It's the same old story, you leave one bunch of blokes in power for too long and they start to think they belong there."

"Was it Holden's doing that it was sold?"

"No. But it's landed in his lap. Poor bastard."

Michelle's lawyer's name was Daniel Levine and the lights were on at his bungalow in another fashionable seafront suburb that Sydney seemed to have an endless supply of. I think it was near Double Bay, but it was dark and I had trouble getting my bearings although we were definitely heading east.

Frank got Daniel Levine's address by calling his office and asking someone called Annabelle to track it down. She did so in less than five minutes and we didn't have to leave the car, which I liked. I was beginning to find this small space so reassuring that I had a hard time thinking about going anywhere else.

Frank knocked briskly. There was no reply. He punched the doorbell. We heard a distant ringing, then silence. He rang again. We heard a crash, the sound of footsteps.

The rattle of locks. The door opened. A dishevelled man with curly hair stood on the other side. He had pouchy eyes, booze breath. It looked like we'd interrupted a meaningful session with a bottle. He had his wallet in his hand and was extracting a note.

"You're not the pizza."

"Frank Webster, *Sydney Star*."

Daniel Levine looked us over. His eyes narrowed when he saw me.

"You might as well come in," he said.

We followed him down a dimly lit corridor into a dimly lit living room.

"Drink?"

We said yes.

Daniel Levine shakily poured two shots into heavy crystal glasses. He looked at me hard. Turned to Frank.

"Don't tell me who your mate is," he said. "I don't want to know."

"Well then you know why we're here," Frank said. "We want to know if you know anything about why she was killed."

Daniel Levine shot another look at me. Said nothing. Still there was silence. Daniel Levine studied his glass then drank from it.

"Can you tell us anything at all?" Frank asked.

"Of course not. It would breach my obligations to my client."

"Your client is dead," I said.

Somewhere we could hear a dog barking. A car pulling up. Otherwise all was quiet in the suburban night.

"Oh, yes," Daniel Levine said, "how could that have slipped my mind? Well that changes everything, of course."

Daniel's eyes were not in the business of focusing. He seemed to have trouble holding his head up. I thought about offering to make coffee. Figured he'd probably have trouble accepting it from a man who wasn't there.

"Anything you can tell us would be a help," Frank said casually. Like it wasn't a matter of my whole future.

There was another long silence. Frank looked at me and shrugged. Daniel Levine was attempting to marshall his thinking equipment. He didn't look like he went head to head with a whisky bottle that often. As one who has, I can usually spot a kindred spirit. Daniel Levine was a novice drunk. He wasn't handling it well.

"You must have been looking for Vince's money," Frank prompted.

"One way or another," Levine slurred. I felt sorry for him. Found his kitchen and got him a glass of water. Brought it back. Made him drink it. He gulped it down in two swallows and went straight back to the whisky.

"What do you mean?"

"We couldn't find any money. And we looked long and hard. That means Vince either has none or its very well hidden."

"Which is more likely?"

"Take your pick. It amounts to the same thing—if you can't find it then you can't have it." Daniel swilled his glass. Some of the contents slopped on the carpet. It was that expensive wool stuff that's designed to look like cheap sisal.

"When did you find this out?"

"Weeks ago."

"How did Michelle take the news?"

"She took it well. She said she just wanted to be rid of him. Move on and start a new life."

"Did the situation change? She gave me the impression she was coming in to some money."

"Not as far as I know," Levine said. But he was too drunk to tell a proper lie. Frank sensed it too.

"Are you sure?"

"She hated him. She just wanted rid of him."

"They seemed quite pally when they spoke on the phone last night," I said.

The dog barked again. More urgently. Over it we heard the doorbell. "That'll be my gourmet dinner," said Daniel, getting up slowly. He searched his pockets for the money he'd had out before. Found it.

"You guys don't have some change for a tip do you? This is all I've got."

Frank handed him a few dollars.

"Thanks," said Daniel as he made his way slowly to the door.

The door bell rang again, insistently.

"I'm coming!" He went out of the room.

"He's not telling us everything," Frank said. "I say we—"

His next words were swamped in sound. A heavy, damaging sound. Loud and deep, like a bomb blast. I sat utterly still, too shocked to register. Brain too numb to make the connection. Then I heard the pain, the screaming. A death rattle, really. Not human. No living being made that sound. It came from the front door. I was on my feet, running towards the echo of it. It was fading, yet still around us. Surrounding us with shadow.

Wednesday 10:58 p.m.

The front door was open and Daniel lay flat on his back, pinned to the carpet by the expanding red hole in his forehead. Brains and blood all over his broken face.

Frank was right behind me. He gagged. "Dear God," he said, "I think I'm going to be sick."

"Stay here." I stepped over the body and ran down Daniel's front path, crouching. I didn't seriously imagine that whoever had killed Daniel Levine was hanging around waiting for me to catch up with them, but I was raging. I wanted to know what the hell was going on. I wanted to know why two people had been killed within yards of me in as many days. I wanted answers, goddammit, and if it meant confronting a brazen killer with a dangerous weapon, then I would bloody well do it.

A futile gesture, of course. It was a professional job. And professionals don't hang around to admire their handiwork.

The car screeched off into the night. I broke cover, ran after it, not thinking about the uselessness of my action. I ran till I was out of breath and all I saw were the receding tail lights.

I stopped. There were more red lights in my vision. Flashing ones, this time. Cops. Heading to Daniel's house.

I ducked behind a hedge. Flattened myself against somebody's well-tended edges. The lights passed. There would be more soon. People came out of their houses, attracted by the scent of disaster. I lay pinned to the hedge for a few minutes, heart racing. I tried to review my options and realized I didn't have any. There were more people, talking, pointing, speculating. There was only one thing to do; pretend that I was one of them. I got up, brushed myself off and strolled like I hadn't a care in the world.

People streamed out of their houses, attracted to the lights, the sirens, the sense that something they only ever saw on television was happening in front of their eyes. I kept walking. Walking is not only good exercise, it helps you to think. I needed to think.

One thing seemed clear. Daniel Levine had lied when he said he didn't have a clue. He'd had one, all right, and it had got him killed.

More cop cars went by. I was grateful for the dark. It helped me to concentrate. Michelle was going to get money out of Vince one way or another. All I had to do was find out what the other way was.

But the more pressing concern was how to get back to Oxford Street. It wasn't too far but it was still an impractical distance to cover on foot. I needed wheels. The affluent burghers of the suburb had wheels, but I doubted whether they'd lend them to me, even if I asked nicely. That meant only one thing. I was being treated like a criminal, it was time to start behaving like one.

I chose a big house with a double garage. The lack of lights showed there was no one at home. Either that or they preferred to sit around in the dark. The garage lock wouldn't be too hard to circumvent.

I picked the lock and let myself in, lowering the garage door behind me.

It was difficult to see in the dark at first, but after a bit I was able to make out the shape of a small car. The space for the second car was empty. The garage had the usual family clutter—a large freezer, tools, children's toys, sporting equipment. I stepped carefully over a skateboard. A small red light blinked on the car dashboard, letting me know that any attempt

to break in would end in tears. The car would have been useless to me even if it hadn't been, as hot-wiring is not a skill
that I can honestly put on my alternative, dishonest c.v. Besides, I didn't feel up to stealing a car. It would look bad. I
needed something a judge would look more kindly on. Something not as easily noticed if it went missing. I had in mind a
bicycle.

A small window shed faint light on the rear of the garage.
Through the gloom I thought I noticed a shape that resembled
bicycle handles. I groped my way towards it.

The door rattled and half the garage was flooded with light.
A body silhouetted by car headlights. One arm up, still holding
the door handle. Holding a conversation with the person behind the wheel.

I crouched behind the second car.

"Come on, Dad." It was a teenager's voice. "Just five
minutes. Let's drive by and look. There'll be a body and
everything."

The father said something about homework.

"Come on. Five minutes. Please. It'll be cool."

The car engine stopped. "You won't see anything," said
Dad. But he'd lost the fight.

"Let's walk over there. I saw at least five cop cars."

The car engine started again. The driver parked it next to
me. The driver got out, locked the door. "The police won't
let us anywhere near," he said. But the kid was already waiting out on the street.

The garage door closed behind me and I breathed a sigh of
relief that was almost a sob.

My hands shook as I put them on the bicycle handles. I
struggled to lift it out from the other equipment that it was
tucked in behind. Skis, surfboards, scuba gear. This family had
an active sporting agenda. The bike eventually came loose. It
was old-fashioned and heavy and looked like it hadn't been
used for a while. That was all to the better. I checked the tyres.
Soft but not flat. They'd have to do.

I lifted the garage door, dragged the bike out. Tried not to
look too suspicious. The streets were empty. Daniel Levine's
murder site had acted like a big magnet. I got on the bike. It

was wobbly, one wheel frame was crooked and I was way out of practice. I memorised the house address and silently promised I'd return their bicycle when my commitments eased up.

I'd left my bag in Frank's car but I still had my map. It wasn't too hard to get the general direction of the centre of town, all I had to do was follow the skyscrapers. There was a busy main road. I had no choice but to use it. It was hell. A road built with no care for traffic that wasn't on four wheels. I cycled hard, banishing thoughts of cars running me down. The hills were tough. Would have been so even with a modern, properly geared bike. I ignored my body which reminded me every few seconds that I was not cut out for this kind of caper. I pushed on like a man possessed. Which I suppose I was. After a couple of false turns I made it back to Oxford Street. I ditched the bike a couple of streets away from The Dancing Queen and sat down until the waves of nausea had passed.

I needed to know much more about Michelle's background if I was going to get anywhere. And her oldest friend seemed the best place to start.

The guy in the tutu and the dog collar was still on the door at the club but without Michelle he wasn't keen on letting me in.

"We don't need tourists," he sneered.

"This is business. I'm here to burn up the dance floor with my version of 'Disco Inferno.' They'll be talking about it for weeks to come."

"Is that a fact," said Mr Tutu.

"Ask Gracie."

"You're with Gracie?"

"Personal invite." It was partly true. Gracie had offered to show me the sights when we'd met that morning at his gym. And the sights didn't come much more eye-boggling than men in high wigs and white lycra.

"Gracie leaves me a note when he's got guests."

"It's a last-minute thing. Just flown into town."

The guy stood in front of me in a way I didn't care to question.

"That'll explain why you're not dressed for it," he said. His manner did not invite contradiction.

I didn't contradict. I went back to the place where I had left the bike. It was still there, probably because it was too old and uncool to be coveted. In the slightly better light I noticed that the pump was clipped to the frame. I pumped up the tyres. Then I checked the map again. I needed a bed for the night and I had one in mind.

My ex-wife didn't know it, but she was about to offer me hospitality.

Thursday 12:10 a.m.

Mary and husband Grant lived in a place called Rushcutters Bay. I knew the address off by heart because of all the letters I had written Simon.

I had ridden shakily over from Oxford Street, one eye on the map and the other on the traffic. I had no headlights and a couple of cars nearly hit me because they didn't spot me till it was too late. They didn't realise how close they came to collecting a cool reward and being hailed as heroes.

The house was big, split level, obeying the precise lines of modern architecture. It came with a sturdy fence and a bold sign advertising the protective services of a reputable security firm. I walked around, viewing it from all the angles. It was going to pose a problem, all right. I could do locks, but not alarms. Not yet, anyway. I fished out my dwindling supply of change.

"Hi, Mary. It's me."

"Sam? My God, don't you know what time it is?"

"Sorry, did I wake you?"

"You think I can sleep with what's going on? Grant's been trying to find a way to get us out tomorrow morning."

I put a clenched fist to my forehead. "It's best you stay away."

"Sam, you need help. Admit it for once in your life."

"The best way you can help is to keep Simon as far away as you can."

"You can't keep it from him for ever."

"I need some time, Mary. Can you do that?"

"The police called. A nice bloke called Malcolm Wright. He wanted to know if I'd heard from you."

"What did you say?"

"I said you'd called."

"Thanks a bunch."

"I'm not perjuring myself for you, Sam. One of us has to stay out of jail for Simon's sake. Anyway I told them I didn't know where you were."

"I'm outside your house."

"How clever. That's the first place they'll look."

"They must have looked and gone. Probably saw the alarm and figured there was no way for me to get in."

"You haven't rung my lawyer, have you?"

"I'm getting around to that."

"I don't understand you. Not now. In fact I don't think I ever have. Why do you always insist on playing by your rules? Why the hell aren't you doing what any person with a shred of common sense would be doing now?"

I couldn't think of a reason, so I said nothing.

"You think you're some sort of giant boy scout." Mary was warming to her theme. "Well, grow up, Sam. This is the real world, not some comic-strip adventure. Think of Simon, if nobody else."

"He's all I think about," I said, but not to Mary. To the inside of my head. To the gods, if they were listening. And I was increasingly suspicious that they were not.

"Sam? You still there?"

"Yep. Still here."

"You haven't been listening. Jesus, why does that not surprise me?"

"I listened."

"In one ear and out the other, and now I'm starting to sound like my mother. That's what you do to me Sam, you make me feel like my bloody mother. Always telling you off, always trying to drag you out of adolescence. Raving on, listen to me now. I never rave. Only you make me do this."

"Sorry."

"No you're bloody not—God, what difference does it make? You don't listen."

"I listen."

"You see, you could have made a go of your life. You've got talent—there I go again. See? I can't stop myself."

"Vince . . . ?" I prompted.

"Right. Vince O'Donnell."

Mary drew a deep breath and went into professional financial analysis mode. "I did manage to find out something. A friend of Grant's knows someone who worked with him and Vince is broke."

"I heard that."

"It's true. One of the main reasons is he developed a big tourist resort up the coast a few years ago. Built it on a swamp. There were terrible problems. The mosquitoes refused to leave. He sold it in the end but the Singapore consortium that bought it got it for a knock-down price. He's finding it harder to get his hands on the money he needs. New Harbour has to pan out. If it doesn't, Vince O'Donnell will be finished.

"Another thing, Sam," said Mary. "The gossip is that Michelle was insured for three million dollars."

"Wow."

"Yes. You get a lot of wow for three million."

"Can Vince collect on that if she was murdered?"

"Who knows? It sounds like a risky proposition to me. Since he'd be the beneficiary the insurance company would be all over him like a rash. They're not going to say, 'Sorry your wife's dead—the cheque's in the mail.' They're going to dig until they uncover every sleazy thing he's ever done."

"Unless someone else takes the rap."

"They're still going to check Sam. I'm sure they trust the cops even less than you do. Three million is not exactly loose change."

"I'm not intending to take the rap."

"I hope not. I don't want to have to explain this to Simon. It'd break his heart."

"Thank you for your endless compassion," I snapped. "No man is an island, I read that poem too."

Mary just snorted.

"Can I stay at your house tonight?"

"It's locked up. You won't get in."

"I think I can. Just tell me what the alarm combination is."

The house was dark, warm and smelled of eucalyptus. I drew back the curtains to let some ambient city light in. I didn't turn on any lights. Mary had told me the neighbours preferred other people's business to their own.

The house was spacious, modern and expensively decorated. I recognised some pieces of furniture from Mary's and my days together, but the main stuff was new to me. Asian antiques—very solid and expensive looking. Aboriginal art that looked like it cost more than my annual salary. A sleek and shiny dining table big enough to hold field sports on.

An antique chest of drawers held silver-framed pictures of the family—Mary and Grant tanned and laughing aboard a yacht. Simon in a school uniform I didn't recognise on the front steps of the house. Simon and two other, older boys whom I assumed were Grant's contribution to the composite family, playing volleyball on a beach. The biggest photo was all five of them at a beach barbecue. They looked good together—handsome couple with toothy kids.

I couldn't look at it for long.

The kitchen was space age. The counters gleamed, even in the dark. No knick-knack or coffee jar interrupted the smooth line of the benchtop. There wasn't snackable food in the fridge but there was a bottle of wine. It looked expensive. I opened it and drank some. It was the least they owed me. I inspected the freezer. There was a giant-sized box of fish fingers. I shovelled them into the microwave oven and drank some more wine while they got zapped. Found some ketchup and doused them. Ate standing up at the stainless-steel kitchen counter. Left the dirty dishes in the sink. Just like home.

Glass in hand, I continued the tour of the house. It went on for ever. Simon's bedroom was upstairs at the end of a long corridor. It was bigger than my whole flat. His clever decorating managed to make it look as though I'd strayed into another house altogether. Here was clutter on a grand scale. The walls were hidden by posters of pop stars and actors. His bedside light was the shape of a football. School text books, adventure stories, comic books were jammed into an overcrowded bookcase. And there was a photo of me and him taken about three years ago in Regent's Park. I held a softball bat and had one arm flopped over his shoulders. He held a mitt and was pulling a face. The sun shone, the grass was green and the whole thing sucked me back to another time.

Mary and I had still been married. Things weren't going so well. I had known that, but I'd chosen to do nothing about it. Neither had she. She worked hard, I worked late. We both were extra nice to Simon to make up for the fact that we weren't speaking to each other. Using my patented Sam Ridley hindsight-o-meter, I could see that it had not been too late then to do something about our sickening marriage.

I stared at that photo and imagined myself going back in time. I would break into the alternative universe called the past and give the former me a stern talking to. Adult, sensible talk. I'd tell him to protect what he had and lay out the miserable options that the future held. I'd include the part about breaking into his ex-wife's luxury harbour-side home. I'd even tell him about the fish fingers. Nobody should be put in the position where they're forced to steal their ex-wife's fish fingers. Perhaps then the former me would really listen and make some changes that would involve not ending up like this. More likely he wouldn't. I felt sure he'd prefer, when faced with the choice, to learn things the hard way.

"Shit," I muttered and shuddered. The way I often do when the out-and-out foolishness of my behaviour creeps me out.

A car drove past and I went to the window. There was not much to see except the green-grey leaves of a eucalyptus tree. I opened the window a little to let in the sweet green smell.

But the photo drew me back. I looked at it again and realised that it wasn't me at all, but rather a stranger. A confident, laughing man who bore but a passing resemblance to the person I had become. If it was true that the past was another country then my past was another planet. The Sam-like person in the photo had no inkling of the swamp of despair that his life would sink into.

I lay down on the bed, suddenly cold. Pulled the duvet around me. Breathed in the smell of my son. Heard the sound of his laughter and fell dead asleep.

I don't know what woke me. Nerves probably. Or the tape in my head that was replaying the evening's action-stuffed agenda. Why had Levine been killed? Did he know the same thing as Michelle? What was that thing? Something to do with Vince? Something to do with New Harbour? Something else that I knew nothing about?

I toyed with the luxurious idea that Levine's death would make the police realise that Michelle's killing was more than just an unpremeditated crime of passion. But not for long. I know what cops are like. I know how much they like to make a quick arrest on a high-profile case, no matter whether the suspect is the right one or not. I had to find the right one.

I checked my watch. It was four-thirty in the morning. Not too late to go asking questions.

I washed my face in one of Mary's bathrooms and ignored the fact that I looked like Freddie Kruger with stubble. I put my dark glasses back on. They covered up enough.

Mary had an office. A smallish room with a powerful computer. It was bare and functional, the way she likes to work. The exception was a couple of small Picasso etchings that I remembered her buying one year when her bonus cheque had accumulated an impressive number of zeros.

I went through her drawers. The car keys were where I expected them to be. A leather strap with a VW badge told me what make of car to look out for.

I took the keys.

I closed the window in Simon's room and checked the house for dead bodies. There were none. Things were looking up.

Mary's car was parked on the street about twenty feet from the front of her house. She had never driven anything else except VWs. When she was a student, we'd taken a trip to

France in a purple Beetle. Her taste had evolved more practically as her earnings increased. This year's model was a punchy Golf convertible.

I prayed that the nosy neighbours weren't night owls as I slid behind the wheel and started it up. It had a throaty diesel engine that I thought would wake the whole neighbourhood. But nobody came running after me as I tooled down the street and back towards The Dancing Queen. I almost knew the way. Apart from a potentially disastrous incursion the wrong way down a one-way street, I got there with almost no trouble at all.

Driving back to the club, the radio news carried reports of Daniel Levine's killing. A pizza-delivery boy had seen someone who looked a lot like me leaving the area. The slender hope that the cops would start looking elsewhere became anorexic, then died.

I parked outside the club. A handful of people were leaving. The bouncers had gone, which meant I didn't have to invent another smart line that would fail to impress them. Smart was the last thing I felt.

A solitary waiter slowly cleared glasses from the sticky tables, loading them into a wire rack to be put into a dishwasher. I made for the dressing rooms.

Harry's door was open.

He was packing yards of pink fabric into a suit carrier. He was wearing street clothes—crisply ironed jeans, a black tee-shirt and boots. He looked up when he saw me but didn't stop packing.

The room was a mess. Someone had gone over it pretty thoroughly, moving things from the surfaces on to the floor. Make-up jars had been opened, clothes strewn everywhere. The place reeked of perfume. Harry ignored it. He packed his dress.

"Some party," I said. I began picking up stuff.

Harry zipped up the bag, pushing the last two inches of frothing tulle gently into the bag. He then hung it on a clothes rack. He started putting cosmetics in a large plastic tool box.

"What's going on?" I asked.

"You tell me." Harry's voice was monotone. He moved

slowly and stiffly. The lithe performer I'd seen the previous evening was gone.

So I told him about Daniel Levine as I scooped up an armful of wigs and put them back on the dressing table. I told him about Michelle's conversation with Vince and I told him that I hadn't killed his old friend. All the while he went on cleaning, picking up, trying to undo some of the damage.

"Who did this then?"

Harry rubbed his eye. "Look I'm tired, okay? It's been a bloody stressful day and you're pushing your luck, mate. I should have you arrested."

"Go ahead." I could afford to be nonchalant because I didn't think he intended to do that.

Harry threw the last eyeshadow pot into the tool box, lifted it up, put it down on the floor next to a shoulder bag.

"Bugger you. Look, I don't know anything . . . I . . . Michelle was my friend." He crumpled. Sat down on a fluffy stool and looked about to break down and sob. I waited. He pulled himself together.

"But I think you do know something. The people who made this mess have probably reached the same conclusion."

"How do I know it wasn't you?"

"I would've cleaned up."

Harry wiped his eyes with a tissue. Stood up. Looked me in the eye. Then for some reason I think he decided he could trust me.

"Let's go and find Gracie."

Thursday 5:30 a.m.

I helped him carry his dresses out to his car. Then we walked around the coffee shop I'd visited when I was looking for him the morning before. The coffee bar was about half full.

"I shouldn't go in," I said. "Have him come out."

Harry kept walking. "You think this bunch of queers is friends with the cops?" Harry said as he pushed the swing door open. "Besides, Gracie won't budge. Nobody interrupts his breakfast."

Gracie was sitting in a back booth reading the menu and sipping black coffee. The same imaginatively dressed clients were in place, slurping down big cups of coffee and manhandling plates of cholesterol.

"If it isn't the Pommy tourist!" Gracie cried as he spotted us. I flinched. His voice was powerful and carried across the room. Customers looked up. Took in me and Harry and my flimsy disguise. If any of them recognised me, they didn't show it. Maybe it was too early in the morning for such agile brain work. Or maybe Harry was right, they just didn't care. I ducked into the booth anyway, willing every cell to fold itself in half, to make me smaller, less obtrusive.

"How's your holiday going?" Gracie asked brightly. Maybe he didn't follow the news.

"Next year I'm going to Barbados," I said grimly.

"Why? You don't like Sydney? How can you not like Sydney?"

"It doesn't like me."

"We want to talk to you about Michelle," Harry said. "And keep your voice down, for God's sake."

"Oh." Gracie looked down. Studied his pink fingernails, flaked a piece of polish off.

A waiter slouched over, notebook in hand. "You must eat," said Gracie, pushing the menu at me. "Eat for both of us. I can't touch a thing, well maybe a slice of melon, the weight you know. But you must have everything. I'll watch."

Harry shrugged a "see what I mean?" shrug. I didn't need much urging, the fish fingers seemed a long way back. I ordered bacon and eggs with the lot. Harry did the same. Gracie's eyes grew round as the plates arrived.

"Oh!" he said faintly, as if he'd just spied an artwork of great beauty for the first time. "Oh!" And he looked down at his melon. It was a nice melon, but it didn't measure up to the heart-attack festival that Harry and I were about to confront.

Coffee arrived scalding and too strong, just the way I like it. Gracie stirred some artificial sweetener into his and then poked at the melon with his fork. His eyes were on my plate. "A good breakfast. Just what one needs to start the day."

"Why don't you have some?" I asked. "Once won't kill you."

He shuddered. "Got to keep our fighting weight. Us artistes."

I tucked in. It was the best breakfast I had ever eaten.

"Michelle's photos," Harry said. "Tell Sam what happened."

"But she said—"

"Just tell him."

"Are you sure?"

"For God's sake!" Harry hissed.

Gracie recoiled. Sighed. Tapped his fingers on his coffee cup and looked imploringly at me. *See what I have to put up with?*

"I have a day job. Processing photographs." Gracie began by looking at me, but his eyes slithered lasciviously towards the bacon. He breathed deeply. "It's shit work, but only part-time, thank God. Couldn't stand it there any longer than twenty-five hours a week and I don't have the time anyway. What with the gym and rehearsing, I'm always busy. People think I must have a boiling social life but I don't. All I do is perform and work out. Perform and work out. There's no time for anything else. And as you know, the older you get, the more maintenance is required. You let up for a minute and everything sags, you know what I mean?"

"I was saying the same thing just the other day. Have some." I pushed a rasher across the plate.

Gracie paused over it, one hand lifted delicately, fingers bunched as if to pluck it from the plate. Then the moment passed. The fingers straightened. Came to rest around the coffee cup.

"No, no. I mustn't. I used to weigh fifteen stone," he said by way of explanation. "Jenny Craig is my patron saint."

"Wow," I said, trying to imagine Gracie half as big as he was now.

"Yeah," he sighed. "But I could go back to it like that, you know." He clicked two elegant fingers. "Every day it's the same struggle. Get through the day without falling face down in a plateful of spaghetti carbonara." He shot a sharp glance at Harry. "*He* has no idea what I endure."

I nodded as understandingly as I could given the fact that my mouth was crammed with toast, bacon and egg.

"Michelle," prompted Harry. He looked like he was running out of patience with his friend. "Just tell Sam what she told you."

"Hey! I'm grieving for her too," Gracie snapped. "I liked her."

"Keep your voice down," Harry said calmly. "Sam would appreciate it."

I liked Harry more and more. He was a man of good sense. But almost anybody would have seemed that way in contrast with Gracie.

Gracie pushed his half-eaten melon aside, picked up a pack of cigarettes. Lit one and tossed me the pack.

My fingers scrabbled for the cigarettes. I lit one. Sucked deep. It felt good. The nicotine hit my brain at speed, shook it around, put it back together again. The quiver that had developed in my hand stopped. Endorphins danced in my brain, spreading rosy good cheer.

"As I was saying before I was so rudely interrupted . . ." Gracie breathed smoke in Harry's direction, lowered his voice discretely. "Michelle had some photos of a rather . . . incriminating nature. She wanted them copied. She came to me, asked me to do them on the quiet. When I saw them I understood why. There was no way you could have taken them to a chemist shop, uh-uh." Gracie leaned back, folded his arms over his chest, shaking his head and waiting for me to feed him the line.

"What did the pictures show?"

Gracie grinned. "They were very, very naughty."

"To do with her husband?"

Gracie nodded. "That's what she said."

"Vince in bed with some woman?"

"Uh-uh."

"Vince in bed with some man?"

Gracie looked pained.

"Well what? Animals? Rubber sex toys? Under-age boys?"

"No, no. Much, much worse."

"Gracie, I can keep guessing, but we'd be here all day."

Gracie leaned forward again, dropped his voice. "We're talking serious crime here. We're talking," he paused, stabbed his finger on the formica table top, "about murder."

Thursday 6:04 a.m.

Somewhere, deep in my heart, something stirred. It was Hope. Getting up, dusting itself off. Getting back in the race.

"Murder?" I whispered hoarsely. Some fried bread was stuck in my throat.

"It was about three months ago," said Gracie. "She came to see me one morning. We met at my gym for a carrot juice, and she said she had these photos that she wanted me to copy. She said it was to do with her divorce and it was very serious and maybe the police would have to get involved. I assumed it was Vince, who else could it be? Anyway, she warned me before I looked at them that they were ugly. She slid them out of her handbag and across the table to me. I was pretty well prepared for the worst, but this . . ." He shuddered.

"It was a woman's body. She'd been strangled. She was swollen, grotesque. Her face . . . blue. Her eyes were nearly popping out of her head . . . and her neck. It was a mess.

"There were four photos, all showing much the same thing. Some were a bit wider than the others. She was lying somewhere, near a wall. It was dark around. Lit by a flash judging by what I could tell."

"Did Michelle say where she'd got these photos?"

"She didn't say. She asked me not to mention it to anyone and I didn't."

"Was there anything identifying the victim?"

"No."

"Nothing written on the back?"

"They weren't exactly holiday snaps."

"Did you recognise the person?"

"No."

"What'd she look like?"

"She had short, dark hair and wore an orange striped jacket and a beige suit and there was a handbag. Cheap, beige leather. There was a cross too. A delicate gold cross on a chain. Let's see, what else? She was youngish, I seem to recall. Early twenties, probably."

"And you didn't recognise her?"

"Darling, I'm sure her own mother wouldn't have recognised her."

My mind raced, tripped, stumbled over itself to assimilate the new information. "You didn't keep copies by any chance?" The cops wouldn't have much to go on, and the word of one cross-dressing night-club dancer probably wasn't going to weigh heavily.

"To pin on my bulletin board?" Gracie arched an eyebrow in a practised way.

"Tell me what happened after Michelle brought you the pictures."

"We went to the lab that night. I ran off copies for her and she left. I didn't see her after that, apart from at the club."

"Can you remember anything else she said—how she came by the pictures, anything at all?"

"All she said to me was that she needed copies made before the owner found out they were missing. She asked me not to mention it to anyone, not to talk to anyone. She said it could be dangerous. For me as well as her. So I kept my mouth shut. I can do that, you know." He shot a defiant glance at Harry.

"Did Michelle seem nervous or frightened at all?"

"No. She was calm and very down. Very serious. Usually she was more outgoing and bubbly, you know, a party girl. But the day she brought those photos to me it was all business.

It was kind of creepy too. Copying them at night and every-thing. Especially given the subject matter."

"You have no idea at all who the woman was in the pic-tures?"

"No. The only thing that struck me was that they weren't recent. The woman was wearing out-of-date clothes . . . about a decade out of date. The other thing that backed that up was the quality of the prints. They were Polaroids you see, which aren't stable. They break down after a few years. They fade away, literally. And these weren't in that great a shape."

"So that's what Michelle was doing," I said. "She said she was going to make Vince pay. Maybe she was going to use the photos to blackmail him. Levine could have been in on it. Maybe he even helped her plan it."

Gracie shrugged. "It's a pretty powerful incentive to come up with the money. A couple of snaps for a few mil in ali-mony. I'd pay that to keep out of jail. If I had it, of course."

"This is all supposition," Harry said. "You don't know anything."

"What's your theory then, Einstein?" Gracie asked.

"I just don't think Michelle would get mixed up in some-thing like this. She played fair."

Gracie shrugged as he languidly lit another cigarette. "Maybe she was sick of playing fair. Maybe she didn't like Vince parading his strumpet around town. Fair only gets you so far. I'd go for revenge myself." He blew smoke. "And the money, of course."

"I wouldn't expect you to understand a thing like honour," Harry said angrily.

"Oooh," Gracie recoiled in mock horror. "Well we know one thing. She's dead. So those photos must have had some-thing to do with it, I'd say. But it's just a rough guess. What would I know about anything?" He glared at Harry as he stood up. Put down a few dollars to pay for his fruit and caffeine. I thanked him. He shrugged. "Always glad of a little excitement. Gotta go now. The gym calls."

Harry and I paid the bill. Walked back towards the car.

"My best friend is murdered and he calls it excitement,"

Harry fumed. "Sometimes I wonder why I bother with the little trollop."

"Did Michelle tell you what she was up to?"

Harry squinted into the distance. "She knew the combination to Vince's safe," he said. "He didn't know that. She found it out ages ago and kept it to herself. She said you never knew when it would come in handy."

Then he was gone, striding back to his car. Then he turned. Came back. "I don't know if this is relevant. It's kind of weird. But Tiffany and Michelle had a public barney a while back."

"I heard that."

"It was a put-up job."

"How put-up?"

"Vince knew it was going to happen. He rang Michelle and told her what restaurant he and Tiffany were going to be at for her birthday and what time. I was there when she took the call. She wrote it down on a pad."

"How do you know it was Vince?"

"He has such a loud voice I could hear what he was saying. Personally I don't think Michelle cared at that stage about Tiffany. That was the other thing that made it so odd. She knew what the score was. She knew Tiffany hadn't been the first. She'd found that out quite a while ago."

"That's not what she told me."

"Take it from a professional. They were putting on an act."

"To what end?"

Harry shrugged and walked away.

I went to Mary's car. It was grey, I noticed in the daylight. There was kid paraphernalia in the back, probably Simon's. I ignored it. I debated calling Mary to tell her that I was the temporary owner of her car but decided against it. As she herself had told me, she had enough on her mind.

Instead I rang Frank's newspaper and asked for him. He wasn't in. The woman on the other end of the phone assured me he'd be in at eight. It was just gone six-thirty.

I decided to fill the time by staking out Vince's place. As housebreakers everywhere know, you can learn a lot by hanging around outside someone's house for long enough.

The phone directory obligingly supplied Vince's address. I
was filled with warm feelings for a country that made things
so accessible. That was the easy part. Finding Vaucluse, the
suburb where he lived, was a bit harder. I got lost several times
before I found that Mary had a street map in the glove compartment.

I had thought Mary and Grant's house was big. Vince's
place dwarfed it by several hundred square feet. It was white,
stuccoed. The original inspiration had been Spanish, but it had
grown cancer-like into a mish-mash of styles that didn't say
much about anything, except the owner's financial status. Even
if the building hadn't said "I am very rich," loud enough, the
view certainly did. The sign on the gate spelt "Bella Vista,"
in curling brass letters. And the vista was about as bella as
they come. It included every feature that Sydney was famous
for. It was a view that said "I have arrived" with an added
soupcon of "nah-nah, nah-nah nah."

I parked across the road and down a little where there was
a reasonable line of sight for the house.

The sun got brighter and hotter. Insects made a racket.
Vince's neighbours arose and went about their well-paid busi-
nesses, judging by the luxury cars that transported them. I
fixed my sunglasses, pulled down my hat. I wished I had a
paper to find out what people were saying about me. Looked
through the glove box to see if it contained anything interesting. There was the car manual and a bag of melted toffees. I
took one and sucked on it, enjoying the sugar rush.

I sat there for some time, half dozing. Mulling over the
things that I'd learnt about Michelle and Vince: publically
staged fights, blackmail. Dead bodies. At least no one could
say they were divorcing because the excitement had gone out
of their marriage.

It was some time later when a car drew up, a late model
MG convertible in British racing green. Vince's girlfriend Tiffany was at the wheel. She tooted the horn and the automatic
gates swung open. I wasn't sure whether the surge of lust I
felt was for the car or the sundress-clad woman at the wheel.

The gates took a while to swing shut. Whoever was pushing
the button had to make a couple of attempts before they closed

all the way. The stuttering closure made me tempted to try and slip in until I noticed the security camera trained on the drive. Not worth the hassle. I popped another toffee.

Tiffany unfolded from the car, ripped her sunglasses off and strode angrily up to the front door. She kicked the tyre of the black Range Rover parked out front. She banged on the door. Vince answered it. Judging by the arm movements, she had a bone to pick. He tried to calm her down. It didn't work. He stood back from the door, trying to get her inside—there was probably a by-law preventing public raising of voices in this suburb—she refused. I rolled down the window to see if I could hear anything. There was a babble of anger, but it was indistinct and I couldn't risk getting any closer.

I looked at the view some more. It hadn't changed since the last time.

Moments later Tiffany came flouncing out. She drove off at speed. Vince remained on the doorstep, hands on hips, looking into the middle distance. Then he went back inside. He emerged a few minutes later and got into the Range Rover.

The front gates swung open smoothly this time. Vince swept out.

"Atta boy, Vince," I said and I set Mary's car in pursuit.

A Volkswagen was probably not the best for discreet tailing. Most of the cars on the road were either Japanese or Australian. European models stood out. The upside was that the Range Rover was equally distinct and I could keep it in view from quite a distance back. Vince drove steadily and within the speed limit. We climbed the hills of the posh eastern suburbs, going west. Back into town. I relaxed a little. This was my turf. I was almost getting to know it.

The morning traffic had started to build up but that suited my purpose. I kept back, drove smoothly within the speed limit. We passed King's Cross and threaded through one-way streets until we ended up outside the Central Railway Station. Vince parked his car on a meter. I parked about fifty yards down the street. It was early enough so there were spaces. I didn't feed the meter, there was no time.

I followed him into the station.

Thursday 7:41 a.m.

The railway building foyer was jostling with commuters. Vince threaded his way patiently through suits and their owners. He moved smoothly, hands in pockets, stopping and starting, standing back to let others through with a smile. A man used to working a crowd. Used to getting what he wanted. He was probably skimming six foot. Wore a well-cut suit that discretely complimented his worked-on physique. His skin was ruddy. He looked as if he'd spent a lot of time in the open air ignoring advice about hats and SPF numbers.

He avoided the ticket counters and went straight for the luggage lockers. There were fewer people in this part of the station. I held back further, tried not to look suspicious.

Vince didn't waste any time. He extracted a key from his pocket and opened one of the smaller lockers. I craned to see what he was doing. He had his back to me so it was hard to tell. He put something inside or took something out. He re-locked the compartment and palmed the key. I dodged behind a backpacker and her companion having a loud discussion about whether they could afford to stow their spare bags for a week or not.

Vince was doing the pavement two-step with a harassed woman commuter coming in the other direction. She had on a wide straw hat of the type recommended to keep skin cancer at bay and dark glasses. She was clutching on to a wide-mouthed bag for dear life that way some women do and was trying to make her way through the crowd from the other side. Because of the people and their bags there was only a small by-way. Vince stepped one way at the same time she did. Then they both stepped the other way. Then they laughed. Vince put out his arm in an open handed "after you" motion. Gratefully she stepped around him. She had a train to catch.

Vince didn't. He strode nonchalantly out of the terminal. I was torn. Should I try and get into the locker? A dodgy prop-osition in such a crowded place. Or should I follow him and see where he went next? I decided on the latter.

Walking into bright sunlight after the gloom and cool of the terminal was like being punched in both eye sockets, even with the help of my Raybans. I squinted as I tried to keep Vince in view. He climbed into his car. I hung back. Vince pulled out and I made a dash for Mary's car.

Something made me stop. The car was where I had left it but surrounded by cops. Two or three and probably others on the way. I didn't think it was because I hadn't fed the meter.

I turned slowly, jammed my hands in my pockets and walked as casually as I could in the other direction. I found a phone box and called Frank at the newspaper.

"My God you're a difficult bloke to keep up with," he said cheerily.

"There are many demands on my time."

"Where are you?"

"A place called Deep Shit."

"You got that right. The cops are most anxious to speak to you. They want to know what the hell you're up to."

"I'd like to know that myself."

"They kept me hanging around the police station for hours last night. I fed them your line that there might be more to this than meets the eye."

"What did they say?"

"They laughed."

"How do they explain Daniel Levine's death?"

"They're a little confused about that. On the one hand he

was doing business for a particularly sensitive Vietnamese mob boss . . . which is well-paid but bloody risky, and on the other hand a pizza delivery guy saw someone who looks a lot like you running away from Levine's house. So they're in two minds. Was it the mobster or was it you? Was it perhaps the mobster and you acting in cahoots?"

"Were they at all curious about why you were there?"

"Naturally. I told them the truth. That I'd come to interview Levine about his client's death. Nothing unusual about that. Of course they had to hold me for hours while they satisfied themselves about my veracity. They let me go in the end. Didn't you see my front-page story? 'My Assassination Terror.' "

"I must have missed it in my rush to get to the comics."

"It's a beauty, mate. It's got everything. My editor and I don't usually get on, but she's starting to wonder that she ever doubted me."

"I'm pleased to hear it. Listen. I managed to find out a few things last night." I told Frank about Gracie and the photographs of the dead woman and following Vince to the train station.

"Shithouse," he said. "We're making some progress."

"We?"

"Yeah. Team effort, mate. Team effort."

"Right. I get the mortal danger and you get the front-page leads."

"Hey. That's not fair. I'm doing my bit. Did you see my story? I'm on your side, mate."

"If you're on my side you'll find out who this dead woman is."

"You haven't given me bloody much to go on."

"Use your initiative."

"I'll find out. I'm on a roll," Frank said smoothly. His perkiness was beginning to irritate me.

"You do that. See if you can do something about the Third World debt while you're at it."

"What are you going to do?"

"Find out what Tiffany and Vince were up to. What she said that made him dash off to the railway station."

"Maybe they did it together. She says she was home alone when Michelle was killed."

"Thank you Sam Spade," I said and hung up the phone.

I couldn't risk going back to the railway station so I wandered around until I found a bus to take me to Double Bay. I sat in the back and kept my face behind a newspaper that had been left on the seat. A lot of the stories were about me. I switched to the inside pages. No matter what the story, the newsprint seemed to voluntarily form the words "Sam Ridley is a dead man."

A kid got on the bus. He was Simon's age or a little older. He wore a blue school blazer and a fraying straw boater. The bus was filling up so the kid sat next to me. He looked at me curiously. I looked out the window, shuffled the paper. The kid looked away. I returned to the paper. Tried to take in some news about a new water purification plant for the western suburbs. The kid snuck another look. I turned, smiled at him. Trusted the stubble and the hat would be disguise enough. My beard is grey, something that I've never had much cause to rejoice about until now. It would help to separate me even further from my passport photo which showed me at a youthful twenty-eight.

The kid smiled uncertainly. Now he wasn't so sure. He looked away. Hunted in his bag for a book and began to read. I allowed my breathing to return to normal. Folded the newspaper so that he couldn't see the photo of me festooning the front page.

I got off a stop earlier, nevertheless. The kid didn't look back.

Double Bay was as chirpy and expensive as it had been the day before. The shops were open for business, the street cafés crowded with people eating calorie controlled breakfast fodder.

I strolled jauntily towards Tiffany's house, trying to look as though I fitted in with the general well-to-do milieu. Ignoring my dirty, crumpled clothes. I found Tiffany's place just where I had left it. I pressed the buzzer at the gate. The god-like pool boy let me in. If he recognised me, his milky-blue eyes gave no sign.

"Yeah?" he mumbled.

"Tiffany in?"

"No."

"Know where she is?"

"She's out."

"Remember me? I was here the other day."

He nodded, not really caring.

"Mind if I wait?"

He shrugged. Pointed at one of the recliner chairs clustered around the pool. He had the "just visiting" air of someone who's taken so many drugs that he didn't know to regret it. I peered into the pool. It was sparkling clean. Yet the boy picked up the vacuum cleaner and pushed it across the bottom nevertheless.

"What's your name?"

He regarded me quizzically. Turned the question around in his mind, examined it from several angles. "Joe," he said finally.

"How long have you known Tiffany?"

"She's my sister." Now that he mentioned it, I could see the resemblance.

"You live here, Joe?"

"Sometimes I stay here," he said. "Tiffany likes having someone around. You never know, she says. You never know in the city."

"That's true, you never do. Is Tiffany worried about her safety?"

Joe looked as confused as if I'd asked him to hold forth on one of the more abstruse concepts of semiotics.

"Has someone threatened her?"

"I dunno." He shook his head and went back to sweeping.

"What's happening with Vince?"

"Nothing. Vince is a good guy."

"But they had an argument this morning. Do you know what it was about?"

"No." But Joe was incapable of dissembling. He looked shifty.

"Yeah you do. What were they arguing about?"

"It's not my concern, that's what Tiffany says."

"What else did she say?"

"That we'd find somewhere else to live."

"You're moving away from here?"

"It's Vince's place. And now he wants to sell it. He told me he needs the money. Tiffany can buy it off him if she wants. But she doesn't have the money." Joe turned the vacuum off and stored it neatly in a miniature shed. "This place is worth a lot."

"I can imagine. Are Vince and Tiffany having problems?"

Joe closed his eyes tightly as if concentrating hard on his answer.

"When was the last time you saw them together?"

"They had a big fight," Joe said.

"When?"

"A week or so ago. Tiffany said Vince had been ignoring her. She told me that he didn't love her any more. But Vince said it was just because of his work. He has a lot of problems with work and the divorce. He didn't have as much time with her. Tiffany said he was spending too much time with his other woman. He said he had to because of the divorce. It was serious because she wanted all his money. Tiffany didn't believe him."

He scooped a single insect out of the pool and glared at it before casting it into the shrubbery where no doubt it would hotfoot it straight back to the water the first chance it got. That's the trouble with nature, you can't trust it to behave.

"Tiffany won't be back till after lunch," Joe said after he'd dealt with the insect. "You can wait, but it'll be a long one." I could see he was warming to me and I felt pathetically grateful. But I couldn't hang around just because one burnt-out ex-junkie thought I was okay. That would have been sad. I got up to go.

"If you need a pool cleaner," Joe said, following me to the gate.

"You'll be at the top of the list," I assured him.

I called Frank from a phone booth and asked him to call me straight back. I was down to my last twenty-cent piece.

"I've been trawling the murder files all morning," he said.

"Nothing so far. Nothing fits the description you gave of the woman."

"Is there anything even close?"

"Nope. Got any other ideas?"

I thought I heard someone knock on the phone booth. It was my despair telling me to get off the phone and go and hand myself in to the police.

"Maybe it was earlier. Did you check earlier?"

"I checked everything. From twenty years ago up to yesterday."

I suddenly felt very tired. I leaned against the wall of the booth, massaged my temples. Tried to get some inspiration from the collective unconscious. It told me to go to the police.

"The pictures could be fake," Frank said. "Have you thought of that? There's no record of anyone like her dying this way. She could be anybody. We don't even know if she was reported dead. She might have just—"

Somewhere around me there was a noise. The sound of a penny dropping.

"Frank—"

". . . I mean, we don't have anything to go on here . . ."

"Frank—"

"If she were dead I'd have found her. I looked everywhere, mate. Our files are the best in the city. If she's not there . . ."

"Frank!"

"What?"

"We know who she is. We saw her picture. We know this woman."

"What do you mean, we know her?"

"We know her. Get the files—the newspaper files you showed me. From your colleague who died. What was his name?"

"Jennings."

"Right. Get the one with the whole page that he clipped on the Bondi development. There's a picture of her there."

Thursday 10:30 a.m.

Frank came back on the line gurgling with satisfaction.

"I've found her!"

I let him have the moment. Journalists love telling the rest of the world that they know more than the common man. That's why most of them are in the business.

Frank cleared his throat. "Her name was Victoria Reid and she was an office temp. She disappeared one night after work, seven years ago. Hasn't been seen since. She'd been working for the city council. She lived with her mum, Elspeth, at Manly. There's a photo here, it's kind of blurry. She had short, dark hair and is wearing a gold chain and a white frock. It's got to be her. So what d'ya reckon? Are we hot or what?"

Frank and I arranged to meet at a park in town so he could give me the photo and I could show it to Gracie. I had severe misgivings about continuing to use public transport. But I had no choice. Fortunately, the bus driver was so bored I don't think he would have taken a good look even if I'd come dressed as a toreador in pink sequins. There were a handful of other commuters but they appeared absorbed in their own universes. My anonymity, it appeared, was safe.

The park Frank had directed me to was well-patronised with

the drunken homeless of the neighbourhood. They were clustered in conversational groups, shouting at each other and arguing over bottles of booze wrapped in brown paper bags. A fight broke out. There was a lot of wild swinging after which the person, who'd missed his target, would fall over and the person he'd taken a swipe at would help him up and the fight would start again. They were all too pissed to do much harm to each other. It was like watching moon walkers attempt an expressive form of modern dance.

"Fancy a snort, mate?" One of the fighters had taken refuge on my bench. He grinned shiftily as he held out his offering. A green glass bottle poked out the top of a grimy brown bag. The glass was chipped and my putative drinking partner had cut himself. There was blood on the bottle and on his face.

"No thanks, mate." I smiled to show there were no hard feelings.

"Go on. You look like you could do with it." He shook the bottle and some of the liquid spilled out on to my jeans. I half expected it to burn a hole.

I smiled again. "You have it. I'm fine, really."

"Go on," he said, urgently this time. "Ordinary working man's booze too good for ya?"

I got up. "I'll pass, thanks anyway."

"What's the matter with ya?" The drunk stood up too. For some reason, I'd pissed him right off. "Too bloody posh to share a drink with ya old mate? Is this any way to treat me after all we've been through together? The ordinary working man's too good for you now, isn't he? Now that you've come up in the world, Mister Bloody Upwardly Mobile. Well who will ya mates be when ya on ya way down again, hey? Answer me that? Who will ya bloody mates be?"

It was a good question, possibly worthy of debate, but I didn't have time for it right then. My own downward spiral already had a fair head of steam. It was heading in a different direction than his, but it was plummeting all the same.

I scouted the edge of the park for a sign of Frank's Mini. It wasn't there. I didn't want to go back to the streets, so I walked around the park. The drunk got up to harangue me some more. I kept walking, eyes down. Got back to the bench just as the Mini lurched up to the pavement, another catchy opera tune making the little car quake. Frank got out, adjusted his designer specs and surveyed the park. He spotted me. The drunk's attention had been snagged by two men conducting a strenuous argument whilst squatting on their haunches. It seemed safe to return to the bench. I strolled over, sat down.

"Sorry I'm late. The editor wanted to have a deep and meaningful about my story. Actually, it was more of a screaming match. Well, it would have been a screaming match except she never raises her voice. She's the passive-aggressive type," Frank said cheerfully.

"What did you tell her?"

"Just what I told the cops. She's got me working on a Daniel Levine follow up today. She doesn't like me. She thinks I'm an over-educated ponce with no real tabloid instincts. This morning's story was just a fluke. I happened to be in the right place at the right time." Frank adjusted his expensive-looking glasses and beamed as he handed over an envelope. "I can't wait to prove her wrong. Who's the guy you're getting to i.d. this woman?"

"Gracie's a temperamental, cross-dressing, gay night-club singer."

"The witness of my dreams."

"He's all we've got." I slipped the photos out of the envelope. There were two of a serious-looking dark-haired woman with a face of such regular contours that at first one didn't realise how beautiful she was.

"Victoria Reid hasn't been seen for seven years," Frank said. "She went missing the day the first sod was turned on the Bondi project."

"Could be a coincidence."

"Could be the world is flat. But I don't think so."

"Me neither," I said. "Maybe I'll go and visit her mother. Where did you say she lived?"

"Manly."

"Manly, right. Where's Manly?"

We split up. Frank went back to his office and I walked down to Darlinghurst and Gracie's gym.

The same receptionist and the same beefy bodyguard were on the door. I asked if I could see Gracie.

"You look familiar," said the steroid-enhanced one as he blocked my way into the gym.

"I'm Al Pacino's twin brother."

He squinted at me.

"Really?"

"Not really." I sighed heavily for theatrical effect. "I was here yesterday. You must have a good memory for faces."

It was the little compliment that did it. He let me through.

Gracie was easy to spot in pink, white and green. He looked like a candy cane on the exercise bike.

"Have you come to join me for a workout?" he asked, unsurprised to see me.

"Thanks, but I'm following my own rigorous programme. It's called 'On the Run.' "

"Sounds delicious."

"You'll be able to but the video in the shops by Christmas. It's going to make me a fortune." I held up the photo of Victoria Reid. "Does she look familiar?"

Gracie studied it, shook his head. "Should she?"

"You tell me."

Gracie didn't let up the pace as he studied the photo some more. He wiped the sweat from his face with a striped towel that matched his outfit.

"It's so hard to say. The photos I saw were taken at night. And she was pretty banged up, you know? Someone had done a job on her. The hair looks the same, though. I think.

"Hang on," Gracie held his hand out for the photo, studied it again, eyes narrowed. "That could be her," he said. "She was wearing a cross, see?" He pointed a well-formed nail at the photo. "The woman in Michelle's photo had the same one. It's unusual, isn't it?"

It was unusual. A Coptic cross with a wealth of curling detail that made it look more like a small key than a crucifix.

"Are you sure?"

Gracie was sure. "I remember that cross. Aren't I clever?"

·

Thursday 12:15 p.m.

Steroid Master was on the desk when I went back out. I smiled breezily. Waved in the way Al Pacino's brother might have done.

It was risky returning to Circular Quay where there were crowds and almost certainly cops. But the reckless fatalism had descended and set hard. I bought a ticket for Manly as Frank had told me to do.

Nobody bothered or noticed me as I waited for the fast ferry to arrive. Nobody stared in my direction as I got on board and sat up top. Almost everybody was wearing sunglasses, the light was so bright as to be unbearable without them. I didn't look so out of place with my hat and shades.

It threw out some incredible sights this city on the water, if naked glamour was your thing. I imagined the good life that my former wife Mary was living here with Simon and their new family. I fleshed out the events hinted at by Mary and Grant's photo collection. Then I worried them like a hurt tooth. I tried to pick out their flash place in Rushcutters Bay. Compared it to my cramped flat in London. Mary had said that I didn't have much to offer my son and she was right. If the judge had chosen me the package deal would have in-cluded a grimy upbringing, an indifferent education at a par-

lously funded British state school and no sun-filled weekends
cavorting at designer beaches. The more I thought about it in
the burning southern light, the clearer it was to see that I was
not much of a father to Simon. Especially now—on the cusp
of adding a criminal conviction to my already unimpressive
c.v.

Elspeth Reid lived in a thirties-style house on a hill, spread
out below was another beach a lot like the one at Bondi, making me wonder if the city had ordered a job lot. This one was
fringed by Norfolk pines, but it still had the requisite blinding
beauty.

Mrs Reid's bungalow was red brick. The garden was neat
and the plants grew profusely. They probably had no choice
in this climate. I was hot and sweaty from the walk from the
ferry.

I rang the door. There was no reply. I rang again.

"I'm around the back."

There was a side path with a low gate. I unhinged it and
went through. Elspeth Reid was digging in her garden. When
she heard my footsteps, she turned and lifted a hand to shade
her eyes. She was early fifties tops. Her arms in a short-sleeved
shirt looked strong.

"Mrs Reid?"

"Yes." She looked puzzled.

"My name is Sam Ridley. I've come to talk to you about
your daughter."

She was silent for a moment. Then realisation dawned.
"You're the one . . ."

"No I'm not."

"Who are you working for?"

"Nobody. Can we sit down and talk?"

Mrs Reid stared at me. Fists clenching and unclenching.

"Who are you working for?"

"Look, I . . ." I took a step towards her which was the
wrong thing to do. She charged me with the fork.

I've never been attacked by a middle-aged woman wielding
a garden implement before. It took me a few seconds to figure

out what was going on. I dodged to one side a fraction too
late. The fork grazed my arm.

"Hey!" I said, but she was already coming back for another
round. Now I knew how the bull felt in the middle of the ring,
facing up to the guy with the tight pants and the sharp weap-
ons.

She aimed for my head this time. I ducked and scrabbled
sideways. Looked around for something to defend myself
with.

Elspeth Reid lunged at me again. I tried to grab the fork
but missed. One of the spikes grazed the top of my fingers.

"There's really no need," I said.

We were circling each other. I backed away. Came up
against something solid. It was a door. I yanked it open. Shut
it smartly behind me. Found myself in the kitchen.

She broke the glass in the top of the door with the fork like
a regular Arnold Schwarzenegger. Came in after me. Got me
pinned against the sink. She picked up a kitchen knife and
aimed like she knew how to use it. Then she skirted around
the kitchen, commando style, making for the phone that hung
on the wall next to the refrigerator. I made an executive decision to ignore the knife and leapt for the phone. I got there
first and ripped the receiver from the wall.

"Sorry," I said. "Desperate measures and all that."

She lunged at me, knife first. I've had people do this to me
before and it's quite easy to avoid if you step out of the way
quickly enough and use your opponent's momentum against
them. I grabbed Mrs Reid's knife arm and twisted it just
enough to persuade her that dropping it would be a good idea.
The knife clattered to the floor and I left it there. I couldn't
afford to bend down. There was no telling what a well-aimed
kick from this woman would do to my already delicate body.
Instead I held on to her arm in a friendly yet firm manner.

Mrs Reid stomped on my foot. The pain distracted me from
keeping a grip. She went for the knife again. I reached it first,
kicked it away.

She glared at me, half-hunched. She looked like she was
going to make another bid for the knife.

"Please," I said. "Someone's going to get hurt and I'm afraid it'll be me."

She sneered at that. So much for humour defusing the situation. She picked up the toaster, one of the heavy old-fashioned English ones, snatched out the cord and threw it at my head. I ducked, the cord whipped across my cheek. It stung like hell.

"Hey! That's enough, okay?" I have my limits and being toaster-whipped by a middle-aged woman is one of them. I grabbed her by both arms, she kicked and spun but I held firm. I forced her to sit down.

"I could hold you against your will but I'm not going to. I could put that knife to your throat, but that is not my style, despite what you might have heard on the news."

She stared. Said nothing. She was cooking up another plan, I feared.

"So we're just going to sit here and chat like civilised adults. No throwing things, no knives and especially no garden forks. And when I've asked you a few questions, I'm going to leave. I'm not going to hurt you. All I want is information. I want to find out what happened to your daughter. If you want to find that out too then you'll help me out. Do you understand that?"

She was silent for a long time. I could hear the clock ticking.

"Right then," I said. "Let's have tea."

I made the tea strong and poured it into two mugs depicting the coronation of Elizabeth II. They were hanging from a mug tree that had similarly themed crockery on its other branches. The inside of the house told you that Elspeth Reid was the sort of person that one would never have any difficulty buying presents for; anything that had a motif of the British royal family would be warmly welcomed. The place was a shrine to the Windsors. Plates showing various esteemed couples and former couples hung on the walls and were propped up in rows on a rail around the kitchen. There was a large portrait of the Queen Mum and a calendar depicting Windsor Castle hanging from a cork board. To round out the design concept, a corgi was sunk in a snuffling sleep in a dog basket in one corner. Not much of a guard dog, patently.

"Drink this," I said. I handed her the cup and she grasped it with both hands till her knuckles went white. "Have you got any biscuits?" I realised it was a while since I'd eaten.

"In the tin on the bench."

I helped myself.

"Some weeks before Michelle O'Donnell died she had some photographs copied. I'm fairly sure they were of your daughter. She was dead."

Elspeth Reid seemed to take this news in her stride.

"I think Michelle's death and your daughter's are connected somehow. I'm trying to work out how."

"Have you got the photos? I want to see them."

I told her what Gracie had told me.

"How can we find them? I want to see them."

"I'm working on that. Perhaps we can start by you telling me as much as you can about Victoria."

"There's some gin in the cupboard, can you get me a glass please?"

I kept an eye on her while I found the gin and poured it into a glass. She took it gratefully, her hands shaking. Maybe she'd had enough tough-guy action for one day. God knows, I had.

"She was working for the council when she went missing. She was a temporary secretary," Elspeth Reid said. "She'd worked there for about a month. She was actually employed by an agency. She went to lots of different offices in the course of a year." She watched me closely, seeking out signs of criminality, no doubt. Searching for the clues to why someone would end another human being's life.

"But when she disappeared she was only working for the council."

"That's right."

"What sort of things was she doing?"

"Typing and dictation, I suppose. What else do secretaries do?"

"Did she talk to you about her work?"

"We'd discuss some things, at the end of the day when she got home. We'd sit in the kitchen." Elspeth gestured around the now messy scene. "Vicky would have a cup of tea or a

drink while I made dinner. She would tell me about the people
she worked with, some of the funny characters, little stories
she'd saved up to amuse me. She liked being a temporary
secretary. The people were varied, she liked that. She was very
observant, she noticed details.''

''What happened the day you last saw her?''

''Nothing much different. She got up at six-thirty, same as
she always did, and she made me a cup of tea. Then she got
ready for work. She left about seven-thirty to catch the ferry
into town. I expected her home about nine or ten that night.
She was going to have a drink with a co-worker but she didn't
show up. I'd made shepherd's pie. I gave it to the dog in the
end.''

''Was Victoria having any personal problems, anything that
might have caused her to run away?'' I asked.

Elspeth looked stricken, as if I had accused her of a crime.
''No,'' she said quickly. ''She was a good girl. She didn't . . .
she wouldn't have done anything like that without telling me.''

''What about boyfriends?''

''There weren't any. Not that she couldn't have had any,
but she was a bit shy. A late starter. She'd only ever been to
girls' schools. She wasn't used to mixing with men, especially
after her father left. I suppose that was my fault. I sheltered
her.''

''When did her father leave?''

''She was ten years old. Barry just left a note on the hall
table. Said he wasn't coming back. We never saw him again.
Victoria was hurt by it. She was only a child. She didn't understand.''

''Where does her father live now?''

''North Queensland. He shacked up with a woman half his
age—they live in a New Age commune thing. All free sex
and lentils.''

''Did Victoria ever express any interest in finding him?''

''When she disappeared the police first thought she might
go to him, but she never showed up.''

''Are you sure?''

''Barry would have told me that, at least.''

''Did Victoria's habits change at all before she disappeared?

Did she appear nervous or worried about anything?''

"No. She did everything the same as before."

"But she was planning to meet someone for a drink after work that night?''

"She was going to stop off and see one of her colleagues. He had an artists' studio in Camperdown," Elspeth said. "They'd seen each other a couple of times that week but they were just friends though. No funny business going on." I wondered if this poor woman had ever had a friend herself apart from her daughter and the symbols of family as represented by the House of Windsor.

"Do you have a photo of Victoria?"

Elspeth hoisted herself out of her chair. She went to a drawer and rummaged. I watched carefully in case she was fossicking for another weapon, but she pulled out a snapshot.

"This was the most recent one," she said. An attractive, dark-haired young woman smiled back. The same one as was in the newspaper clippings. She had on a white sun frock and her skin was tanned. It set off the tiny gold crucifix around her neck.

"Was she wearing that cross the day she went missing?" I asked.

"She never took it off."

"What else did she have on?"

She was wearing a linen jacket, a nice peach coloured one that we'd bought in a factory-seconds place in Surry Hills, and a beige linen skirt and white sandals and white handbag."

That description tallied roughly with what Gracie had told me. I felt Hope stirring again. Back on its feet. Punching, shadow boxing, ready to go.

"Did Victoria ever talk about meeting Vince O'Donnell?"

"No, I don't think so. She had a very humble position. A temporary secretary doesn't have much status, although as I say, Victoria liked it that way, but I don't think she met any important people. She was just in the typing pool."

Elspeth finished off the gin. "But when I go over these things in my mind I wonder if I ever knew her at all. That's what I think about at three in the morning when I can't sleep, which is most nights. Did I let her down in some way? Is

there possibly anything I could have done that would have
kept her alive?''

"You can't think that," I said, reaching out to touch her
arm. "She wouldn't want you to think that."

Elspeth froze. Looked down at the hand on her arm.

"The telly says you killed Michelle."

I was about to tell her not to believe anything she saw on
the telly when a thought struck me.

"You knew Michelle?"

"No. Why would I know her?"

"You called her by her first name."

"English rules of etiquette don't apply here."

"Michelle thought her husband was mixed up in what happened to Victoria. She never came to see you?"

Elspeth shook her head. "No. I haven't spoken to anyone
about Vicky in months.

"You get a lot of cranks after something bad happens. People write and say the most unthinkable things. But that stopped
a few years back."

"Nothing since then?"

Elspeth shook her head. "I can't stop hoping that one day
Victoria'll walk back in here, sit down and ask what's for tea.
It's a little luxury I allow myself. It helps me to keep going.
Do you understand?"

I did.

"But I think the time for that is past. She's not coming
back, is she?"

"I don't think so."

"I'd give anything to know, you know. Anything to know
where she is."

She looked at me almost defiantly with her clear blue eyes.
Not investing any hope in me because she'd done that too
many times before.

Thursday 2:41 p.m.

Elspeth drove me into town. She said it was the least she could do. She felt a bit bad about the toaster. I let her feel bad. My cheeks still stung.

"Where are you going now?"

"To see the artist. The one Victoria was supposed to meet."

"Larry Winter. I'll take you there. He lives in Camperdown."

We drove past Darling Harbour and Frank's office and a spaced out collection of buildings that advertised itself as Sydney University. Then we wound through some streets with row upon row of detached cottages.

Elspeth stopped the car outside a brick loft.

"First floor is his."

I got out.

"You'll let me know if you find anything?" Elspeth asked.

I said I would. She drove away.

The artist was in. He answered my knock by bellowing, "It's open, ya bastard."

I trooped up a flight of narrow, paint-stained steps into a studio the size of a football field.

"Who are you?"

I looked around. The voice didn't appear to be coming from

anywhere. There was certainly no body I could see to attach it to. The space was big and white. There were hundreds of paintings, stacked one on top of the other and leaning against the wall. It was the Jackson Pollock type of artistic vision. In other words it made absolutely no sense unless you had a few hundred grand to plonk down so that all your friends would know how rich and cultured you were.

"I'm on the bloody dunny," the voice shouted. Sure enough, I heard the sounds of ablutions being completed and a door slamming. A man came out, one hand doing up his paint-smeared fly. "Jesus," he said. "I get no peace anywhere. Who are you? Whaddyawant?"

I told him my name and gave him Elspeth as a reference. The words Sam Ridley didn't seem to conjure up any lawless visions. Larry Winter stared at me for a bit, harrumphed, scratched his crotch and offered me a beer. I accepted. He shuffled over to a fridge in one corner and swiped a couple of cans. There were no chairs so we sat on the floor and drank. Larry studied my face carefully, like he was checking the proportions.

"How's Elspeth?" he said finally.

"Fighting fit."

Larry nodded. "Yeah," he said. "Must call her. Haven't spoken in ages. I get carried away in here. Don't get out much."

I looked around at the paintings. There must have been two hundred of them.

"Going through a creative patch," Larry said, with some pride. "Gotta make the most of it. Can't just stop in the middle of something."

"I won't stay long."

Larry took a thoughtful sip. "Doesn't matter. Got to rest sometime. I've been up since five." He rang a surprisingly delicate finger under his pouchy eyes and then shook his shaggy head, as if to wake himself up. "You want to talk about Vicky, I suppose?"

"Yeah."

"You're a journalist?"

"Yeah."

"That story's over, mate. Dead and buried, like her."

"That's your theory?"

"You got a better one?"

"I'm more interested in yours."

Larry crossed his legs awkwardly. "Alright. I think she was killed. I don't know who did it. But someone did. And they hid her real good. Cut her up into tiny pieces and stuck her in an industrial furnace, bundled her into the boot of a car and drove out into the bloody desert and left the birds to take care of the evidence. Took her out to sea and let the sea worms have a good feed. I don't know, there's a million ways."

"What makes you so sure?"

"Because I didn't know her very well, but I did know one thing about her. She told me once what had happened with her father, how he'd just pissed off, and she'd been seared by it. I tried to explain this to the cops. She wasn't the sort of person who would walk out. She loved her mum. She never would have treated her the same way as her father did—just up and buggering off. Vicky was still trying to deal with that example of parental devotion more than twelve years later, there's no way in the wide world she would have treated another person the same way."

"But the police thought she'd run off?"

"Yeah, well thousands of people go missing every year in this country and for every one of them there's four or five people who say the same thing as I did about Victoria. Sure they looked for her, but not for long. Problem was there was no evidence to suggest any other option. She literally vanished, nothing was ever found. Not a shoe, not a bag, not a bloody thing."

"What were you doing at the council?"

"I was in one of my straight phases, trying to pretend I was a respectable member of society. I was sick and tired of starving for my bloody art. I needed money. I was so bloody broke I was living on Vegemite and beer and didn't have enough to buy paints and canvas. So I got a job. It was very surreal— so dull that I thought I'd have to open a vein, just to see if anybody would react."

It was extremely difficult for me to imagine this bear of a

man hunched over a typewriter, but one never could tell—
perhaps he'd stored up the necessary skills because his mother
had wanted him to have something to fall back on.

"Victoria and I hit it off immediately, God knows why, we
couldn't have been more different. She didn't know what to
make of her life. She'd had the full-on Catholic upbringing,
girls' school and all that, and I think she really bought it—
the whole spiel about the Virgin-fucking-Mary. She wasn't
even Catholic, but her mother wanted to hide her away. And
then she got out in the big wide world and she's intelligent,
so she sees that things aren't exactly adding up, and she
doesn't know what to make of it. If she accepts what she's
seeing now she has to junk all of the old ideas and to junk all
of the old ideas she has to admit that they were wrong. She
was juggling it all when I met her. Very convinced about some
things, very uncertain about others. But we had a few laughs
together."

Larry leapt up and began rummaging through a stack of
canvasses. "I painted her," he said over his shoulder. "Here
it is." He pulled out a small square canvas maybe a foot in
diameter. It consisted of a series of slashing lines starting at
the opposite top corners of the canvas and meeting in the centre. The palette of colours was pink, green and purple. I looked
at it, pretended I was concentrating on the work while I
searched frantically for something that would not betray my
complete ignorance of art.

"I did it from memory. It represents her cheekbones,"
Larry said. "She had great bones."

"I see that now," I said, thankfully. Larry slid the canvas
on to an empty easel. "Let's keep her out for a bit and see if
she has anything to say to us." He backed away from the
painting, apparently transfixed by it. I wondered if the next
step was a makeshift seance using the beer cans.

"Did you sleep together?"

Larry turned to face me, dragging himself out of his reverie.
"Tried it once. Asked her back here to see the etchings and
all that. Didn't get close. She needed a long warm up, yes sir.
I learned that lesson pretty damn fast. I was young and wanted
to bone everyone I met. Hell, who am I kidding, I still want

to. Anyway I didn't have three months to invest in a shag. If she'd been a drinker, it would have been different, but she was a bit of a wowser, which ruled out getting her rat-arsed and just going for it." Larry scrunched his beer can regretfully. "She was a good-looking girl, though. She smelled good too. Only Catholic school girls smell that good." He smiled and wrinkled his nose at the memory.

"Did she ever have any contact with Vince O'Donnell?"

"What the property bozo? Hard to imagine, why should she?"

"I heard they might have been . . . involved."

"Involved in what way?"

"She might have known him. Perhaps met him through work."

"It's possible, I suppose. She was always darting off to different departments to plug gaps, so she might have been in with the planning guys. And Vince had that application in to wreck that bloody building out at Bondi, but that had all gone through . . . almost sure of it, signed, sealed and stiched up before Victoria ever turned up to work there."

"What happened the night she disappeared?"

"Jeez, I'd chucked a sickie that afternoon, so I left about one." Larry saw my puzzled look. "I pretended I was sick," he explained. "I needed time to paint. So I came back here and started work. Victoria rang me about three and asked if we were still on for that night. I hadn't seen her outside of work for ages and we were both looking forward to it. We arranged that I'd meet her at a bar in the Cross at six."

"Her mum said you'd met up twice already that week."

Larry looked puzzled. "No we didn't."

"That's what Victoria told her."

"She must be confused. I didn't see Vic outside of work that week. I spent every free hour in here. I was painting like my life depended on it."

"Did Victoria sound any different when she rang you?"

"No. She sounded just the same. So I spent the afternoon here and about six I headed off. I was late getting there, about six-twenty I suppose. She wasn't there. I waited about an hour and then I left. Got some Chinese and came home."

"You didn't call her?"

Larry looked a little shamefaced. "I started painting. I forgot all about it," he said. "Also we'd had some arguments about my always being late. I thought she'd got pissed off with waiting and had just left. I didn't think much about it until the next day."

"What happened?"

"She didn't turn up for work. Her Nazi boss was going ballistic. A creep called Brian Patrick. He was flouncing around, the effete little prick, threatening Vicky with all sorts of things when she finally did show up. So I phoned her mum and she told me Vicky hadn't been home. She'd called the cops. And that was that. They didn't take it very seriously at first. Told her to wait another day."

"Did this guy Patrick and Victoria get on?"

"Nobody with half a brain gets on with Patrick. He's one of those poor, sad fucks who thinks his job makes him important. Victoria thought he was a laugh, the clichéd civil servant. She got under his skin because she didn't respond to his petty tyranny the way a lot of the others did. He gave her a hard time. He used to say it was because he had a "regard" for her or some bloody stupid thing. He fancied the pants off her, that was the truth of it. He used to follow her around, the cretin, with a hard-on the size of Queensland. He'd have done anything to get into her pants. He was always trying to impress her. He used to get her up in his office and tell her that he was much more important than she realised. That his was the kind of power that was wielded behind the scenes. The usual crap." Larry swept his arm out in an arc, knocked over the beer can. "Rasta!" he yelled, making me jump. A big dog came loping out from a corner and slurped obediently from the beer puddle. "Good fella. Good Rasta," crooned the artist.

"What did Victoria do about this Patrick?"

"She was pretty cool about it. She treated him firmly. He was always inviting her into his office to perform 'special tasks.' I know what special tasks he wanted from her and it had nothing to do with office equipment." Larry scratched the huge animal's head vigorously. "Or maybe it did. That would fit right in with his twisted mentality. Boning on the photo-copier.''

Larry grinned like he'd got the mental picture in technicolour. Then he jumped up. ''The Muse won't wait. Gotta get on with my work,'' he said by way of goodbye.

''Patrick, does he still work at the council?''

''Sure he does,'' Larry began mixing paints. ''He'll be there till they cart him out feet first.''

Thursday 3:29 p.m.

I called Frank from a phone booth near Larry's studio. I'd filled him in on my conversation with Elspeth Reid, leaving out the part about the toaster and the knife.

"There's a chap called Brian Patrick who works for the council who might be worth checking out. Victoria worked for him and apparently he had the hots for her. Might be worth checking."

"I've got one for you," Frank said. "My impeccable source at Cop HQ says a private eye called Marvel has been asking about Victoria Reid."

King's Cross was busy with its own nefarious business when I showed up. I was glad to be there. Getting in from Larry's place had been a drag. I'd started walking and gone in the wrong direction. I'd approached someone for advice and they'd advised me badly. Eventually, I found a bus that was going sort of near. I hiked the last half mile up a steep hill. I was in no mood for pleasantries.

Marvel's office hadn't changed much since when I'd been there the day before. Lusty Louise was teaching a lesson to some poor bloke who hadn't done his homework. The stairs were just as dirty, and dingy, and there was the same, sweet smell of dead meat outstaying its welcome.

Marvel's office door was open, I went in. I didn't bother to knock. Marvel was behind his desk in almost the same pose as last time.

I say almost. His hands rested on the bench. Palms flat down. His forehead was on the blotter. There was something else on the blotter too. A big red stain. I didn't think it was yesterday's ketchup.

Someone knocked at the door. I looked up sharply.

Frank stood there. He'd started to take his hands from his pockets. His practised nonchalance had deserted him. Horror froze on his face.

"Frank, Marvel. Marvel, Frank." I walked around the body. Marvel had been shot in the head. I didn't need a pathologist to tell me it had been some time ago. He was cold, stiff and starting to smell.

"Marvel worked for Vince," I went on, to fill that awkward gap in the conversation

Frank didn't move, but the "O" shape his mouth was making got bigger and it was starting to assume accusatory tones.

"Don't look at me like that. I just got here. Marvel hasn't drawn breath for some time. He's stiff, see?" I poked Marvel's corpulent torso to demonstrate, but Frank wasn't taking in the details. "I'm starting to wonder about you," he said.

"I'm wondering too." I searched Marvel's pockets. "I'm wondering if I'll ever see the light of day again and let me tell you that it concentrates the mind. Besides, do you think I'd have told you I was coming here if I'd been responsible for this?"

"Three corpses in two days?"

"I can count."

Frank began edging towards the door.

"Don't go. Marvel might finally be able to tell me something. I'd hate to think his death had been in vain."

"You've met this guy already?"

"Yesterday. He wasn't very forthcoming."

I began searching the office. Marvel was a low-tech kind of guy. He didn't have a computer and his filing cabinet consisted of three drawers that didn't give much resistance.

"Don't you think the person who did this would have removed any incriminating evidence?" Frank asked, looking more and more like he'd rather be somewhere else.

I used the cuff of my shirt to open the file drawers. They didn't contain much. Two half-empty bottles of inferior whisky. Some demands for overdue bills.

The bottom drawer contained a pair of worn Adidas trainers, a new shirt still in its cellophane wrapper and a very large handgun. I wrapped my shirt around my hand before picking it up. Frank took another step back. He was practically out in the hall. I sniffed the gun barrel. It didn't smell as though it had been fired recently, but then I'm not an expert.

"You think he was shot with his own gun?"

"No. But I like to keep an open mind." I closed the filing cabinet. There wasn't much else of interest in the room. The drawers to Marvel's desk held the usual stationery supplies, along with a handful of condoms. Perhaps the proximity to Lusty Louise's School of Pain was more than a geographical accident.

"Let's go next door," I said. "Find out what the lesson is for today."

Lusty Louise's student was just leaving as we arrived. He was younger than I would have expected, clean-cut and wearing an expensive suit. He straightened his tie and looked at us with guilty conspiracy as he ducked out. Frank wished him a nice day.

Louise was dressed, predictably, I thought, in a gym slip and push-up bra. Her hair was dyed black and pulled back in pigtails high on her head. The look was accessorised with black boots and a matching leather whip—as if an SS stormtrooper had morphed into Pippi Longstocking.

"Come in," she said. We followed her into a small room. It had a couple of small windows and the blinds drawn tight. The light came from table lamps. There was a wooden chair attached to a sloping desk. Just like school. I sat on the desk. Frank leaned against the window sill.

"Which one wants to go first?" Lusty Louise was British.

She had a flat, esturine accent and a dull look in her eye. She primped her hair. It had pretty ribbons. She even snapped gum. I was impressed. A woman who cared enough about her work to think about the details.

"I charge more for a threesome."

Frank and I looked at each other, he, still a little green from what he'd seen in Marvel's office, gestured in my favour.

"You cops? I give a special rate to cops."

"Journalists."

"Same applies."

"We just want to talk."

"That's what they all say, first time."

"A few questions."

"You still pay. I don't discriminate. My time is my time."

"What happened to the hooker with the heart of gold?"

"She's next door. Here it's a hundred bucks every fifteen minutes."

Frank got out his wallet. Peeled off some notes. "Do you give receipts?"

"I give everything," said Lusty Louise. "That's why the world beats a path to my door."

"Been in Marvel's office lately?" I asked as she picked up the money and slipped it into her boot.

"No. I've been working my fingers to the bone."

"Heard any sounds? Like gunfire, for instance?"

"What are you getting at?"

"Your neighbour's dead. He was shot."

Louise's jaw sagged. For one awful minute I thought she was going to drop her bubble gum, but she came to. Worked the pink wodge back between her teeth.

"Why?"

"Why indeed. See anybody go in or out? Hear anything unusual?"

Louise slumped into a chair. Shook her head.

"He was working for Vince O'Donnell," Frank said. "Following his wife."

Louise shrugged her shoulders. The name clearly didn't mean anything to her.

"Did he ever talk about his cases?"

"No. He was much more interested in getting me to tell him about mine. I used to tell him he was an old perv." Her voice sounded hollow. "I used to tell him and he'd laugh. Said he had to be a pervert to be in his line of work. He had to enjoy watching."

"What did he tell you recently?"

"We hadn't spoken. He was always out."

"Do you know where he kept his records?"

"What records?"

"He must have kept some documents."

"I wasn't his secretary."

"Did he mention any threats against his life?"

"Not in casual conversation, no. He said his last client stiffed him his fee. That's about as exciting as it got."

"How well did you know him?" asked Frank.

"We had an appointment once a week."

Frank and I exchanged glances. We weren't getting anywhere. Louise sat between us, limp like a cloth doll. The sound of us opening the door seemed to rouse her.

"You could try his room," she said. "One floor up."

B. S. Marvel did indeed live in one room. And it was a mess. The sun filtered in through dirty windows. The carpet was a dump of old newspapers, coffee cups, and clothing. There was an unmade sofa bed, a small kitchen bar. Dirty dishes piled high in the sink. The cooker had stains dating back to the palaeolithic era. I felt instantly at home.

"Do you think it was ransacked?" Frank asked.

"No, I think he lived like this." I was warming to Marvel.

Frank stepped gingerly into the tiny kitchen. A startled cockroach ran across the floor. Frank jumped back, his face had gone white. "Hate those bloody things," he muttered.

"I'll take the kitchen then."

"What are we looking for?"

"We'll know when we see it."

We searched for maybe half an hour. Through every stack of newspapers, in every kitchen cupboard. Under and around every piece of furniture. We even looked down the back of the sofa, unzipped the cushion covers. Frank found it in the end. On the top of a stack of TV guides. "Hide it in an obvious place," he said. "Like 'The Purloined Letter,' you know? Edgar Allan Poe?"

"Unless they made it into a movie, I probably didn't catch it."

Frank held the envelope out to me. It was a manila A4, reinforced on one side with cardboard.

The kind of envelope used to send photographs.

Thursday 5:32 p.m.

We spread the photos out on the table. They weren't the photos we were looking for. They were mostly of Michelle. Marvel had been following her close. We saw Michelle out shopping, Michelle going to restaurants, driving in her car, visiting her beauty therapist and otherwise living the life of a wealthy and idle woman. Some showed her with a bandage on her wrist—a souvenir of the tussle she'd had with Tiffany that had got the fashionable of Sydney so excited. Some didn't. They must have predated the Big Event. There were several of her wearing the natty purple suit that had wowed me on the plane.

There were a couple of Michelle visiting a house that I recognised. In Manly. And even more of her talking with a woman that I recognised.

"Call me a big girl's blouse," said Frank, "but shouldn't we be making a speedy gateway?"

"Just a minute." I shuffled through the other photos. Elspeth had not only beaten me up. She'd also taken me for a ride.

Frank danced up and down on one leg like a kid who needs to go to the toilet. "Louise will've called the cops," he said. "We're gonna get caught here red-fucking-handed. Then we'll both be in prison. I won't be able to help you if I'm inside too.''

Michelle had visited Elspeth Reid. Marvel had the photos to prove it. Why had she lied about it?

''I think I heard footsteps,'' Frank said, his voice rising in panic. ''We've got to get out of here now.''

There were more photos. Of a rangy, sandy-haired man with a mouth too big for his face. I held it up. ''Recognise this guy?''

Frank barely looked at it. ''Come on. Bring the photos. Let's just go. I think I heard a door slam.''

''Just look, Frank.'' I held up the photo. ''Any ideas?''

Frank looked, edging back into the room as though he were walking on eggs. ''It's Brian Patrick. He works for the council. Can we go now?''

''Are you sure?''

''As sure as I can be given that I looked him up in our files less than an hour ago. Look, I'm just going to go, okay? I can't be found here—''

He reached for the door, but someone opened it before he did. Frank stepped back.

''Oh, Jesus,'' he said. ''This is the last thing I need.''

Thursday 5:53 p.m.

It was Elspeth Reid. She came in, nodded at Frank. Cast her eye over the mess and then fixed it on me.

"Where's the file?"

"What file?"

"Marvel's file on this case," she snapped. "It's not in his office, I've already looked."

"It's not here. We haven't found anything."

Elspeth acted like she hadn't heard me. She began searching, quickly. Frank and I watched her, saying nothing.

"Whoever killed him probably took it," I said, with my talent for stating the obvious.

"No kidding," Elspeth said and kept on looking. And then, "I was counting on Marvel being a bit smarter than that."

"We found the photos."

"I've seen them. They're no use to me."

"Why did you lie?"

She straightened up. "Why do you think? I had no idea who you were or who you were working for. I still don't know."

"Nobody. I'm working for nobody."

"Well, the *Star*, but only tangentially," Frank smiled and

held out his hand. "Frank Webster, *Sydney Star*. And you are?"

"Lady Mackbeth." Elspeth ignored the hand and the question.

"Suppose you tell me what's really going on?" I asked.

"Suppose we get the hell out of here," Frank said.

Elspeth was searching in the refrigerator. Poking past food that was old and mouldy. Suddenly I could see that she was crying.

"Don't cry," I said. "We'll figure something out."

On the way out I took one last look at Marvel's office.

"I thought we were leaving?"

"We are." I scanned the room one last time. Elspeth stood beside me, wooden. Frank had given her one of his large embroidered linen handkerchiefs. She'd recovered herself pretty quick.

The phone.

It was a fancy one. It had a screen showing the numbers called. I picked up the receiver. Pressed the redial button.

"What are you doing?"

"It's an old trick I learned from Princess Diana." The phone dialled dutifully. I waited for somebody significant to answer. Tried to ignore the dead private detective to my left. A dead private detective who was beginning to smell.

"Hello?" An adult, male voice.

"Hi. My name is Charles Miller. A friend, a private detective gave me your name."

"Whaddya want?"

"He . . . ah . . . said you . . . ah . . . might be able to help somebody like me." I hoped my fishing would seem like nervousness.

"Yeah, mate. I can help you. It's not cheap."

"I was told it wouldn't be."

"And I need a hundred percent deposit in advance. Cash only."

"That can be arranged."

"I'll need a photo and a copy of your old passport. Plus your drivers licence and any other stuff you need done. It'll all cost extra, of course.'' He named a figure. A preposterously large figure. ''That's just the base rate. For the passport.''

''That sounds just what I'm looking for,'' I said. ''I've got your number. I'll call you tomorrow, Mr—''

''Kelly,'' he said with a laugh. ''Ned Kelly.''

I put the phone down. Gave a silent cheer. It felt good. It felt solid. Maybe the gods had decided I was worth a punt after all.

We stepped out into the busy sunshine of King's Cross and merged into the crowd. There was a cop on the pavement.

''Just keep walking,'' Elspeth said, suddenly regaining her composure. She put her arm through mine as though we were mother and son out for a stroll along the byways of vice.

The cop stood there. Looking straight ahead the way they do. He saw us as we walked past, but by then I was in profile. Elspeth was chattering about a garden that she had visited. Frank looked as guilty as sin. The cop stared at us. Elspeth's monologue required no response, as she'd intended, so I nodded in a bored way as though I'd heard it all a hundred times before. I didn't think he'd seen us come out of Marvel's office. I prayed that he hadn't.

''I mean, hydrangeas are all very well, but I really think they could have done with something more imaginative in that corner . . . it's not as if they don't have the money. But then I always say people with the most money don't always have the best gardens. Sure, they went for the obvious, flashy things, but the whole picture did not say 'inspired' to me . . .'' Elspeth burbled.

We got past the cop. He looked at us, but not with recognition. He didn't come after us. I felt no tap on the shoulder. Heard no words that presaged the end of my freedom. I broke into a sweat. I could have hugged Elspeth. And Frank. I didn't. I kept my grip on Elspeth.

''Lets us both have a chat,'' I said. ''We've got such a lot to catch up on.''

''Not with him here,'' Elspeth said, looking at Frank.

''What? Me? What've I done?''

''You're a reporter. I don't trust reporters and I don't like them.''

"*He's* a reporter too," Frank glared at me.

"Sorry," Elspeth said. "That's the way it is. Last time I confided in a reporter I ended up on the front page. I won't make that mistake again."

Frank sniffed. "Give me back my handkerchief then."

Elspeth handed it over.

"It's all right," Frank said, peeved. "I've got things to do. I'm working this story too, you know."

"Come on," Elspeth said after he'd left, "let's get the car. I've probably got a ticket by now." We walked down a hill, where the sex shops and restaurants gave way to apartment buildings.

I was working it out as we walked. "Vince put Marvel on Michelle's trail—I know that from Vince's daughter. So he followed her when she came to see you. When was that?"

"About three months ago."

"And then he knows about the photos. He sees Michelle go to Gracie and get them copied. Or he makes an educated guess. He reports to Vince and Vince confirms it by going to Michelle and pulling some sort of deal."

"Probably. I never heard from her after that one visit."

"So she did get the photos from Vince. What did Michelle tell you?"

"Not much. That she might have some evidence about Vicky. Not what it was or how she got it."

"The prostitute said Marvel's last client stiffed him out of his fee. I'm assuming that was Vince. So Marvel comes to you. Offers you what he knows. Which is a good way to finish what he's started and collect his fee. Am I right?"

"He said Michelle didn't care about finding out what happened to Vicky."

"So what made Michelle suddenly play ball with Vince? Did he pay her off?"

"That's what Marvel was trying to find out," Elspeth said.

"And then there's Michelle's trip out of the country. Maybe she acted as a courier for Vince for some deal or other. With all the heat on him he couldn't leave Sydney at the moment. Yet she could go. His estranged wife. Did Marvel know she was going away?"

"I don't know. He didn't mention it. He said he was following a couple of things up and he'd be in touch when he had something."

"Whatever it was, looks like he found it."

Thursday 6:35 p.m.

Elspeth's car had a parking ticket fluttering from the window. She took it, looked at it and started crying again.

"Marvel was my friend," she said. "My friend and my only hope of finding out what happened to my daughter."

I got the car keys from her. Opened the car door. Got her seated in the passenger seat. She stared straight ahead. I got in the driver's seat and turned the key in the ignition.

"You've got me now."

"You can't help me. You don't know anything."

I decided to ignore that. "You don't fancy a spot of house-breaking?"

I turned the car around and drove back the way we had come. Then I retraced the route Marvel had taken the day before when he'd visited a large house in Paddington.

Elspeth and I strolled up to the front door of the old house and pushed the bell. I could hear a tumbling arrangement of tinkling chords in response, but no footfall. I waited. Pressed the bell again. Looked casually out into the street to see if anyone was paying above average interest. A car drove by but the driver didn't look our way. A young mother wheeled a toddler in a pushchair. There was no one else about the street.

I rang the door once more, for luck. And just in case whoever was inside had fallen asleep or been in the shower, still nobody came. I had the feeling there was nobody to come. The place felt empty. I told Elspeth to wait and I'd let her in. There was a side path with a green wooden gate leading to the back yard. It was about five foot high and locked so I hoisted myself over it with one deft movement.

I wasn't deft enough. I got about halfway and fell the rest. I landed on one foot and stumbled face first into a small border. I made a note to work on my fitness. It's not strictly necessary for journalism but I could see the advantages for burglary.

The garden was narrow and long. There was a small shed and a lot of grass. A tiled area featured a barbecue and a set of cast-iron tables and chairs. Best of all, there wasn't much view for the neighbours. Tall trees sheltered me from the two houses on either side.

The barbecue had been used recently and by someone who wasn't skilled in suburban procedure. A charred mass of something lay in the grate and the smell of starter fluid was unmistakable. I poked it with a tool that lay nearby. There was nothing left to see.

The back of the house had a joyful feature: a glass conservatory. I let myself in by breaking a pane of glass. Went to the front of the house and admitted Elspeth.

"Who's place is this?" she asked.

"There's a prize for the first person who finds out. Marvel came here yesterday."

The place was under-furnished, even by my standards. There was a cane sofa in the conservatory and a rubber plant that couldn't decide whether to live or die. A matching cane and glass coffee table bore a collection of fashion magazines.

On the ground floor a dark hallway connected a kitchen, a dining room and a reception room which looked out on to the street. There was no food in the fridge and only a couple of boxes of packaged diet meals in the freezer. One cupboard turned up a couple of tins of baked beans, a jar of Vegemite and a packet of Swedish crispbread.

The middle room had another sofa, a coffee table and a small television. A small bookcase held a collection of racy paperbacks about go-getting young women who got what they wanted by being very accommodating towards rich and powerful men.

The front room had probably been the main reception room in days gone by. It had been turned into a makeshift office. There was a large wooden desk with an old-fashioned blotter, a bunch of filing cabinets, another sofa and several more pot plants. Built-in cupboards revealed boxes of vitamin supplements, a powdered formula that had an additive list that would barely fit on the label, and pamphlets promising a healthier, slimmer life to the person who combined the two and participated in a calorie-controlled diet.

The filing cabinet was filled with correspondence between a company called Sunvale and various suppliers and customers. They were tagged at the bottom by Michelle O'Donnell's name. Judging from it all, it looked as if Michelle was the Avon lady of vitamins. I shoved the letters back in the cabinet, and as I did, I noticed another one that had slipped out of the folder.

Dear Michelle,
This is to advise you officially that I'm handing in my notice. My great aunt, who I've told you about, is getting worse, so I have to go back to Adelaide and take care of her. I'm her only relative and she refuses to go into a home. I'll be leaving Sydney as soon as I can. I don't want to go. I've had a good time working for you and I am very grateful that you took me on. I'll never forget your kindness. I'll write and let you know how things go. Thanks again for everything.
Karen McArdle.

"Marvel tell you about this?" I asked Elspeth.

Elspeth shook her head.

"Maybe this was the business Michelle was referring to with Vince." I told Elspeth about the phone call that Michelle had made to Vince the night she died.

The letter was dated ten days ago. It seemed unlikely that Karen McArdle was still in Sydney, but I made a note of the name. Perhaps Frank could track her down in Adelaide. Meanwhile, there was the rest of the house to search.

We took the stairs. There were three large rooms on the first floor. The first, which looked out over the back garden, was furnished with a double bed. It was covered by a candlewick bedspread but had no sheets or blankets. A tangle of wire coathangers lurked in the wardrobe. There was a small dresser with a lamp and a lace doily on top. The dresser drawers were empty. The middle room contained a few empty apple boxes. The front room, the largest, had another bed, a morning chair and more built-in wardrobes and bookcases. I sat on the chair, looked around, absorbed the atmosphere. The delicate fragrance of perfume hung in the air.

"A whole house, just for this?" Elspeth said. "These places are expensive. Nobody in their right mind would use it just to run a small-time business. You could do that from your bedroom."

"Maybe she liked to do things with style."

Elspeth was not convinced. "Think about it. How many pills would she have had to sell just to make the rent back? Not to mention employing a secretary. It doesn't make any kind of business sense. And why not have a place a bit nearer home? She'd had to trek across the harbour every day. Most people avoid that if they can."

We went back down the stairs. I went through the office drawers again. The telephone was in one of them.

The phone had a built-in answer machine. There were no messages. I rewound the tape and listened to the recorded messages, inviting callers to communicate with a company called Sunvale. The voice was Michelle's. I punched the redial button. It called a travel agency where I got an answer machine inviting me to leave a message. I declined.

The sun was losing its edge when, finally, we got back out on the street. The new light softened shapes and brought people out to play. Their voices carried from backyards I couldn't see. I could smell woodsmoke and barbecues. It nudged my hunger. I hadn't had a decent meal since breakfast and that had been a while ago.

Behind us, footsteps moved fast. I turned. Saw what was

coming too late. A dark shape burst into my firmament, grabbed me roughly around the neck. I felt pain but could not quite locate its source. Then I knew. My arm was twisted up my back in a way that suggested bones would soon break. I tried to relax, forced myself to relax. It's not easy when Jonah Lomu's big brother's got your writing arm.

Thursday 7:15 p.m.

It was Chook, Michelle's driver. The avenging, twenty-stone rugby player. Elspeth hit him across the back. He swatted her off.

"What do you want?" she demanded.

"I wanna talk to him," he said.

"Take your hands off him," Elspeth did not seem to register the disparity between her size and Chook's, "do you want to bring the cops here?"

Chook edged my arm further up my back. It felt as though my shoulder and its socket were going to part company.

"He got away from me once," he said. "Made a fool of me. I got hassled by the pigs."

"Oh, for God's sake," Elspeth said. "Let's discuss this like adults shall we?" She planted herself right in front of him. "He's not going to tell you anything until you let him go." Elspeth folded her arms across her chest. "So which is it to be?"

Chook waited a time before he dropped my arm. A sensation like an internal waterfall started up as the feeling returned.

"I have an idea," Elspeth said. "Why don't we drive back to my place and I'll make some food?"

"She's bossy, like my mother," Chook grumbled as we

parted company with Elspeth. At his firm request, I'd agreed
to drive with Chook. Elspeth would lead the way in her car.

We joined the rush-hour traffic streaming to the north side
of the harbour. I sat in silence. I wasn't too worried about
Chook becoming violent again, Elspeth's stern manner seemed
to have calmed him down.

It took us half an hour or so to get back to Manly. We dived
under the harbour by way of the tunnel and climbed steeply
up the other side, traversing the smart suburbs of the North
Shore on a ribbon of main road. Chook didn't say a word and
I was grateful for the rest and the silence. I watched the other
cars. I watched the boats on the harbour when we stopped at
a lift-up bridge. I tried to empty my mind, hoping that something relevant would pop back in when I wasn't watching for
it. Something that would give me a clue to what was going
on. Was the Sunvale vitamin business what Michelle and
Vince were working on together, or was it something to do
with New Harbour? Mary had told me that a Singapore-based
consortium had bought Vince out of an earlier project. Was
he planning the same sort of escape deal with this one? I
remembered John Holden talking to Frank about jobs for Aussies. Perhaps Michelle had been doing negotiations on the sly
so that nobody would guess what Vince was up to. If she'd
been his assistant before they married, presumably she knew
the drill. But why had she been killed? I wasn't any closer to
knowing.

The traffic backed up while we waited for the bridge to
lower. Yachts sculled by, their masts rocking on a slight chop.

Chook had his eyes fixed dead ahead.

"Why'd you do it?" he asked.

I sighed. An exaggerated sigh, for effect. "Let me tell you
something, Chook. I may look stupid to you. A lot of people
make that mistake about me. But if I had set about to kill
Michelle, I'd have made sure that the whole world and his
immediate family hadn't seen me out with her that night. I'd
have made sure I didn't get eyeballed by a taxi driver escorting
her indoors blind drunk. I would not have had sex with her
and I'd have made damn sure I didn't leave any evidence like

my fingerprints on the murder weapon. Do you follow what I'm saying here?''

Chook appeared to be paying me no mind. He'd fixed his eyes back on the water. He did not take his eyes off it. I couldn't be sure that he was listening but I went on anyway.

''And another thing. If I had killed her on the spur of the moment. I'd have needed my passport to get me on the first plane out of here to somewhere there's no extradition treaty. I would have wasted no time doing that. I would not have left it in the house so the cops would immediately know everything about me except my blood type. And I would not be running round the bloody city trying to find out just who the hell set me up.''

Chook wrenched his attention away from the sea. He squinted at me while he reached for the brake handle, interest in his deep-brown eyes. ''Why would anyone set you up?''

''I don't know. Because I was there.''

''Cops took me apart. They like getting their hands on a Maori fella, especially when he's got a record.''

''What sort of record?''

''Assault.'' Chook said it impassively. I looked at him with new respect. ''It was a long time ago, alright?''

''Of course,'' I said quickly. The cops would be interested in anyone with a record. Maybe my prospects weren't so dim, after all.

''Do you have an alibi for the night she was killed?''

''Went home. Watched the footy on telly, had a few drinks and went to bed. Had an early start. Michelle wanted to be taken to the gym.''

''Why was a woman with a sprained wrist going to her gym?''

Chook didn't answer. Instead he handed me a cigarette and I sucked on it greedily. I occasionally make halfhearted attempts to boost my chances in the longevity lottery, but this was clearly not the time.

Ahead, Elspeth made a right turn. We followed her.

• • •

"Anyone want coffee? Or something stronger?" Elspeth said brightly as she let us through to her still-sunny kitchen. Chook and I both opted for beer. I opened the bottles while Elspeth rustled up kedgeree in a well-used frying pan.

"What were you doing at Marvel's?" I asked her.

"I hadn't heard from him in a few days. I had a bad feeling."

"Did you know that Victoria wasn't out with Larry the artist those times you thought she was?"

"Yes," she said. "I knew. I just didn't think it was any business of yours." Elspeth smiled to show no hard feelings. The smell of kedgeree filled the kitchen. Chook stared at his beer bottle. Elspeth had given him a glass to drink out of with a picture of the Queen on the side. He preferred the bottle with the kangaroo on the side.

"Have you got any theories about who she was with? Larry mentioned a boss who'd taken a shine to her."

"The cops checked him out. He was somewhere else."

I remembered I had to call Frank about the note left by Michelle's secretary. Two dead women, several years apart. I was running out of time and there were too many loose ends waving gaily in the breeze.

I got Frank on the first ring. "Where are you?" he demanded.

"I need you to check something out. A woman called Karen McArdle. From Adelaide."

"It's not much to go on," Frank grumbled.

"So prove your editor wrong about those tabloid instincts."

"Do you think Elspeth Reid will do an interview? I could use something strong for tomorrow."

"Don't be greedy, you've got a dead private eye."

Elspeth chucked the kedgeree on to plates and we scoffed it with toast. The corgi, roused from its stupor came sniffing for tidbits.

"Tell me why you were at the house in Paddington," I asked Chook. To my surprise he blushed.

"Karen helped me get the job," he said. "We were staying in a hostel. She'd just arrived from out of town, like me. We went out together and got a bit pissed. I told her everything

about me. She was easy to talk to. Then later she called me
and said someone she was working for someone who needed
a driver. I spoke to Michelle and that was that. She said she'd
give me regular work. I had some shearing money saved up
so I got the car on lease.''

"Did you tell Michelle about your record?''

"Up front. That way if they're going to say no then I
haven't wasted my time.''

"What did she say?''

"She said it didn't matter. She believed in second chances.''

"When was this?''

"About six weeks ago.''

"And now Karen's gone back to Adelaide?''

Chook looked glum. "She left without saying goodbye.
That's what Michelle said. She showed me the letter. But I
couldn't believe she'd do that 'cos we were mates. So I
thought I'd try the office and see if she'd left an address or
something.''

"And did she?''

"She just vanished,'' Chook said.

I looked at Elspeth. We were both thinking the same thing:
Karen McArdle had simply vanished, like Victoria Reid.
Maybe in trying to figure a connection I'd been concentrating
on the wrong two women.

"She's really cute,'' Chook said. "Skinny but not too
skinny. And great legs.''

I helped Elspeth clear the plates and stack them in the dishwasher. Chook played with the dog while he worked on his
second beer. Elspeth made tea. I drank several cups of it and
then stood up.

"Know where Michelle's gym is?''

"Course,'' Chook said. "I took her there all the time.''

"Let's go,'' I said. "I think I might be able to figure out
what happened to your friend.''

The phone went. Elspeth answered it. Spoke briefly and put
the receiver down.

"It's the cops,'' she said. "They found out I was Marvel's
client. They'll be here any minute.''

I called Frank before I left and gave him the address of where we were going.

Then we got the hell out.

Chook wasn't keen on driving me anywhere else. "If the pigs stop us, I'm finished," he grumbled. "They'll send us both to jail."

"Then I'm abducting you. That's what you tell them. I'm a dangerous criminal, remember." I punched Chook lightly on the bicep. It felt like concrete.

"The cops are giving me hassle, you know?"

"Only too well."

"With my background, I can't afford another mistake."

"Me neither."

"You really didn't do it? You really didn't kill her?"

"I really didn't kill her."

"Fair go?"

"Fair go."

"Who did then?"

I sneaked another look at this hulking guy as he guided the car out on to the street. Had he murdered Michelle for some twisted, secret reason of his own? He caught me looking.

"Watcha staring at?"

"Nothing," I said quickly.

"Don't stare. I don't like it."

"I won't."

"You think I did it?"

"No," I said too quickly.

"You do. You do think I did it. Fucking Pakehas. You guys see a brown face and you think murderer, rapist. Well you white fellas seem to forget that you've done far more shit to us than we ever done to you—"

"Who do you think did it?" I said, to avoid the lecture. "You know her better than me."

"I just drove her places. She didn't tell me things."

"You said that before. Where did you drive her?"

"Places."

"What sort of places?"

"Shopping, restaurants. Delivering her vitamin pills. The airport once or twice."

"Where was she flying to?"

"Dunno."

"She didn't tell you?"

"Like I said—"

"What about . . . ?"

"Adelaide. That's where she flew to, I remember. I helped her carry her bags. She went to the counter and picked up her ticket and the woman said it was to Adelaide."

"When was that?"

"A month ago."

"She went to Karen McArdle's home town?"

"Lots of other people live there."

"What was she doing there?"

"Dunno. I just drove."

"She didn't chat about the trip."

"Nope. What do I know about her business?"

The car slowed. Chook followed the signs for Neutral Bay. Chook made a couple more turns and pulled into a side street.

"Here's the gym. What are we doing here?"

"You ever think about why she wanted you to take her there yesterday morning?"

"Aerobics?" Chook said hesitantly as if it were a trick question.

"With a sprained wrist?"

"Maybe she was addicted to exercise. I read an article about that. Y'know, people who train even when they're injured. Maybe she was like that. Maybe she was going to do the stairmaster or something. Don't need two hands for that."

"Maybe," I said. "But I think she had another reason."

Thursday 8:58 p.m.

The gym was housed in a two-storey concrete block building. Spartan but with a few flourishes that told the members their exorbitant fees were not entirely for nothing. A sign outside said it was for women only. We scouted the building. Two walls faced the street. There was an alley running down the side and a car park out the back for the patrons.

"Expensive, this place," said Chook, lumbering after me like a giant primate.

I made a note of the staircase that clung to the back wall. It had a sign above it marked fire exit. The main entrance was round the front. Trim women were walking to their sleek cars.

"You ever come here with Michelle?"

"You bet," he said. "She couldn't get enough of the place. Should have had a bunk bed set up in the changing sheds."

"I'm sure they're more than mere sheds," I said, eyeing another expensively clad body slipping between leather steering wheel and seat.

"Michelle didn't do things by halves. What are we doing here anyway?"

It was a fair enough question. Acting insanely would have been a fair enough answer. Apart from this latest difficulty that I found myself in, I am generally regarded, by those who know me, as someone who cruises the edges of laws from time to time but rarely breaks them. Burglary is the exception to this rule. I can go months and months without forcing an entry into somebody else's property, but once the scent is in my nostrils I find it impossible to walk away. Perhaps it's part of being a journalist, all those years of forcing myself on people who don't want to talk to me, don't want to answer my questions. Housebreaking is a natural extension of that, digging round in peoples' private space for information they don't want to give me. Or perhaps it's just the sheer thrill. I had tasted the jolt of sheer joy that an illicit entry could provide, it was cheaper than booze and I liked it a lot.

The gym was closing down for the evening, which suited my plan. We went back to the car, which was parked across the road from the main entrance and I tried to call Frank's mobile number. His line was engaged. Chook listened to the radio.

"She's hidden the evidence in there, I'll bet you anything you like. Evidence about Victoria Reid."

"Who's she? I've never heard of her," Chook said. We watched the last few fitness-seekers leave, shouldering bags and primping their just-dried hair.

"It's a long story."

A moist blackness had settled on North Sydney that didn't seem to have any perceivable effect on lowering the temperature. It was hotter than a British mid-summer. I smelt like the inside of a shoe. I could all but see the layers of grime stacking up on my skin. The prison-issue carbolic scrub was looking more and more inviting.

I wound down the windows. Exotic food smells sashayed past. Couples hurried hand-in-hand to evening engagements. Cars cruised, tops down. Somewhere near was a noisy bar where drinkers were watching a sporting event judging by the periodic cheers and groans that punctuated the air.

The gym remained brightly lit. I thought Chook would have left me by now but he didn't seem inclined to. We sat in silence. I concentrated on staying awake.

"What do you think she'd got there?" Chook asked eventually.

"I'm just guessing. If I were being followed, as Michelle was, I'd hide my valuables somewhere nobody would think of. Somewhere I went so often that nobody gave it a second thought."

Some more time limped by on crutches. To help it along, I bummed some change off Chook and called Frank again. This time the reception was better.

"This story gets better," he said gleefully. "I found out that Vince has the lease on that house in Paddington. But there's no company registered under the name Sunvale Health Products. So what do you reckon they were up to? Him and his soon-to-be ex-wife?"

I started to say something. Then I saw my chance to get into the gym.

Thursday 9:35 p.m.

My chance was a contract cleaning crew. They'd parked outside and were unloading equipment from the back of the van. There were five of them. Three men and two women. I went back to the car.

"You wait here. If anybody comes, create a diversion."

"She went to the dentist," Chook said.

"Who? What?"

"Michelle went to the dentist. In Adelaide. She rang Karen and said her tooth was giving her gyp and could she recommend her a dentist. So Karen gave her the name of hers. I know that because I was in the office when she rang."

I reached in the window, punched Chook on the arm. It still felt like concrete.

"You're a good chap," I said. "Don't let anyone tell you different."

By the time I'd crossed the busy road, the crew were inside the gym. The van, with doors open, provided my chance to get authentic props. I grabbed a mop from the van and hoped I didn't meet any of them on the way. There was a woman on the front desk, doing paperwork. She saw the mop and my business-like attitude and I got a clean pass on her radar screen.

The main fitness area was beyond reception. It was the size of about three tennis courts and was studded with complicated-looking machines. A jungle-gym for grown-ups. Three of the crew had already started polishing the equipment and a vacuum cleaner hummed across the floor. A portable stereo blasted aural encouragement. I propped the mop up against a wall. If I ran into any of the crew it'd be a dead giveaway.

There were stairs to the first floor. I took them at a steady pace. The stairs led to a hallway with various therapy rooms off it, judging by the signs. The changing rooms were last on the right. There was only one set because this was a single-sex establishment. I went in. The lockers were lined up in rows perpendicular to the wall on one side. A mirror and dressing table ran the length of the facing wall. It was difficult to tell if there was anybody in there, I had to take a punt. I listened hard before I made my move. All was quiet.

I began searching. The adrenalin which had spiked my bloodstream was also informing my responses.

Five minutes later, I had to concede that I'd been a little optimistic.

The locks were no bother, they weren't that sturdy. Even as an amateur in the breaking-in business, they didn't present much of a challenge. The problem was there were just so damn many of them. About two hundred at a rough count and nothing to distinguish whether they were concealing a smelly jog bra or evidence of murder. No names, no helpful signs, just a plain numbering system that didn't help me one whit. I considered dashing back out to the car to see if Chook could provide any clues, but discarded it as too risky. I had to move quickly. The cleaners would be through here any second. It was either that or wait until they left, but then I had no way of getting out of the building undetected. Just for the hell of it, I hit one of the lockers.

The door to the changing rooms opened. I ducked behind a row of lockers.

"Jude, are you there?" piped a female voice.

I said nothing, focused on a sticker dead ahead of me that

advertised vitamins and prayed to the god of housebreakers that the voice would go away.

It didn't. It came into the room. "Jude?"

I held my breath. There was silence. The voice didn't leave, but it didn't come any closer either. I concentrated on the vitamin sticker that promised new vitality. I'd settle for the old if I could just get out of there in one piece.

After what seemed several slow eternities, footsteps sounded, the door opened and I was, I imagined, once more alone. I let out a slow breath, noticed how fast my heart was beating, flexed my hands a few times and looked more closely at the sticker. Throughout the few minutes of sheer panic a memory had surfaced. A memory of a bathroom cabinet with its rows and rows of tablets. Michelle's were the same brand.

It was the only shot I had. I worked the lock. After a few seconds the door sprung open.

The locker was filled with the things you'd expect. Small bottles of shampoo and soap, a toothbrush and paste and hair gel took up the top shelf. On the bottom a towel, a leotard and some underwear lay neatly folded. I lifted the towel and let out a small whistle.

A buff-coloured envelope was tucked into its folds.

I was about to zip on out of there when the door opened and one of the cleaners entered. She plonked the portable stereo on a seat and turned it to full blast. She swiped her dusting cloth from her shoulder and started polishing to the rhythm of one of those bands that always makes me think that all music is starting to sound the same.

I was trapped. The music banged my eardrums, reminding me that sleep was sorely lacking from my life. I slunk back to the protection that the lockers afforded, briefly considered putting the envelope back. At least I'd know where to find it.

The cleaner sang along to the music. I risked another peek. Her cleaning was moving her inexorably in my direction. There was one escape route. Around the next column of lockers lay the entrance to the pool and saunas, but I couldn't even make a dash for there while her back was turned because the mirrors would give me away.

The stereo had moved on to another song. It sounded tediously like the first. I snuck another look. The energetic cleaner was giving the tops of the lockers a dusting. That kid was going to get her reward in heaven. I made my decision. It was a flimsy move but it was all I could think of with that racket going on.

I slipped around the column of lockers and through the door marked "swimming pool." She hadn't seen me. She was working on the top of the lockers and they didn't have mirrors. I gave a silent cheer. Then I turned around and came straight back out again.

"Hiya," I said to the girl, who was still showing a bracing expanse of bare back as she reached. She stopped. Turned.

"Hi," she said uncertainly. At least I suppose that's what she said. The music continued at levels high enough to make you wish for an early death.

"Sorry, didn't mean to startle you. Checking out the spa pool. The pipes have packed up. May need to be overhauled again." I tapped Michelle's envelope as if to indicate that my mission had come via a sealed document. "It's been more trouble than it's worth," I went on, praying that my makeshift Australian accent fooled her. In that respect the music was a blessing.

"Right," she said.

"Catch you later, then." Moving confidently towards the door. I whistled like I had every right to be there.

"Right," she said and went back to her job.

It was almost too easy. I walked back along the corridor, descended the stairs, crossed the foyer and put my hand on the front door. Emotional string music welled in my ears. My bid for freedom. Over the wire. My hand fastened on the door handle and I pulled. Nobody tapped me on the shoulder. Nobody saw me even.

I opened the door and walked out. I took a deep breath of sub-tropical Sydney air.

I could get to like this place, I thought.

Chook's car was still parked across the road. I yanked open the door and got in. "Found it!" I said jubilantly. I slid into the seat and shut the door.

"T'riffic," said the driver as he fired up the engine. He pressed a little button that locked all the doors.

It took me a good three seconds to realise that it wasn't Chook.

Thursday 9:59 p.m.

decided to start with the simple questions. "Where's Chook?"

The driver rode the bumper of the car in front, pumping the accelerator so that the car moved forward in spurts. "He has a nasty headache. He needed to go and lie down."

We drove back along Neutral Bay's main road and negotiated the tangle of approach lanes for the bridge. Sydney lay before us doing the dramatic harbour number from yet another angle. The bridge was lit by green lights. I entertained the idea of throwing myself out of the moving car and dismissed it almost immediately. We were moving at a fair clip and it was like the Grand Prix as busy drivers jostled for position. There're lots of stupid ways to die, and making your big exit as human roadkill is one of them.

The driver sped down the steep approach to the harbour bridge and dropped a coin in the toll basket at the other side. We were heading west, that much I knew. I recognised a few landmarks—Darling Harbour, the Entertainment Centre. I looked in the rear-vision mirror to see if there was any sign of Frank. He knew I was going to the gym. It was a faint hope, but it didn't stop me giving it an airing. Especially when we were driving right past the newspaper offices. I prayed for miraculous, divine intervention. Anything would do but preferably something flashy and over the top. A helicopter, a bolt of lightning, even a traffic cop with an infringement notice.

None of those things happened. We were followed by a black Ford, but I sensed it was not the type of escort that was going to benefit me in the long run.

We were following signs for the western suburbs. We turned off the main road and curved around some back streets. The driver slowed the car on a stretch of industrial land. A disused building stood on the side of some sort of bay or inlet. We drove around the water for a bit and through the gates of a builders' yard. On the other side was a wall and a few feet below that, I guessed, was the water. It was dark and I felt as though the temperature had dropped a few degrees. Or maybe it was just me.

The driver jerked the handbrake and turned to me. The engine was still running.

"Envelope please." He held out his hand.

I didn't look over my shoulder. There was no real need. The black Ford was somewhere behind us. I had the envelope balanced on my left knee. It didn't take much imagination to figure out what was going to happen next. I would hand it over and then get dispatched to a cold, wet place that would seriously interfere with my breathing. It was that part that helped me decide. I've never been what you'd call a happy swimmer. I couldn't see the point of it, what with God having invented motorboats and everything. I can swim, but prefer to only under circumstances of my own choosing. Usually the criteria involve a well-shaped azure pool and one of those tiny inner tubes to float your cocktail in. It was apparent that nothing like that would be in the immediate offing.

So I picked up the envelope delicately as if it were fine china and held it between the thumb and forefinger of my right hand. When he reached out with his left, I poked him hard in both eyes using my free hand.

He recovered pretty damn quick, I have to say. Or maybe it was sheer fighter's instinct that made him reach out blindly and grab me round the throat. One thing was for sure, he couldn't see anything. But that was small consolation to my lungs, which were having to think up creative ways to get oxygen so they could stay in business. I jabbed his jaw with my elbow. Quite hard, I thought, but it didn't have any perceivable effect on his grip. I plucked ineffectually at his arm. Not much joy there either. Then I had a brainwave. I used my free arm to let off the handbrake. The car started rolling quickly towards the water. The slope was steep and slightly greasy. It got his attention immediately. I could tell from the panic on his face that the watery finale had been intended for me only. He grabbed at the handbrake and stomped on the footbrake. The car slowed a little, but didn't stop. The slope was too steep, too slimy. We slid towards the water. Behind us, I could hear people running, shouting.

The driver panicked. He fumbled for the central locking button and the locks popped up. He yanked hard on the door as the car, which had gathered a bit of momentum by virtue of its size, sailed into the water. The thug grabbed the envelope as the car hit the water with the grace of a fourteen-stone belly flopper.

The driver was making good his escape, I couldn't say I blamed him. But he had responsibilities to attend to first. I grabbed him.

"Give me the envelope," I hissed, my arm around his neck this time.

"The car . . ."

"Give me the envelope," I said, more slowly. Repeating a simple idea several times is the most effective way to get people to do what you want. I once read this in one of my ex-wife's self-assertion manuals. I hadn't imagined at the time that it would come in so handy.

"Sinking . . ." he croaked.

"Very observant. Now give me the envelope." The sinking process was actually taking much less time than I had imagined, but there was no time to think about that. I had the high ground. My opponent's future freedom didn't depend on the contents of that envelope, but mine did.

He handed it over, wound down the window and wriggled out faster than I would have thought possible for a man of his size. I wound the window back up before the water started to lap around it. The car continued to sink. And I prayed to the gods of the underworld that they would reject me one more time.

Thursday 10:15 p.m.

It got much colder and I got much wetter. But there was still air in the car when it landed at the soggy bottom of the lagoon. That air was my escape route. A foolhardy, some would say downright stupid, plan that I had formulated while my brain was half-starved of oxygen.

Wait till the pressure in the car equals the pressure outside, a fire fighter had once told me. He'd described this theory over a few drinks when we were both warm and dry and it had seemed to make perfect sense at the time. Now, with the water creeping around me, it seemed like an absolute act of lunacy. I fought with the panic. Forced myself to stay calm. Panic won out: I tried the door handle, it was sticky and several hundred pounds of water were confidently pressing on the other side. I shoved with my shoulder. Nothing. I tried the window, but the electronics had died when the car took a bath.

My terror level was keeping pace with the waterline. I tried to talk myself into calm, but it didn't work. I couldn't distract myself. It was cold, wet, dark and I was never getting out.

I scrabbled in the glove box for a plastic bag to put the envelope in. The gods hadn't completely deserted me, the car manual came in a ziplock bag. It wouldn't keep my cargo completely dry, but it was better than nothing.

The water edged up around my chest. It smelled like an old sewer. I tried the door again, it was jammed. The handle wouldn't work. So much for the theory of equal pressure. I thought about my friends in London and the urge to cry became almost overwhelming. *Why not?* I thought. No need for a macho facade any longer. It was not as if anyone would see me, and hell, I was for the Styx ferry any moment now.

The fetid water lapped at my chin. I put my hands up to protect the envelope and then I felt it. My escape hatch.

The sunroof.

I fumbled with the catch. It was plastic but sturdy. I jiggled it and it moved. The water slimed higher, pushing the air bubble and me against the roof of the car. I counted to ten, just for the hell of it. I counted back down to one again. There was maybe one inch of air. Then, using all the strength I had ever possessed, I slid the latch open, grabbed the last of the air and kicked up as hard as I could.

The water was salty. I took in a lungful and broke the surface coughing and gagging. I made it back to the shore using a very odd stroke to keep the envelope above water. I crawled up the slope. There was no one there to meet me. The driver and his cronies had probably given me up for drowned, which was good. Things maybe were starting to go if not my way, then at least not in the complete opposite direction.

I sat down gingerly and opened the envelope. It was wet but I hoped not damaged beyond repair. As I prised out two photographs, a small gold chain dropped out. It was a Coptic cross, so light and delicate that I could barely feel the weight of it. I closed my hands around it while I looked at the photos. The light was faint, for which I was grateful. The young woman had been battered so effectively that it wasn't possible to make out her features. But she was wearing the clothes that Elspeth described and there was the crucifix. I slicked my hair back, wringing some moisture out so that I didn't drip on the photos.

There was something else in the envelope: a photocopy of a handwritten letter from, I assumed, a council official to Vince O'Donnell. Dear Vince, it said (I'll paraphrase this bit), We know that you really badly want to take a lovely old building in Bondi and impose your own particular post-modern vision of the horrors of urban living on it. Other companies want to do that too. But you have made your point much more succinctly with your generous offer. The contract is yours.

There was another document, the minutes from a meeting of the planning committee the day that it met to consider who was going to be the lucky winner of the contract. The minutes listed the participants and the organisations they represented. There were names that I recognised. Then I compared the dates of the two documents. Like the old Soviet elections, the winner of the Bondi development had been decided in advance.

The last document was a small diary. It didn't take much imagination to work out whose it was. I turned to the page that corresponded with the dates on the papers. There wasn't anything interesting. Then I remembered Larry the artist saying Victoria had arrived later, after the Bondi project had been settled. I turned the pages until I found the name that I had assumed I would. It was there, all right. The night she went missing and a couple of nights before that. I whistled. I knew all about what happened to Victoria Reid. I knew so much I could go on *Mastermind* with it as my specialist subject.

I stood up stiffly. Tucked the wet envelope in my sopping pocket, thought the better of it and took it out. Half hunched I made my way up the precarious slope. The last thing I needed was another meaningful interface with that damn lagoon. My movements were stiff and careful but my brain was singing. I had it. And when I got back on solid ground I was going to leap in the air and do a little dance. I was wet and cold and probably a walking tenement building for water-born bacteria, but I didn't care. I wasn't going to spend the next twenty years in a cell. I could become a semi-respectable citizen once more. I thought happy thoughts as I scrabbled the last ten feet. The first verse of "Singing in the Rain" tra-la-la'ed through my head.

After I saw the gun, I forgot the rest of the words completely.

He was standing in shadow, but I could see the barrel

clearly enough. It was small but that only made it look more scary.

"Hello," I said. "We haven't met officially, but I know your work."

He laughed as he stepped out of the shadow.

Thursday 10:59 p.m.

"I see you're right on top of things," John Holden, the government minister said smoothly. Here was a man at his ease. A very bad sign.

It was the question I should have asked when I first heard about the pictures. Why did Vince keep this incriminating record in the first place? It was the only evidence that showed that Victoria Reid hadn't run away. A smart guy would get rid of everything, not keep happy snaps of the event.

But a blackmailer would hang on to them. For insurance purposes. And Vince needed someone in government to keep his career dreams alive. John Holden had killed Victoria Reid because she found out, probably via Brian Patrick, that he'd brokered an illegal deal with Vince.

"Hand over the stuff."

Had Victoria stumbled upon this while she worked for Patrick? Patrick could have kept the note as insurance for himself. Elspeth had said that her daughter noticed details. That had been one instance where she could have more safely been less observant.

I slipped the papers back into the envelope. Started talking a wall of words at him. Hoping that something would come to mind while I did so.

"I suppose you figured Vince owed you. You got him the Bondi project. So when Victoria found out about it what did you do? Try and charm her? Take her out for a few drinks and try and screw her or something? But she wasn't that kind of girl, was she? She didn't flop into bed with every handsome guy she met. So when you killed her you didn't plan it so carefully. Then you needed Vince's help to take care of the body."

"Hand them all over," Holden smiled. I edged back without thinking and almost tumbled back down the slope. He was close now. He stepped away, to avoid my flailing arms.

"It's slippery," I said. "Like you."

Holden laughed some more. "Sticks and stones may break my bones."

I swivelled my feet, trying to get purchase. My Doc Martens did the best they could. I didn't feel secure, not one little bit.

"No one's coming to help you," Holden said. "Frank Webster thinks he's pretty smart but he should know that mobile phones are easy to listen in on. He should learn not to boast so much."

"You'll take care of Frank like you did Marvel and Levine?" I pressed on desperately. If I could keep talking, I could keep breathing.

I suppose Holden figured he didn't have much to fear from me. I cut a pathetic figure, dripping wet and bruised. No way of defending myself. No back-up. No reputation. I didn't mind. It might work to my advantage.

"No more amateur theatrics, I get enough of that in politics." Holden pulled a weary face. "Please give me the envelope. I've got work to do."

I was in a bind. If I gave him the envelope he would kill me. If I didn't he would kill me. Either way, I didn't like my chances of going home to London with a suntan.

"If you let me go, I can hurt him. I can hurt Vince. Let me go. You've got the evidence. I'm wanted for murder—who's going to be listening to me?"

Amazingly, Holden appeared to consider it. It must have been tempting. If Vince was guilty of Michelle's death, then

Holden would get some revenge for having been blackmailed for so long.

An idea occurred to me. I tried not to smile. Sometimes when my brain works it really, really works.

"See, I think the plan was that Vince and Michelle would fake Michelle's death and collect on the insurance. Vince is broke, New Harbour may fall flat on its face and Michelle is worth more dead than alive."

Holden raised one eyebrow.

"I think it was Michelle's idea. She and Vince found someone who wouldn't be missed, someone who looked roughly like her. Her name was Karen McArdle. They gave her a phony job and a place to live. She was new in town so she probably didn't have any friends. So when she disappeared no one would notice. She'd be just another young woman who'd vanished. One of thousands. And when 'Michelle' turns up dead, the cops discover she has a driver with a dark face and a record of assault. A perfect fall guy."

I hoped Holden wouldn't spot the flaws in my logic. I felt like a court jester working for a tyrannical monarch, having to create the diverting story that will save my life.

"Michelle went to Adelaide, Karen McArdle's home town. When she got there she faked a toothache, called her assistant and said 'recommend me a dentist.' She stole Karen McArdle's dental records. Swapped them with her own for the autopsy.

"The private eye, Marvel was on her case. And he'd found out about the forger. You put it together. The forger has arranged Michelle's new identity. She would have to lie low somewhere nobody knew her for a while. Till the payment came through. Singapore or somewhere near. Somewhere nobody knew her."

"A fantastic tale, told with ingenuity and flair," Holden drawled.

"I'm sure you had some part to play. You get to make one final pay-off then the evidence that incriminates you is yours for ever. Perhaps a friendly word in a corrupt cop's ear. Or a sweet bribe to the coroner to overlook any inconsistencies. The offer of a little something to ease his retirement."

I stopped after that because I didn't want to overdo it. I held out the envelope.

"Chuck it down," Holden said.

I threw it like a frisbee. It landed at his feet. He picked it up, keeping the gun trained on me. He looked inside.

"Vince told me that these are the only set now. Which is fortunate. I don't have time to be running about town." Holden smiled. I wondered what Elspeth would make of that smile.

"There's a woman who doesn't know whether her daughter's dead or alive."

But Holden just walked away. Got into the black car. The wet thug glared at me from the back seat.

"It's been a pleasure doing business." Holden waved the envelope. "I'm off home to relax in front of a big open fire."

"Don't sit too close."

As he drove away, I felt in my pocket. The tiny, elaborate crucifix was still there. I closed my hands around it, feeling the sharp point dig into my palm.

Thursday 11:15 p.m.

I walked in the direction of town. Cold, angry and uncertain what to do next. I should call Frank. Warn him about Holden. But Holden had everything he wanted now. Holden was safe, so Frank was safe.

My clothes smelled, my shoes squelched. The water in the lagoon had not been fresh. I'd lost my wallet. I had a handful of change and Victoria Reid's crucifix. It wasn't going to get me far. I kept walking.

The road became busier. Cars flicked past. My walk had slowed to a plod. I fantasised about a big, clean bed in a dark room where I would lie, comatose for days. No one to disturb me, no one to come and charge me with foolish things like murder. I didn't even know what to do next. My eyelids sagged, my knees buckled and I fell limply on to the pavement, face down.

Two Dali-esque faces hovered over me. I started, blinked, my heart filled with lurching fear. Where the hell was I?

The faces were talking, but I couldn't make out what they were saying over the roar of the traffic. I blinked more. The shapes settled down, looked more human. There were two of them, a young woman and a man. Fresh-faced, clean-scrubbed, smiling, but still concerned. The woman held my hand, patted it. I noticed the badge on her lapel; a stylised fish. They were proselytes for Christ; doing God's work. I smiled woozily. "Where am I?"

"You're in Glebe," the young woman said, which made me none the wiser. She had a slight lisp, I like that in a woman. "Can you remember what happened?"

"I . . . I don't know," I said, playing it up a bit. I was greedy for a bit of sympathy. "I was attacked . . ." Well, that was kind of true. "By these two big guys . . . they took my car and all my money, threw me in the water. Left me there. I dragged myself out, I don't remember how. Somehow I must have got here."

The woman's dark eyes widened with concern. "We should get you to a hospital," she said. She stroked my hair and checked my forehead for a temperature. I willed that small, white hand to stay on my face a little longer but she took it away. I noticed a shiny wedding band. Brand new. She turned to her husband. He nodded. Hospital was the best place for me.

"I'm fine," I said. "I should be getting home. My family . . ."

"We'll ring them from the hospital and let them know you're okay."

"There's no need. I can go straight home. I'm fine."

"We insist," said the man. "You could have internal injuries."

"No really, I must get home. Please no hospitals. I hate hospitals."

"Come on, Jamie," she said. "If he doesn't want to go . . ."

"It's not a case of wanting to, Margaret," Jamie said.

I struggled to get up. "I'm okay, see?" I stood, toes clenched to stop me swaying. "I need to get home. My family will be worried. I'll call a doctor in the morning."

Jamie relented. I would have too. If I'd been him, I'd have wanted to spend as little time with me and as much time as possible with my luscious new wife.

"We'll drop you home," said Margaret. She had dark, curly

hair and soft-brown eyes. I could have dived into those eyes.

They led me to their car, small Japanese hatchback. It was piled with suitcases. She lent in, moved a few things around. The fabric of her jeans stretched tight with that movement. I pretended I wasn't looking at her arse. That was no way to repay their kindness.

"There you go," she said, straightening up. "I've made room."

She stepped aside for me as I made the same movement to get out of her way. We laughed, stepped the other way, still blocking each other's path. I stopped, in surprise. Then realisation.

Things started to fall into place. The things that had bothered me when I spun Holden that yarn. And I had the answer. I knew the story.

I got in the car.

"Been on a trip?" I asked as I buckled up.

"A retreat," Margaret smiled shyly at the memory of all the sex, no doubt. "In the Blue Mountains. Perfect peace and quiet for a whole week." Which would explain why they weren't frogmarching me to the nearest police station. I said a small prayer of thanks to God for all his followers who don't keep up with the news.

"Where can we drop you then?" Jamie fired up the car.

"Paddington," I said firmly.

Jamie guided the car through the light-soaked streets. He and Margaret didn't make small talk. She would reach over to stroke the back of her husband's neck every now and then which made me jealous. I wanted a woman like that. This guy, however high his standing with the man upstairs, didn't deserve a goddess.

I must have dozed without realising it, because soon Jamie was asking me where in Paddington I lived. I sat up quickly, rubbed my eyes as an aid to thought. I was trying to remember the location of the house in Paddington. I looked around, desperate for some sort of clue. Nothing rang any bells. I searched my brain for the number of the street, or a nearby landmark, none would come. Margaret and Jamie looked perturbed.

"Sorry," I said. "I fell asleep. I'm still a little confused."

"Let's drive around a little," Margaret said. "To help you get your bearings." But the look she shot her husband was full of concern.

We drove and nothing came to me. I'd followed Marvel to a house in Paddington, that much I remembered. All else was a blank. I couldn't even remember what day it had been. Jamie became a little impatient. He turned on the radio. I stiffened, expecting news about me to come tumbling over the airwaves. But instead we got an announcer explaining that the station only broadcast the Good News, which ruled me out by a wide margin. I relaxed a little. The announcer played a soothing song.

Jamie drove slowly. Margaret looked back from him to me, a small frown creased the skin between her eyes. I could tell she was starting to have doubts. How come I didn't know where I lived? Was I loony? Sick? Lying? I smiled reassuringly. The corners of her mouth lifted in response, but she looked away quickly. I checked my watch, it was coming up to the top of the hour. I didn't have much time. I was fairly sure that the station's policy of glad tidings would get the elbow during the news bulletin and then I'd have some questions to answer.

I closed my eyes, concentrated on what had happened: It had been only this afternoon I was last there, I was fairly sure. That it felt like ten years ago added to my sense of discombobulation.

It flashed into my head, the name of the street. I'd read it on Michelle's company letterhead. I said it out loud.

They both seemed relieved. Jamie made a turn, said that it wasn't far. We drove a quarter of a mile or so. The Christian singer sang about how well he knew Jesus. Then he stopped. I tensed, waiting for the news sting. I was tempted to have Jamie stop the car and let me out, but that would have looked suspicious. Instead I waited. Maybe they wouldn't even have the news, maybe they didn't report on the heinous deeds that people do to each other.

The station's news sting launched into full trill. It was a bubbly, frothy thing that promised listeners their sensibilities would not be aggrieved in any way. In the time that it took the sting to play we covered about a hundred yards. We were at the street that Michelle's office was on. On impulse I told Jamie to let me off there. No point in leaving a trail of breadcrumbs.

The news report began. A low-key woman who promised certainty of outlook with every syllable, reported on a plan to fund a Christian school in a place called Annandale. I allowed myself to breathe.

"Here we are," Jamie stopped the car. Margaret got out to help me. I struggled with the seat belt. I couldn't find the button to release the catch. The newsreader passed on to the second story about a visiting evangelist and his promise to win Sydney for God.

I couldn't get the buckle out. A curse sprang to my lips but I remembered my hosts and didn't say it.

"Let me help you," Margaret said. She found the buckle and freed it with one movement.

"Thanks," I said. "I really—" I stopped. Heard someone say my name. But neither Jamie nor Margaret knew my name. It must have been on the radio then. I looked at them both for a moment. They were frozen, as was I. They knew from my reaction that the news report was talking about me. We heard other words; *dangerous, must not be approached, police manhunt*. Margaret took a step back. She swallowed, I saw the muscles on the side of her throat move. I got out of the car. She stood still, her hands balled into fists. Jamie stood up very slowly. I was closer to his wife than he was; he didn't want to take any chances. I was perversely glad that the news report said I should not be approached. That had its advantages. They stood still, looking at me, not each other. Wondering what I would do.

"Thank you for your help," I said. Then I ran like hell.

I stopped at the end of the street, out of sight of their car. They didn't follow me. I was dangerous and should not be approached. They drove to safety. They would call the cops, let them do the chasing.

There wasn't much time left.

Thursday 11:55 p.m.

There were no lights on in the house I had gone to that afternoon with Elspeth. I got in the same way I had before: through the broken window.

The place was dark: I left it like that.

I went through to the office, sat behind the desk and took out the phone book that I found in the bottom drawer. Dialled Vince's phone number. Took a big breath.

"Hello?" The voice was raspy. Maybe I'd got him out of bed.

"I've got some information and I want to do a deal." As I spoke I picked up a pencil and started doodling because I like to do that when I'm on the phone. The blotter, big, clean and white, was an open invitation.

"Who is this?"

"You know who it is. The guy whom you and your girl friend set up."

"What information do you have?"

"I found your wife's hiding place. I found the hiding place."

Silence. Then: "What d'you want?"

I told Vince where to meet me. Then I prayed that Holden

had gone straight home to his log fire like he'd said he would and not called Vince to gloat.

I turned on a light. There seemed no point in sitting in the dark when Vince knew where to find me.

Frank answered my call on the first ring.

"Where the hell are you?" he demanded.

"Find anything on Karen McArdle?" I asked, because I didn't have time for small talk.

"Not a dickey bird," Frank grumbled. "The only Karen McArdle I found died ten years ago, according to official records. And I looked everywhere, mate. I'm in debt to every contact I have."

I drew a big circle on the blotter and then another one inside it. I shaded in the lines, making a thick band. Thought about putting ears on it to make a face.

"Do you mind telling me what's going on?" Frank sounded grumpy. "Since I'm running around doing all your donkey work? Where did you go to after Elspeth Reid's? She's pretty worried about you, she even rang me. And did you hear about Chook? He's in hospital after somebody clocked him on the head and stole his car. Did that happen while you were with him? I'd appreciate it if you'd give me a clue about what's going on here. I mean, it's not like I've got to put a story together or anything. And we do have a deal . . ."

The pencil flew across the paper but the shading wasn't smooth. There were bumps. I shaded some more. The bumps started to assume a pattern. Frank grumbled on in my ear but I'd stopped listening. I kept right on filling in the blotter with my pencil.

Before too long some words rose off the page. And some letters followed by some numbers. An airline flight, and a name. A name that represented a new, prosperous life for a resourceful killer.

I made a couple more calls while I sat there. I called the airlines to enquire about departures. And I rang Ozzie. Told him where I was. Asked him to help me out one more time.

I felt in my pocket for Victoria Reid's crucifix. It was pink gold, old and quite worn in places. Maybe Victoria had rubbed it a lot; like a talisman I stroked it a couple of times for luck. I didn't believe half the story I'd told Holden. Well, maybe half because half was all it was. And I didn't honestly know what I was going to do now I had more or less the full idea. So I sat and waited for Vince to show up. If nothing else I was curious to meet him. It had only been a couple of days but I felt like we'd been through a lot together.

It seemed like no time at all before I heard the sound of a key in the front door.

Friday 12:15 a.m.

He wore a black waterproof jacket, blue shirt and brand-new jeans. His arms were crossed casually and a cigarette dangled from two fingers. I had my feet up on the desk. Just to show him.

"I like all this," I said, gesturing around. "Whose idea was it? Michelle's or your girlfriend's?"

He dragged a couple of times on his cigarette. "I'm thinking Michelle's," I said as though I had all the time in the world. "Know why? Because I think you're an opportunistic kind of guy. I think you take ideas when they're given to you. So Michelle comes to you and says, 'Let's fake my death and go halves on the insurance. And I know you've got those lovely photos so let's have John Holden smooth the way with officialdom.' And you know that a plan that half-arsed is never going to work. But if you let her set everything up; this office. Get her to hire a secretary, who's really your new amour, then you can turn the tables at the last minute. Am I right?"

I knew an answer probably wasn't in the offing, so I pressed on. "Chook was supposed to be the fall guy. Karen McArdle hand-picked him, didn't she? But when Michelle told you she'd brought me home you decided to bring the thing forward. A little bonus for you both. But it wasn't quite all in

place. So you dropped something at the train-station locker—
your girlfriend's forged papers—and you passed the key in
full view of everyone. That was cool. I didn't even know what
was going on and I was ten feet away. So your girlfriend, or
accomplice or whoever has a new identity"—I held up the
blotter with the name and the airline flight etched on it—"and
you are free and clear."

I took my feet off the desk. I'd just thought of something.
Another loose end.

"What do you want?"

"My good name back."

Vince barked laughter.

"Turn over your girlfriend. She killed Michelle and Marvel
and Levine. Poor Levine, gets offed just because he's privy to
Michelle's original idea. You think she's going to stop there?
I'd say you're not safe, especially with a few million dollars
hanging around. You'll get done for aiding and abetting, but
you'll be out before you know it. Maybe if you get a smart
enough lawyer he'll extricate you completely. You won't get
the insurance money, but no plan is perfect."

"That's simply not possible." Vince smiled, took a final
drag on his cigarette and tossed the glowing butt in the bin.

"That's how accidents start," I said primly.

"What do you have in the way of proof exactly?" Vince
rasped.

I held up the envelope. I'd found it in the filing cabinet. It
was the same as the one Michelle had used to collect the
evidence about Victoria. I'd stuffed it with blank paper.

"Michelle went to a lot of trouble to collect this."

His eyes uncrinkled slightly. He was cool. I started to get
a crazy feeling in my gut. It was the loose end. Damn, I wished
I could pin it down.

He was relaxed and smug. Maybe he was going to kill me.
I had been banking on the fact that he needed me alive. That's
what fall guys are for. But perhaps not. A dead Sam Ridley
would close the case quite neatly. As I began sifting through
the options, one piece of the puzzle came loose and presented
itself to me in startling clarity. I'd made a mistake. I'd left
somebody out.

Friday 12:42 a.m.

I stared at Vince. He knew that I knew.

A slender knife came out of the folds of his jacket. The sort that I'd only ever seen in movies about the Mafia. And a loop of thin cord. I hate it when crooks come prepared.

"I'm going to have to hold you here until the cops come."

The sharp point of the knife hovered close to my neck. I thought about my arteries and how much I like having them in working order. I sat in the chair and let him tie my hands.

"I'm a good citizen, you see," he said as he yanked the knots too tight.

"In my day good citizenry didn't include bribery, blackmail and accessory to murder."

"This is Sydney," he said and smiled.

Vince picked up the phone. He was dialling when Ozzie arrived.

"Sam! What's going on?" Ozzie had stormed in as though it were a media scrum and there were ten other camera people jostling for the shot. He had his Sony camera on his shoulder. Paula brought up the rear.

Vince's knife disappeared. He sat on the edge of the desk. Picked up the envelope that I tried to bluff him with. "He's going to be arrested for the murder of my wife."

I looked at Paula. She'd seen the knife. And me tied to the chair.

"What's going on?" Ozzie asked.

Paula sighed. Crossed the room and started to untie me.

"I wouldn't do that." Vince stood in her way. "You're committing an offence."

"There's no need to tie him up," she said. "We outnumber him." She worked on the knots. I could feel her breath on the back of my neck. Ozzie was a lucky guy.

Ozzie seemed to catch on. He turned his camera on Vince. Smooth and professional like I'd seen him at the New Harbour site, a million years ago.

"Got anything to say for the camera?" he asked Vince.

In the distance I could hear sirens.

Vince said nothing. He didn't need to. He was in a pretty fine position. I was about to be his personal Jesus Christ, taking the rap for all his sins.

Paula freed my hands. "Let's go, shall we?"

We walked out of the room, Ozzie bringing up the rear. He never let that shiny artificial eye off Vince's face.

The car was outside. Door open, keys in. I dived in the driver's seat, Paula slid in beside me. Ozzie crashed in the back.

A car with a flashing light turned into our street.

Friday 1:03 a.m.

It started to rain. The rain was so heavy it seemed as though it was not just falling from the sky, but was spurting out of the ground as well. The Volvo's wipers struggled feebly and then gave up. The deluge surrounded me.

"I've been meaning to get those fixed," Ozzie said from the back.

I pushed on, blindly.

"What's the quickest way to Double Bay?"

Paula peered at the opaque glass that was our windscreen. She gave directions.

I fancied that the cop siren had dropped back but maybe the rain drowned it out.

"Where are we going?" Ozzie asked.

"We might be able to lose him if we nip down here," Paula said. I swung into a side street, managed not to hit anything. We took a couple more turns. Blind all the way.

"We lost him," Ozzie said. "At least I think we did. Bloody hard to see. What's happening?"

Paula guided me back out on to a main road. I picked up some speed. Signs looming out of the swirling lake that was the Volvo windscreen reassured me Double Bay wasn't far.

I picked up speed again. Ran a red light. Nearly lost it when the Volvo hit a puddle. The engine groaned, but ploughed on. I patted the dashboard encouragingly.

We crested a hill. Hit the swanky suburb of Double Bay so fast that I missed Tiffany's turn-off by a good hundred feet. The Volvo squealed in protest as I jammed it into reverse, barely using the clutch, and backed up.

I stopped at the end of the street. Described Tiffany's house. Told Paula and Ozzie to find a phone and call the cops. Paula slid into the driver's seat.

"I thought we were escaping the cops," Ozzie said.

"Things have changed."

"Shouldn't we come with you? As back-up?"

"I'd prefer the police, thanks all the same, Oz."

I sprinted the hundred or so yards to Tiffany's house. Maybe the Fates had finally come around to my side because as I reached her front gate the rain stopped.

Friday 1:49 a.m.

It was only after it stopped that I realised what a racket sub-tropical rain makes. The silence quivered in the wake of the deluge, still picking up vibrations.

Tiffany was packing. She was mad, judging by the way she was flinging things around. Her gate had been closed but not locked. I had walked straight in.

"Going somewhere?" I asked.

"Lying shit," she said. "All men are lying shits. God I should have known."

"He was two-timing you, wasn't he?"

Tiffany threw something at a large packing case, there was a ripple of crunching glass, it seemed to give her pleasure. She looked up, recognised me. Another liar to add to those she knew. But my crimes against her were further down the list than Vince's.

"It was a straightforward relationship," she said. "I brought the glamour. He brought the cash. We weren't in love. But we could have been. And we had good sex. Or he did. The size of his dick, I can't pretend that the earth moved for me. Although I did. Pretend, that is. It was good training in a way. For acting."

"How did you find out about her?"

Tiffany sighed. "I knew there was someone else," she said. "I just knew it. Got to learn to listen to the inner voice. Note to Tiffany: listen to the fucking inner voice."

"Did you tell Vince this?"

"He denied it, the pygmy. We had a big fight when he told me I couldn't keep the flat. I love this place. I want to keep it. Vince said there was no more money. That's when I knew there was someone else. No more money is Vince's shorthand for 'hasta la vista, baby.' I confronted him. Went to his house in the morning. I half expected to see her there with him, but he's too clever for that."

I picked up a vase and wrapped it gently in tissue. Moving is hell. Almost as stressful as divorce, they say.

"Do you know who she is?"

"I saw her once. Michelle was out of town. That's how I tripped him up. He said he was seeing Michelle to talk about the divorce. But he'd been saying that a lot, I was suspicious. I used to work in the airline business and I have a few contacts, so I checked. She flew to Adelaide that weekend. So I followed him to this restaurant. And there he was helping this woman out of the car. She looked familiar. It bothered me for ages. Then I remembered. We'd flown to Ayres Rock for this big do. A new hotel opened there and she was there. Vince and I spoke to her. It struck me at the time that she was working the room like a pro."

"When was this?"

"About a year ago."

"What did you do after you saw them eating together?"

"I sat on it. Until he told me about the flat. Then I decided it was time to play a little rough."

"You're in danger."

"He's the one in danger," Tiffany said grimly. "I won't forget this. I don't take this sort of behaviour lying down."

I placed the vase in the case.

"Want to know what I think? I think you should get the hell out of here right now. Vince's friend is a very dangerous woman. The thing that made her safe is that no one even knew she existed. She came to Sydney and pretended to be Michelle's secretary so they could kill her. They've kept their affair very, very quiet. Nobody knows for sure except you."

Tiffany continued with her aggressive packing.

"I say you can't afford to take chances. Michelle's death was very cleverly planned. She thought she was setting up her so-called secretary. But actually it was the other way around."

"Well this is all very interesting. But it doesn't help me get a roof over my head." Tiffany stopped packing. "I need a drink," she said. She went to the kitchen, came back with a bottle. "Fancy something?"

"We should get going," I said. "Does Vince know you're here?"

"Where else would I be?" she said bitterly. "I've got to be out by tomorrow."

"Come on then, we'll find a hotel."

"That's the best offer I've had all day," she said and grinned impishly. Perhaps I'd misjudged Tiffany. If I had I was glad. I was always pleased to forgive beautiful blondes. I took her arm.

The shot caught Tiffany in the other elbow. Flung us apart. I heard the crunch of bone. Blood splattered over us both. She fell. I dropped on top of her. Covered her. Tried to think. We'd stepped out on to the patio. The shot had come from outside. She was in the bushes somewhere. With a gun. Tiffany began sobbing. I dragged her inside. There was a big silence in the wake of the sound.

"Where are the lights for the backyard?" I whispered.

"In the kitchen, beside the oven," Tiffany gasped, shock in her voice.

I found the switch and plunged the yard into darkness. I picked up a carving knife. Not much protection against a bullet, but it made me feel braver.

Regretting the day I had ever thought a trip to Sydney would be a good idea, I went into the garden.

Friday 2:10 a.m.

I walked as softly as I could. Straining for any signs of another person. I could hear insects and far away the sound of traffic. Not much more. I crept around the pool using my anger to charge up my responses. I was pissed off. I didn't deserve to be treated like this. Someone else, finally, was going to pay.

I heard a scuffle, moved towards it. I held the knife so that it might look like a gun from a distance. Moved as quickly as I could across the paving that stretched between the house and the pool.

The backyard was actually rectangular, but the tricky placement of shrubs had made it seem to mimic the fluid, kidney shape of the pool. Behind the shrubs was a gap almost big enough to walk through, although the shrubs and small trees zig-zagged so it would not have been possible to get a clear view, even in daylight. Behind the greenery, a brick wall. The part of me that wasn't feeling gung-ho hoped Tiffany's assailant had already used it as an escape route. I wove through the bushes, contorting my body to move the branches as little as possible. Ahead I heard some branches move. My eyes began to get used to the absence of light but it wasn't much help, I still couldn't see anything further than about a foot away. Leaves swatted my face. My clothing got a fresh layer of damp. I strained all my senses. None of them gave me any clues.

I reached the garden shed where I'd seen Tiffany's brother working from the first time I'd come. The shed door was closed. I tried the handle. It was sticky, but it opened. I eased the door back. The shed was small, made smaller by the crush of garden-and pool-tending equipment. A quick glance showed there wasn't enough space to hide. I eased the door back, leaving it off the latch.

"Walk this way, please," the voice was low and soft. You don't have to be assertive when a gun can speak as loudly as you need it to. "And drop the knife."

I swallowed. I dropped the knife. The gun barrel pressed against my temple. Attached to the end of it was Karen McArdle, or whoever she was, all business in black. The woman I'd seen swapping keys with Vince at the train station. She had a cool, beautiful face. But the look in her eye made me gasp for breath. "Walk towards the house."

I could see no point in arguing. We began a crablike walk around the side of the pool.

Tiffany had propped herself up and wrapped something around her shattered elbow. Pain had robbed her face of its shape. Blood soaked her clothes. She looked up, clutched her elbow closer to her. Her knees sagged to one side.

"Get over there," Karen McArdle said. I moved beside Tiffany. Put my hand on her shoulder for a crumb of comfort. We stared at Karen. No need to ask her what she was going to do. She was going to kill us both. Maybe make mine look like suicide. Something artsy like that. I'd never get a chance to clear my name. My son would know me as a murderer. The thought filled me with despair, more even than the prospect of death.

Karen raised the gun. Aimed it at Tiffany's face. She couldn't miss from that distance. Tiffany shook. Tears ran.

"Please," she said. "Please don't."

Karen McArdle just smiled.

"Is this wise?" I said. "I mean, shouldn't you just be concentrating on your getaway? I would, if I were you." Karen McArdle's eyes snapped on to me.

"I'd be getting out of here," I continued. "Catch that plane." From the blotter I knew that she had a ticket for Singapore leaving first thing the next morning.

"Cut your losses. You've killed three people and Vince has an alibi. He's not going to share the money. Escape while you can."

"Shut up," she said. The gun moved back to Tiffany.

"Think about it. He's betrayed his wife and his girlfriend. He's blackmailed a government minister for years, helped him cover up a murder. Why should he start behaving honourably now? Millions of dollars in insurance is no incentive to take the moral high road. If he ever gets the money."

"How do you know I haven't got something on him?" she snapped. When they did get to run away together, it was going to be a charming future à deux.

"Just go. Tiffany and I won't know where to find you. We don't even know what your new identity is. Please. I have to get her to a doctor."

"She won't need one," Karen McArdle said, quite calmly. She raised her firing arm, steadied it with the other. Pointed it at me. I heard a roaring in my ears and felt a pain in my head. There was more sound and light. Much too much light.

Friday 2:35 a.m.

The light was at the end of a long tunnel. A shadowy figure stood at the end, in silhouette, gesturing me to join him. "Come on, Sam," I heard him say. Or maybe it was a her. The voice sounded familiar but my brain was too weary to make the connection. My head felt fuzzy and lackadaisical. It was floating. I didn't care. I felt comfortable and relaxed for the first time in days. Maybe I'd just stay in this tunnel, I thought. Maybe I'd just stay right here where no one could bother me. Floating and hanging out.

A sharp slap to my face disconnected any thoughts of nirvana. I opened my eyes. A placid-looking blond head stared back at me. I blinked a couple of times. Was this heaven? If so, why the Aussie accents?

I looked about. Tiffany sat still, nursing her broken elbow. Karen McArdle lay face down on the floor, arms spread out.

"I hit her with the shovel," Tiffany's brother Joe said placidly. "She's not dead. She nearly got you though. The gun went off. Right past your ear."

I couldn't take it all in. Couldn't adjust to life after bracing myself for death. Tiffany and I were okay, I could see that. But I couldn't comprehend it. I should have felt great. Instead I felt sick.

The police came. For once I was glad to see them. They took me and Karen McArdle to the station and Tiffany to hospital.

At the station they took my wet clothes and gave me dry clothes to put on. They were polite and considerate and I didn't see any evidence of rubber hoses. They asked me if I had a lawyer and I said no. I'd lost the paper that had Mary's lawyer written on it.

They put me in an interview room and they gave me a cup of tea. The room was bare. A table, two chairs and a notepad and tape-recorder on the desk with a pencil beside. I drank my tea and awaited my fate. I felt calm and almost relieved.

After about ten minutes an officer came in and introduced himself as Detective Inspector Malcolm Wright. He was portly with curly black hair. He carried a mug of tea in his hand and he groaned slightly as he sat down.

"I've had a bad day, Mr Ridley."

"You and me both." I said it with feeling.

"It's my wedding anniversary. My wife had booked tickets to a show. I was supposed to be there. She is not happy at all. She can count the number of times this has happened before and the number is high. Now she wishes that she'd married someone who works regular hours. Someone with a nice job in a bank, perhaps. Now she says I'd rather spend time with rapists and killers than with her. That, of course, is not true. Given the choice I'd rather spend time with her. But I don't always have the choice."

"I understand."

"So," he said. "Make disrupting my wedding anniversary worthwhile. I want a confession. Tell me exactly why you killed Michelle O'Donnell." He pressed the record button on the tape-recorder and spoke into it, giving his name and the time. "Now," he said, "I haven't got all night."

Friday 3:35 a.m.

Fortified by several more cups of tea, I told the story. Malcolm Wright listened and then asked questions. Hard ones. I told my story again, feeling my brain caving in under the pressure of all the details.

The questions stopped after a while. Malcolm Wright pinched the bridge of his nose and picked up his bifocals.

"I'm not a killer," I said.

"I'm afraid you'll have to let me decide that. You spin a good yarn, Mr Ridley. But then I'd expect that from someone like you."

He left the room. A junior cop collected me and took me to a cell. I was secured inside it.

"No chance of a cigarette, I suppose?" I asked the departing back.

"This is a no-smoking environment," said the cop, sarcastic.

Fenced in on all sides I planned to allow myself the luxury of becoming thoroughly depressed. Instead I lay on the bunk and fell dead asleep.

I was awoken, taken to the interview room, asked more questions. Not the genial Malcolm Wright this time but someone younger and more serious about his career. He went over my story again and again until the words and their meanings started to blur.

I was taken back to my bunk. I lay down. Where was my son. On his way? Here already? Did he know that his father was suspected of murder?

I dozed a little. It took my mind off things.

"Come on." Yet another cop was at my door.

"It's too early for me to receive visitors," I grumbled.

"Wright wants to speak to you."

I sprang out of bed.

"Any chance of coffee?" It was eight o'clock. Optimum coffee time.

"I'll see what I can do," said the cop. He ushered me into Malcolm Wright's office. He had his back to me looking out the window. The sun was up and a bright new day had begun.

"I'm not having a good time, Mr Ridley."

"I'm very sorry to hear that."

"I haven't even been home since last night. Do you know how happy my wife is about that?"

"I'm going to hazard a guess and say 'not very'."

"Are you married?"

"I was once."

"That's right. Your son lives here." He checked a file on his desk, "in Rushcutters Bay."

"You probably know more about him than I do."

"Nice area, Rushcutters Bay. Good views."

Malcolm Wright sat down in his springy executive-model chair.

"I have a few problems," he said.

"I'm sorry to hear that."

"You said that you left the house with Michelle on Tuesday after eight?"

"Yes."

"Now a neighbour saw what he thought was Michelle going back into the house at nine-thirty. But it can't have been her, since she was at the restaurant with you. We know that. We have witnesses for it. Apart from you, that is."

I nodded. I was starting to feel delirious.

"Was there anybody in the house when you got in?"

"I didn't see anyone. But it's a big house."

Malcolm Wright grunted. "Another problem; Michelle was killed in her bedroom, yet the only prints of yours there are on the murder weapon. There are none whatsoever in the room itself. That strikes me as a little odd. You kill a woman after having sex with her but you remember to slip on rubber gloves?"

"I only went into her bedroom after she was dead. I took her coffee. I didn't touch anything."

Malcolm Wright slipped on his glasses. Picked up a grubby envelope that had his name printed on it.

"Barry Marvel was a friend of mine," he said. "We started on the force together twenty-five years ago. He sent me this before he was killed." Malcolm Wright opened the envelope. A file spilled out. "No stamps, the cheap bugger. I had to pay the postage.

"The woman you know as Karen McArdle had many different names and disguises and a rather varied criminal record according to Marvel. The most interesting charges are theft and fraud. I'll be checking all of this, of course."

"Of course."

"Marvel's theory was that she somehow latched on to Vince, an obviously rich man, thinking there'd be money in it for her somewhere." Malcolm Wright held up a scruffy piece of paper.

"He wrote me a little note," he said. "Just in case."

"I like him more and more."

"Marvel somehow got information from a forger who'd doctored some dental records and a false identity. This guy's well-known for his skill in the, er, imitative arts. Vince was definitely on his books. I sent someone round this morning to er . . . check."

He stood up, looked out the window. "The plan could have worked, maybe. But you know sod's law."

"I live sod's law."

That nearly got a laugh.

"You can go," he said and he turned to face me.

I sat there, staring blankly.

"Go?"

"Go, as in opposite of stay," said Malcolm Wright wearily. "We're keeping your passport though, so you're not tempted to leave without saying goodbye."

"But . . . ?"

"Go. Before I change my mind. I do have other suspects to interview. Much more interesting suspects. You are strictly small-time."

"Oh," I said.

"Get a life, Mr Ridley. Don't go round picking up strange women. It's not good for your health."

"What about John Holden?" I said.

Malcolm Wright reached for a manila envelope. Went through a pile of papers. Turned them around so I could see what was written on them. They were copies of the documents I'd taken from Michelle's locker at the gym.

"I met Marvel for a drink last week," Malcolm Wright said. "He boasted that he'd been taking photographs of things in women's gym lockers. I thought he was spinning a yarn to make me jealous. He liked to do that."

I looked at the papers. There it all was. Marvel had helped save my life.

"This means a murder inquiry," Malcolm Wright sighed.

"Yes."

"An old one. I hate those." Malcolm Wright sounded even wearier. "Everyone's forgotten."

"Not everyone's forgotten," I said, thinking of Elspeth Reid.

"A government minister." Malcolm Wright seemed ready to break into tears. "Do you know how much aggravation this is going to cause me?"

I shook Malcolm Wright by the hand. I felt as light as if someone had filled me with helium. I stood there, like a chump. A foolish grin spreading across my face. I had to resist the temptation to hug Malcolm Wright. I had the feeling he wouldn't appreciate it.

"Well, I'd love to stay and chat, but you know how it is."

Malcolm Wright just nodded.

"Be seeing you."

"I hope not," he said.

It was a blur from there. The cops let me have a shower
and dug up a razor from somewhere and they gave me back
my clothes. And my suitcase last seen missing in action.
They'd recovered it from the airport. I looked half presentable
as I stepped out into the relentless sunshine, blinking like a
mole.

Friday 9:10 a.m.

"**S**am! Over here."

"Sam! I'd like a word."

My colleagues, the distinguished gentlemen and women of the media, descended on me like disease-bearing insects. They shouted questions, pushed cameras in my face. Called me by my first name even though we'd never met. I stopped, in shock, also because they blocked my path.

"What happened that night? Tell us in your own words . . ."

"How does it feel to be hunted by the cops."

"What's your opinion of Sydney now?"

One of them even reached out and grabbed my arm. I shook it off. Then there was another one on the other side and suddenly we were moving forward.

"I'm sorry, guys," Frank said. "But Sam's signed an exclusive deal with the *Star,* so if you'd just get out of our way . . ."

"Not that exclusive," growled Ozzie. Journalists. You can always trust them to show up when you need them.

The questions and the crowd followed us to the Mini which lurked in a no-parking zone.

I looked up. Someone caught my eye. Elspeth Reid was

standing a little way off. Looking unfamiliar in smart street clothes. Clutching a small handbag. I went over to her. Took her by both hands.

"I've been speaking to Malcolm Wright," she said.

"Me too."

I hugged her as she burst into tears of relief. Every photographer and news camera operator in Sydney was witnessing our private moment, but it didn't seem to matter.

"Come and see me," she said. "I promise not to attack you with my toaster."

"I will."

I felt dizzy with relief and exhaustion as I walked over to the Mini.

"Right, let's get breakfast," said Frank. "I know this great little place. We'll have champagne. Maybe take a few snaps, start going over the story. I think we must emphasise how important my role was in helping—"

"We're going to the airport," Ozzie cut in.

"Airport? You're not leaving already? Your holiday has just begun," Frank said.

"Sam's son is arriving in about twenty minutes," Ozzie said.

"Simon? How do you know?"

"Your ex called Lyall in London and he called me."

"But—" said Frank.

"We'll pick up the kid and then we'll make plans." Ozzie squeezed my shoulders. "Me and Paula are taking you surfing."

"She's really having you back? And I thought I had a miraculous delivery."

"It's a long story," said Ozzie, grinning.

We crammed into the little car with Frank at the wheel and we flew out to the airport. Frank broke every rule of the road, starting with the speed limit. Other drivers cursed, saluted us with one finger. Frank took no notice. He turned on the radio. An all-news station announced that Vince and his lover Karen McArdle had been arrested.

Ozzie whooped, reached his arm out of the window and slapped the top of the car.

"How does it feel?" he asked.

I just grinned. It felt good as gold.

"This is great," Frank said. "I'll get the reunion pix. Father and son back together. We are a family newspaper, after all." He honked the horn as a car up ahead audaciously blocked our path.

"Frank," I said. "You leave my child out of this, or I will personally make sure you never have any of your own."

"But it's the best part of the story!"

"No pictures of my son."

"But—"

"You heard the man," Ozzie said.

The traffic was heavy. The Mini squirmed in and out of queues and tailbacks. For a decent portion of the journey we travelled on the wrong side of the road. Soon, though, the sprawling airport outbuildings were in our sight.

"See?" Frank said. "I told you I'd get you there."

We screeched to a stop outside the domestic-arrivals terminal. I lurched out of the car, dashed inside.

The arrivals board flicked and flashed. Planes had landed, discharged their occupants. Including the one Simon was on. He was here already. My heart did a dance. The arrivals area was straining with people like me. I threaded my way through the crowd, scanned heads for Simon's curly locks. Sunburned tourists poured out. Simon wasn't among them. I checked behind me, to see if they'd already come out and were waiting for a cab. They weren't there. I went back to the arrivals queue. Nothing.

I'd missed him.

The crowd blurred. I felt tears coming to my eyes. The frustration, fear and anger of the last few days threatened to submerge me. *I'm never going to see him again,* a pitiful inner voice cried. None of this has been worth shit.

I felt a sharp pain in my back. It was Ozzie.

"Over there, mate. Someone's waving at you."

A small boy carrying a backpack came through the double doors. He wore a baseball cap and a T-shirt with a bird on it. He had a bright smile and a knowing look in his eye.

"Dad!"

I began to run.

KAREN KIJEWSKI

___HONKY TONK KAT

0-425-15860-8/$6.99

Country-western singing star Dakota Jones, a friend of Kat Colorado's since childhood, is worried. Like most stars, she has enemies, but someone has been sending her unusually unnerving letters and really nasty gifts...As the pranks escalate into violence, Kat moves quickly to identify the culprit: Is it a faceless fan, or is it someone who knows Dakota more intimately—even a member of her family?

___KAT SCRATCH FEVER

0-425-16339-3/$6.99

A Sacramento attorney commits suicide—and Kat finds a video suggesting he'd been blackmailed. But as Kat investigates, she discovers that the extortionist has a charitable streak, ordering victims to make their payments to an organization that helps handicapped kids. Kat needs to figure out where the truth lies...

< A FELICITY GROVE MYSTERY > THE

DEAD PAST

Tom Piccirilli

Welcome to Felicity Grove...

This upstate New York village is as small as it is peaceful. But somehow Jonathan Kendrick's eccentric grandma, Anna, always manages to find trouble. Crime, scandal, you name it...this wheelchair-bound senior citizen is involved. So when the phone rings at 4 A.M. in Jonathan's New York City apartment, he knows to expect some kind of dilemma. But Anna's outdone herself this time. She's stumbled across a dead body...in her trash can.

BERKLEY
PRIME
CRIME

❑ 0-425-16696-1/$5.99

Prices slightly higher in Canada

PENGUIN PUTNAM INC.
Online

Your Internet gateway to a virtual environment with
hundreds of entertaining and enlightening books from
Penguin Putnam Inc.

*While you're there, get the latest buzz on
the best authors and books around—*

Tom Clancy, Patricia Cornwell, W.E.B. Griffin,
Nora Roberts, William Gibson, Robin Cook,
Brian Jacques, Catherine Coulter, Stephen King,
Jacquelyn Mitchard, and many more!

Penguin Putnam Online is located at
http://www.penguinputnam.com

PENGUIN PUTNAM NEWS

Every month you'll get an inside look at our upcoming
books and new features on our site. This is an ongoing
effort to provide you with the most up-to-date
information about our books and authors.

Subscribe to Penguin Putnam News at
http://www.penguinputnam.com/ClubPPI